Mum Runners

Kathleen Kirkland

Copyright

Text copyright © 2020 by Kath Kirkland
ISBN: Paperback – 978-1-9163035-1-5
First edition published 2017, Xlibris Publishing.

The second edition published in February 2020.
Updated edition published in July 2020.

All rights reserved. No part of this book may be reproduced or transmitted in any form or by any means, electronic or mechanical, including photocopying, recording, or by any information storage and retrieval system, without permission in writing from the copyright owner.

This is a work of fiction. Names, characters, places and incidents either are the product of the author's imagination or are used fictitiously, and any resemblance to any actual persons, living or dead, events, or locales is entirely coincidental.

Acknowledgements

I wish to say a massive, thank you to all my friends and family who have read this book and given me valuable feedback. Those that have enjoyed this book have asked me to write a sequel, which was never my intention when I started *Mum Runners*. There is now a natural sequel, which will be out later in 2020.

Thank you, Tony Piedade from *Joggingbuddy.com*, for the support of my idea.

I also wish to thank Hannah McCall, my editor, from Black Cat Editorial Services.

I must thank Elliot Willis of Willis Design Associates for laying out the jacket cover and Karen Kodish for the amazing profile pictures.

Chapter One

Samantha was having a shit day at work, which was nothing new as shit was the norm at Sprocket and Son's solicitors' office, but today was one of the lowest of the lowest. She sometimes wished she were more proficient in writing wills rather than having extensive knowledge of family law. Couples have bickered over the custody of the dog and even the goldfish in the past, but if she had to write one more letter to the respondents' solicitor on the subject of who should have custody of the signed Manchester United football, she really was going to give up the will to live.

She started to take a sip of her tepid coffee whilst writing the letter when a knock on her door took her by surprise and she spat a mouthful of coffee all over her keyboard.

'Do come in,' Samantha invited, whilst frantically searching through her desk drawer for a box of tissues.

There, stood in the doorway, adjusting his tie, was the new office recruit. He smiled, offering his hand as he walked over to her desk, and she stood. He shook her hand firmly through the rather soggy tissue she was holding and introduced himself. 'Hi, I am Greg Horsforth. It is lovely to meet you and I am looking forward to working with you. I am taking over the building and constructions department.'

'Samantha Lloyd – very pleased to meet you too.' Samantha stumbled the reply, putting her coffee cup down on top of some rather important client documents and trying to make the tissue disappear without Greg noticing. Samantha nearly fell over in sheer delight at this man who was standing before her. Greg was fiftyish, very tall, extremely dark, delectably fit and incredibly handsome – something that Samantha had not noticed in a man since she was divorced some fifteen years previously. Samantha tried to contain her overwhelming urge to imagine him, this gorgeous god who was standing in her office, stark naked. It was hard to continue to look at him with any sincerity.

'My, you are extremely, ummm, what's the word I am searching for...' Samantha stumbled, using a politician's babble technique, so that she had time to think about the words as they left her mouth. Usually, her mouth operated before her brain and this would normally result in her saying the wrong thing. She had visions of saying something like 'My, you are sexy. Would you like to get your kit off?' Taking a few minutes to think about her reply may have made her look like she was illiterate, but it was certainly worthwhile in saving her credibility. She realised she needed a subtle approach to her questioning of his elaborate physique and settled on 'Which gym do you go to? I am sure I have seen you working out recently at the Barge.' Samantha spoke whilst adjusting her glasses and eyeing him up and down to get a better view of the sex god that stood before her. The Barge happened to be the local and most prestigious health club. The fact was that Samantha had never set foot in a gym since she was forced to participate in physical education at school, some thirty-odd years ago. There was a huge possibility that this comment may backfire on her, like a rocket on Bonfire Night.

'I do not go to the gym,' Greg modestly contested, adjusting his tie smugly as he spoke.

'Oh, you look so...' Samantha stumbled again. 'Fit. You look so fit. You must exercise, surely.' Samantha looked Greg up and down, to show how sincere she was.

Greg was starting to feel very uncomfortable with Samantha's verbal and non-verbal behaviour. 'I do,' Greg announced firmly. 'I run marathons. I run practically every day, as a matter of fact.' He was still playing with his tie, as if it were a worry bead.

Samantha gulped, covering her mouth with her hand so this sex god would not notice remains of her chocolate muffin she had eaten for breakfast. Greg was a man of great stamina and commitment and she didn't want to make herself look foolish.

'What exercise do you do at the Barge?' Greg looked her up and down with astonishment. Realising this woman was terribly out of shape, with her protruding middle-age spread that was larger than her thighs and drooping bosoms, he thought she probably only went to the health club for coffee and a natter with her so-called girlfriends but paid the overinflated membership fee all the same.

Samantha rustled her hair in an attempt to make her grey roots disappear against her dyed black hair. 'I am too running a marathon,' she replied quite innocently, trying not to look too smug in case he rumbled her as a liar.

Greg looked horrified that this rotund woman was obviously trying to impress him, as she looked like she could not have run for a bus. Greg thought it best not to embarrass this poor lady and asked, after covering the smirk on his face with his hand and pretending to cough, 'Oh really? That is great. Which marathon are you running?'

Samantha delightedly announced, 'Why the London Marathon of course,' not realising that there were indeed any marathons other than the London Marathon.

Greg tried to contain his amusement with such a comment, holding his hand over his mouth, coughing again, so Samantha did not notice his smile increasing. Again, he played the polite gentleman.

'Wow, you were lucky to get a place – one hundred and twenty thousand people apply each year and you are one of the forty thousand lucky entrants.' Greg tried to stump Samantha as she was obviously out of her depth and he found this conversation the most entertaining he'd had in a long while. Certainly not since Mr Ridgley had stormed into his office one Monday morning, asking if he could sue his neighbour because he continually parked his wheelie bin on his property and was damaging his driveway from the sheer weight of the rubbish.

'Guide dogs.' The words were out of Samantha's mouth before she even realised what she was saying. Whilst rubbing her hands over her waist frantically, as if it were going to shave inches off her over-bulging midriff, she blurted out, 'I am running for the Guide Dogs charity. My mother was blind. She had a guide dog, called Fido, and I appreciate how difficult it is to raise funds. So, I thought that is the best way to get a place and to raise money for such a good cause.' Samantha almost stumbled on her words as she rambled on. Thankfully, she had remembered this information from one of her clients, whose father was blind, and the client told her of her ambition to run a marathon to raise funds for the Guide Dogs charity and they often had places available for runners to join their running team. She'd even invited Samantha to join her one year, but Samantha gracefully refused, making up some story that she was on the NHS waiting list for a ghastly knee operation.

'Is Fido still with you?' Greg smirked, realising this woman was a fake. Having been a solicitor for over twenty years, he recognised a fake immediately.

'Fido?' Samantha replied, looking confused.

'Your mum's dog,' Greg reminded her. 'Gosh, sorry, Mum's been gone for several years now, forgot I had mentioned the dog.' Samantha tried to cover her steps, hoping that Greg did not realise that she had made the whole thing up about Fido. Samantha could not bear the frustration any longer of Greg standing in front of her and questioning her as if she were on trial, so she thought it best to try to dismiss him from her office.

'I am terribly sorry, but I need to get on with my work. A custodial battle going on, relating to a signed football, you know the normal ridiculous world of a solicitor.' Samantha raised her eyes as in jest about such trivial matters.

Greg laughed. 'That is fine, I understand. I had better find my new office and settle in anyway. We must go running one lunchtime, if you are free?' Greg made a running motion with his arms and legs.

Samantha stumbled for the right answer. 'I prefer to run cross-country, not around the streets.' She sighed.

Greg turned and started to leave the office, grinning as he spoke. 'You had better start running on the pavement. London is all through the streets – your knees will not be used to it, if all you do is run on the grass.' Greg retaliated in an attempt to try to score points against this strange woman, covering his mouth to cover his laughter as he left her office.

Samantha called out as he left her office. 'Thank you for the advice. I only said to my personal trainer the other day that I need to start running on concrete and he, too, agreed.' Samantha wiped the sweat off her brow as she spoke; she'd finally got rid of this hunk of a man from her office.

Greg returned, putting his head around the door. 'Samantha, when you have crossed the finishing line, I will be there to take you out, anywhere of your choice as a reward for your efforts.'

'Wow, thank you, that is very kind. Samantha blushed. 'I have always wanted to have afternoon tea at the Ritz.'

'Wise choice.' Greg adjusted his tie. 'Like I said, only after you have crossed the finishing line.' Greg then turned and left, walking towards his office with a huge smug grin on his face, as he knew that this woman was deranged and would never achieve running two yards, never mind twenty-six miles.

'It is a date,' Samantha called after him, not realising that he was too far down the corridor to hear her now, stunned that a sex god had just entered her office and promised to take her on a date: afternoon tea at the Ritz!

Samantha felt rather perplexed after what had just happened, trying to conjure up an excuse as to why she was not training for a marathon when she was next asked by The Sex God. She settled for knee problems, but then she would have to have two weeks' holiday for a bogus operation and could not really come back tanned from the Caribbean if she was supposed to be in hospital under the knife. She sat down to take the load off her legs and then considered what she had just lied about, running in the London Marathon, and thought it could not be that much of a task. It was only twenty-six point two miles, not to the end of the earth and back or anything. Besides afternoon tea at the Ritz with Sex God had to be worth the effort, did it not?

Chapter Two

The bus was in sight and Suzie thought she had best run for it, otherwise, she would have to wait twenty minutes until the next one. She ran as fast as she could, which was not fast enough as just as she reached the bus doors, all out of breath and looking like she had been dragged through a hedge backwards, the bus driver took one look at her, smiled, shut the doors and said, whilst laughing to himself, 'You'll never make a marathon runner. If you did, you would have caught this bus.' He then drove off smiling to himself, like he had done his good deed for the day.

'Bastard!' Suzie attempted to shout at the top of her out-of-breath voice. 'How dare you assume I cannot run very far.'

The bus driver was, however, right; Suzie could not run more than two metres without feeling extremely queasy. She decided that she really did need to start exercising as all she did was sit at home all day watching *Jeremy Kyle* and *Loose Women* and, being only twenty-two, she was getting old before her time. Her mates sat around smoking all day, moaning about the women who live down the road, who they were she would at least search for a personal trainer. Getting fit was going to be more of a challenge than she expected.

She fired up her PC whilst the kettle was boiling to make a well-deserved cup of tea and lit a fag, taking an extremely long, hard drag. She typed into the search engine 'Personal Trainer'. The first result was inviting her to train to be a personal trainer. 'Earn extra income, whilst staying in shape and helping others' the advert read. 'Wow,' Suzie muttered to herself. How interesting, she thought, subconsciously stubbing out a half-smoked cigarette into the overflowing ashtray on her desk. She immediately rang the college that was advertising the course. She muttered the famous words that her late nanny had said so often: 'Why put off until tomorrow what you can do today.' She then had a thought that it must be a sign as she could use the money her nanny had left her. She had kept it in a savings account as her nanny was very specific that she must only use it to improve her prospects one day. She was deep in thought when a robotic voice bellowed at her.

'Good morning and welcome to course admissions, how can I help you?'

'Umm, yeah.' Suzie stumbled. 'Sorry, yes, I've seen your advert online and I am interested in your Sports Science course.'

'Just one moment, please. Can I take your name and I will transfer you to someone who can help?' The robotic voice continued. Suzie was then left listening to the most awful version of 'Wonderwall' she had ever had the displeasure of listening to, being played on the bagpipes. She wondered if the robot had a personality, or did she have to work at sounding so false?

A very enthusiastic voice blurted out, 'Hi Suzie, I am Lucas, how can I help you?' Suzie had visions of this man performing press-ups as he spoke.
'Yeah, uum, sorry, I am…' Suzie hesitated. 'My

colleague said you were interested in the Sports Science course. Is that right?' the enthusiastic Lucas asked.

'Yes, I am. I want to help others get fit,' Suzie muttered.

'Well, you have come to the right place, young lady. We have courses for all sorts of people in different circumstances. We have daytime courses and evening courses...' Lucas rambled on.

'Oh, so many decisions to make.' Suzie took a drag of a newly lit fag, followed by a slurp of her tea.

'Yes, that is not the only decision. Are you looking at a level two or level three?'

Suzie was very confused. 'I have only just had the thought today to do this, so I am not really sure.?'

'No problem, let's start with what is your forte?' Lucas enquired.

'Forte? Sorry, what do you mean?' Suzie started to feel queasy, unsure she had given the correct response.

'Well, what exercise do you engage in? Cycling, aerobics, running – you must have a favourite?' Lucas carried on with his enthusiastic tone. 'Or is it all of the above?' Lucas chuckled to himself.

Suzie was taken aback by the question. It hadn't crossed her mind she'd have to participate in exercise; she had thought she'd just have to learn stuff from books. She realised the error she had made in applying for the course. It was like wishing to train as a childcare assistant and not being able to change a shitty nappy. 'Errm, yeah.' She gazed out the window for inspiration and saw a man running past with his dog in tow. 'Running, I enjoy running,' she lied.

'Wow, so do I. Have you run a marathon before?' Lucas quizzed her.

'Errm, no, not yet. I am running the London Marathon next year though.' Suzie stumbled as she gave her dishonest answer. She had trouble this afternoon, running for a bus and she was telling this over-enthusiastic guy on the telephone she was going to run *the* London marathon.

'Wow, that is so cool.'

'Is it?' Suzie hesitated, chewing her fingers like a schoolgirl who
had been summoned to the headmaster's office.

'I ran the Great North Run last year, that's half a marathon, but I have never been lucky enough to get a place in London.' Lucas rambled on.

'Well, my friend works for a hospice locally and she has asked me if I'd run *the* London marathon to raise funds for the hospice.' Suzie lied, remembering how her mother was always trying to raise funds for the hospice where she worked as a nurse.

'That is great Suzie, you have my admiration.'

'Admiration, why do you say that?' Suzie began to feel unwell.

'Because it is such a long way.'

'Is it?' Suzie answered all innocently.

Lucas gave a polite chuckle. 'You must be an expert in your field, if you dismiss forty kilometres as not being a long way.' Lucas laughed. 'Anyway, what is your name and address and I'll send you some information and I'll call you in a week or so, so we can discuss the options and see if you have had any thoughts on whether you want to learn part time or full time.' Lucas took her details and arranged a convenient time to call her again, next week.

Suzie hung the phone up and felt good about the fact that she was about to embark on a new vocation, but equally she was concerned about the fact that she had just lied to get accepted onto a course to train others to get fit, when she clearly wasn't fit herself. As for running a marathon, she had done some stupid things in her time, but that has to be up there with driving her dad's car into the family's carp pond when her dad was teaching her to drive, her dad admitted defeat immediately after that and advised her to get some professional tuition. What an earth had she agreed to?

Chapter three

Sharon gazed longingly at the pink booties whilst she purchased them for her friend's new-born. With six boys, Sharon longed for a baby girl who she could dress in pink outfits and whose hair she could plait. Sharon turned to her husband and smiled at him as the assistant wrapped the booties in tissue paper, placed them in a bag, added some coloured confetti and handed the beautiful bag to her.

'Don't even think about it,' her husband, Gary, muttered, whilst holding his hand up in Sharon's face. 'We go through this every time one of your friends has a baby. We are not having another baby.' Gary finished the conversation with the voice of determination. 'Come on, I need a coffee.' Gary pulled Sharon by the hand into the coffee shop opposite.

At thirty-six Sharon was concerned her body clock was ticking and her last chance to have another child would soon be over; she pined day and night for a little girl.

'Just one more. If it's a boy then I will have to accept that you are not a real man and cannot provide me with a girl,' Sharon bantered.

'Yeah, yeah, it takes a real man to make a girl.' Gary waved his hand in the air and turned away from her, to dismiss Sharon and her comments. 'You've told me hundreds of times. I'd rather accept that I am not a real man than the possibility of having seven boys, when I should have stopped at two. You got your own way the last four times and I am not giving in again and that is final.' Holding his hand up to signal time out, Gary searched Sharon's face for an expression of agreement, then scanned the almost empty coffee shop for a suitable seat.

Sharon made herself comfortable and whilst searching her handbag and made a comment that Gary would not likely want to hear. '*Morning Chat*, the TV show, were asking for people to go on a segment entitled "I want another baby but he won't let me". I rang them up and gave them my details.'

'What! Gary let out a scream that would easily outdo and labouring mother.

'I told you, *Morning Chat* are looking for couples, where one wants a baby and the other doesn't. So I gave them—'

'Yeah, yeah, I hear you,' Gary rudely interrupted. 'What have you done?' Gary wiped his brow in frustration.

'Don't be angry.' Sharon attempted to put her hand on his. 'The producer is very interested, us having six children already. Although, he thinks I was slightly off my rocker. He thinks it will make a great show. He said he's never met anyone insane enough that has six children already and is desperate for another one. Most people that rang up have one or two children. So I think they are dead keen. I can show the UK public how selfish you are.' She turned away from Gary so he would not notice her childish gesture and poked her tongue out.

'Selfish!' Gary flared up. 'The permanent feeling of being jet-lagged, when the baby wakes all hours needing a feed, or their nappy changing. What is selfish about that? We are almost forty years old for Christ sake. It was different when we were in our twenties, we had more stamina and energy, now we are old and saggy.' Gary nagged whilst reaching over to Sharon's love handles and giving them a tug.

'Would you not like a little girl to cuddle, love and dress in pink outfits?' Sharon probed.

'Of course, I would like a girl, but I don't think I can cope with all the sleepless nights when we already have got six kids to get to school – they participate in different activities, homework and after-school club activities, football, swimming, and the list goes on, when a baby's demands are different,' Gary ranted.

'Just one last time is all I ask. I promise on all our sons' lives that I will not ask for any more, should this next one be a boy as well.' Sharon fluttered her eyelashes as if to plead with Gary to give in.

Gary was getting angrier and angrier. 'I'm having a vasectomy.' He was on the verge of erupting like a volcano. 'Can't have any more then, can you.' He poked his finger in her abdomen.

'You won't let anyone twist and turn your nuts until they hurt,' Sharon teased, twisting her hands as if ringing out a cloth. 'You won't be able to walk for days and your nuts will swell and resemble the size of a rugby ball.' She held her hands wide apart in demonstration. 'I watched an operation on TV once,' Sharon informed him.

'Maybe I won't but, if you don't stop banging on about having another baby, I may have no option but to have two bricks crush my nuts so they don't work anymore.' Gary's laughter was cut short as he soon realised that the waitress was standing behind him with her pad and pen ready to take their order. 'Two cappuccinos please.' The waitress wrote the order on her pad and said nothing and walked away. 'Do you think she heard me?'

'Yes, all of it. What will it take for you to let me have another baby?' Sharon pushed her luck just one more time.

Gary was getting bored of the conversation and started reading the newspaper he had bought. After a few minutes of silence, Gary suddenly piped up. 'Got it.' Gary laughed, pointing to an advert for running trainers. 'You run a marathon, prove to me your determination, and I'll let you have another baby.' Gary smirked as he was sure that Sharon would refuse to run a marathon; she always came last in the boys' sports day events for the mothers as she was so unfit.

The waitress returned with two hot steaming cups of cappuccino. Gary immediately took a sip. 'You're on,' Sharon blurted out.

'Pardon?' Gary gasped, almost choking on his own cappuccino.

'Marathon, you said if I run a marathon. I will, you'll see. I want a girl more than anything in the world and I would climb mountains to get one. Or just run twenty-six point two miles to get one,' Sharon rambled on.

'I didn't mean it,' Gary remarked, realising that his joke had backfired on him.

'You said, if I run a marathon, you'll let me have another baby. I will run a marathon. You'll see,' Sharon continued.

'You can't even run paint down a wall when you are decorating – how on earth are you going to run a marathon?' he said whilst making hand movements as if painting a wall.

'Training, with training. No one is born wearing a pair of running shoes, not even Paula Radcliffe. You have to train to become a great runner and train I will,' Sharon informed him smugly.

'The DFS sale will be over before you cross the finishing line of any marathon.' Gary held his hand out ready to shake Sharon's. 'It's a deal, because I do not think in a million years you could run to the shops and back, never mind twenty-six miles.' Gary laughed.
'Point two,' Sharon corrected.
'Point two what?' Gary raised his voice slightly, enough to alert the waitress who gave him a stern look.
'It's twenty-six point two miles, that is how long a marathon is.'
'You could not run the point two part of the marathon, never mind the other twenty-six miles.' Gary laughed hysterically.
'You'll be laughing on the other side of your face when I finish and you have to give me another baby.'
'You're on.' Gary shook Sharon's hand to agree the bet; it was a safe bet, in his eyes. He knew that his wife would lose interest after she came back from her first run, not being able to move a muscle. Wouldn't she?

Chapter Four

Samantha sat at her desk, unbalanced by what she had just agreed to, and typed into Google 'Training to run a marathon'. Up came some suggested websites, top of the search was *Runner's World* magazine. A great source of information, she thought, and it would look great on her desk if Mr Sex God came in again. She popped out of the office immediately – telling her secretary, Liz, that she had a client downstairs who did not want to come in – and attempted to run to the newsagent. She searched the shelves frantically for the said magazine.

She returned to the office clutching the latest copy of *Runner's World* and desperately searched the pages for help in training to run a marathon. She noticed an advert where an enthusiastic runner had set up a website called *Joggingbuddy.com*. The idea was to put runners in touch with each other, so they could run together. Running alone was very lonely, not very motivating or indeed safe in the dark nights. This filled her with a sense of overwhelming paranoia. She had agreed to run a marathon and a running magazine was spelling out the ghastly dangers. She, however, decided to ignore this fact and typed into the web search bar the address *Joggingbuddy.com* and up came hundreds of fellow runners of all levels and fitness and looking for a running buddy. She added her profile, giving a pseudonym of Henrietta in case Sex

God was a member of the site – she did not want to be rumbled. She found the most gorgeous picture of herself she could find, taken on an Australian beach last summer, wearing sunglasses and a floppy hat, so she was not recognisable. She said that she was very unfit, looking at running the marathon next year and that she needed a fellow runner of the same calibre. She felt like she had just signed up to a dating agency, advertising herself as free and single. She did, however, specify that she wanted female companions; she had no interest in being outrun by men, all macho and physical. She then typed into Google 'Guide Dogs for the Blind' and looked into how she could register to run the London Marathon for their charity. Samantha sat back and started to feel slightly excited but nervous about the possibility of running a marathon. She then began to tingle with pleasure about the fact that Greg, the sex god, may take her seriously if she did manage to run the London Marathon as she had stupidly announced. She had always wanted to have afternoon tea at the Ritz.

The office phone started ringing and interrupted her thought process. It was her secretary, Liz.

'Samantha, I have Garth on the phone for you. If it's any consolation he sounds stressed.' Liz tried to soften the blow a little.

Samantha let out a huge sigh, as she was not looking forward to the conversation. 'Put him through, Liz, thank you.'

'Hi, Garth.' Samantha sounded enthusiastic to hear from him.

'Hi Mum,' Garth bellowed down the phone, with the sound of a party going on in the background.

'Garth, I can hardly hear you. Where are you?

'I'm in the student bar. My friend's band are playing here. They are really good,' Garth shouted louder.

'Why are you calling me whilst you are in a bar listening to your friend's band. Are you ill?' Samantha asked in a concerned tone.

'No, of course I'm not ill. I was thinking I have not seen my old mum for a while and wonder if I can come home this weekend?' Garth tried to sound as convincing as ever.

'Money or washing?' Samantha quizzed.

'What? Sorry, the music is really loud.' Garth raised his voice even louder.

'Money or washing, why do you want to come home?' Samantha shouted back, realising she may have shouted too loud and her fellow colleagues might have heard her down the other end of the corridor.

'Mum, a son does not need an excuse to come home from university. I just have an essay to write and I have too many distractions here. Besides, I miss your cooking.' Garth attempted to charm her.

Samantha lowered her voice. 'You say the nicest things, Garth.' She reluctantly gave in. 'Ring me when you are at the train station. Love you.'

'Love you too, Mum.' With that Garth hung up.

Garth never came home from university unless he wanted something. He was an only child and knew how to play his mum good and proper. He always got his own way. As if the university fees were not costing her enough each term. He was constantly on the want for something else. She was pleased, however, that he wanted to make something of himself and follow in her footsteps and was studying law at Cambridge. Garth would most certainly be proud of his mum's determination to take on a new challenge. Or would he?

Chapter Five

Suzie immediately rang one of her fitness-freak friends, who would know what to do.
'Chloe, it's Suzie,' she announced hastily.
    'Wow, sweetie, you sound stressed. What's the matter, honey?' Chloe asked in a concerned voice.
    'I've just done something really, really stupid Suzie explained.
    'Go on.' Chloe waited with anticipation. Had she run over the neighbour's cat during another disastrous driving lesson?
    'I've kinda told someone I am running next year's London Marathon,' Suzie said reservedly.
    The laughter that came from Chloe sounded like that of a hyena.
'You've done what?'
    'I've told someone I am running next year's London Marathon and they believed me,' Suzie told her.
    'Let me guess, this person was a guy, right?' Chloe quizzed. 'Were you trying to impress him?'
    'Yeah, no, well sort of,' Suzie said, chewing her fingers like a naughty schoolgirl.
'Who is he? Is he worth it?' Chloe asked.
    'No, it's not what you think. I enquired about enrolling on a course to be a personal trainer and he kind of put me on the spot. I said I enjoy running and I

am running the next London Marathon,' Suzie explained hastily, sweating as she spoke.

'Well, honey, you have my blessing, but you are talking to the wrong girl. Aerobics is my thing. I couldn't run more than a mile myself. Running is a different exercise. But that's not to say it's impossible to run.'

'That's why I enquired. I ran for a bus today and missed it – the driver was rude and told me to get fit, so I am.'

'You could train. Nothing like a change to give you a rest,' Chloe informed her.
'Really?' Suzie seemed interested.
'I heard someone talking at the gym the other day about a website called *Joggingbuddy.com* or something like that. You can network with others at the same level as you and run together. Better than running alone, especially with so many nutters out there nowadays.' Chloe tried to offer the poor girl as much help as she could.

'It will be full of athletes, surely.' Suzie chewed her fingers.

'No, totally the opposite, in fact. You find someone to run with to give you encouragement, motivation. Athletes go alone, as they are too good to be held back by others. The website has loads of unfit wannabe marathon runners, all looking for a running pal to give them motivation.'

'Bless you. Do you think I could really train?' Suzie asked cautiously.

'Honestly.' Chloe paused. 'Pack the fags in, get some running pals and you'll be fine. It's six months until race day, they say it takes three months to train, so you should be well fit by the time the marathon is here. The personal training course will do you good too – something to focus on rather than those low-life

mates you hang around with all day long. Really pleased for you, honey,' Chloe went on.
'Cheers, Chloe. I knew you'd know what to do.'

'You're welcome, honey.' Chloe blew a kiss at the phone.

'I best go, I've got to pick Chelsea up from school in a while. Take care, Chloe.'

'Suzie, I love you. Take care and if I can help, just call.' With that Chloe hung up.

Suzie searched the web for *Joggingbuddy.com* and found the site and sure enough it was full of profiles of runners of all levels. Some training to get fit, others to stop smoking, some looking at training for a half marathon and others the full forty-two kilometres. Suzie sat and pondered for a while before she created her own running profile. There was no harm in finding someone else to jog with. They mostly seemed to be in the same boat as her, not being a very fit runner and all. She found a profile of a lady called Henrietta, who also lived in Islington. Her profile read:

Hi, I am Henrietta and I have just agreed to run The London Marathon. Except the only thing I have ever run before is a ladder in my tights. I am looking for fellow runners at the same level to train with. If there are any other women (absolutely no MEN) out there in the same boat, please get in touch. We can have such fun training.

Suzie gasped. 'How exciting! Chloe was right: it is not full of athletes.' She emailed Henrietta eagerly, through the secured website, so she didn't have to give her personal email. If it turned out to be some nutter, she'd never have to see her or correspond with her again.

Suzie wrote:

Hi Henrietta, I am in the same boat, I too have agreed to run The London Marathon and can't even run for a bus. Love to meet up. Suzie xx.

Suzie sat back and waited eagerly to see if Henrietta replied.

Chapter Six

Sharon walked into the kitchen where Gary was frying bacon for his predictable Saturday morning bacon sandwich. He was concentrating on the pan when he asked Sharon, 'Can I make you a sarnie?'

Sharon gave a casual reply whilst removing the boys' breakfast bowls and mess from the table. 'No, I am fine, my love. I had a bowl of muesli earlier.'

Gary turned to Sharon, his mouth dropped and with it so did the spatula he was using to fry the bacon, and he burnt his hand.

'Shit, that hurt. What the hell are you doing eating the bottom of a rabbit's cage?' Gary seemed concerned.

'It is not the bottom of a rabbit's cage. It is good wholesome food, to give you energy and substance,' Sharon informed him as if reading from a book.

'You have eaten a bacon sarnie every Saturday for as long as we have been together – why today have you decided to change your eating habit? You have not turned into one of them soppy vegetarian freaks, have you?'

'I told you yesterday, I am running the London Marathon and I need to change my eating habits.'

'Surely you're gonna need your calories and this bacon sarnie has plenty.' Gary wafted the smoke that was coming away from the sizzling pan.

'My God!' Gary cried.
'What's the matter? You hurt yourself again?' Sharon ran over to him with a concerned look on her face.
'You're dressed,' Gary remarked.
'For goodness' sake, you had me worried there. I thought you'd burnt yourself.'
'No, sorry, when have you ever been dressed before mid-day on a Saturday? It's only nine o'clock.' Gary walked towards her and placed his hand on her forehead to check for a temperature, moving her brown curls away from her face first.
'I am off to the library.' Sharon smirked.
'You can't take the car. I need to take the boys to their football match.'
'Why drive when you can walk,' Sharon informed him smugly, whilst marching on the spot.
'Don't make me laugh. You walk. It's over a mile to the library. You are never going to walk all that way and back.' Gary laughed.
'I am going to be running twenty-six miles – I am sure I can walk a measly one.' 'Point two,' Gary corrected.
'What?' Sharon dismissed his reply.
'You said yesterday that it is twenty-six point two miles.'
'Yes, glad you listened to me for once, you don't normally. I am off.' Sharon turned and left.
Gary called after her. 'What are you going to the library for?'
It was too late. She was out the door before he had finished his sentence.

Sharon arrived at the local library just before ten o'clock. Certainly, the time needed improving. It was being away from the family, on her own and enjoying the outside air. She felt she could get used to this new life. Although she hadn't actually run a single step yet, she could see the advantages. She realised the benefits of owning one of those iPod things her boys were always banging on about. She would add one to her Christmas list and see if Father Christmas would bring her one, especially as she was being a good girl now. She needed some help finding out how to train to run a marathon. Her mother always gave the same response when she asked a question on anything: 'You'll find the answer in the library.' Her mother was a librarian though, so she almost single-handedly campaigned for everyone to use the services of the library. 'If you don't use them, they may close, you know.' She heard her mother's dulcet tones ringing in her head. She needed to ask someone for help. There was a tree-hugger-looking sort of woman putting books away on a shelf in the children's section. Sharon plucked up the courage to talk to her and asked her in a calm tone, 'Can you tell me where I can find books on training to run a marathon, please?'

The tree hugger looked up from her armful of books and replied in a pleasant manner. 'Of course, madam. Who is being stupid enough to run all that way?' the librarian asked.
'Me,' Sharon proudly pronounced.
'Wow, you've got your work cut out for you.'
The librarian looked her up and down intently as she spoke, whilst walking towards her computer.

'I know, but I am doing it to prove a point to my husband,' Sharon informed the librarian who was now busy tapping the keys on her keyboard, searching her computer for information.

'I understand, totally understand. My husband said that I could not change a plug, so I proved him wrong. Okay, I blew the house electrics, but, hey, I changed it. Didn't say I was going to do it right.'

Sharon smiled because she had visions of this young lady living in a house built from mud and sticks, cooking on an open flame, so to save the environment, not with a house that had electrics. She probably uses one of those awful cups that women use during their periods instead of tampons, she thought, although I cannot understand how that is hygienic, seems disgusting having your period blood lolling around below all week.

'The health and fitness section is over there.' The librarian was pointing towards the bookshelf in the corner of the library.

Sharon came out of her dream world and realised the woman was talking to her. 'Thank you.' Sharon walked towards the section.

The librarian followed her. 'Which charity are you going to run for?'

'Caner Research I suppose, Sharon answered immediately. 'I lost my mum to cancer. Only I am not sure how to find out.'

'Have you searched the web?' the librarian asked.

'I don't have the internet at home,' Sharon said apologetically.

'We have computers here. You can use them for an hour for free as a member of the library. Here – there is a free computer over there.' The librarian practically pushed Sharon to a desk and pulled up a chair.

'When you've run the marathon, come back and tell me and I'll give you some sponsorship money.' She tried not to laugh as she realised that Sharon was way out of her depth.

Sharon took a deep breath and searched the web for a charity that she could run a marathon for. She found that Cancer Research had places in the London Marathon. She sent a request to join the running team, telling them about her mum who'd lost her fight with breast cancer and that she'd love to run to raise funds for the charity. It being October, she realised she had six months to get fit for the London Marathon. On searching for ideas on how to train to run a marathon she came across a website called *Joggingbuddy.com*. On there she found hundreds of profiles of runners who were looking for a companion to run with.

'How interesting,' she muttered. She found the profiles of Henrietta, who had only ever run a ladder in her tights, and Suzie, who could not run for a bus. She suddenly didn't feel alone anymore and so she added her own profile. She told the story of how her husband had told her she couldn't even run paint on walls and that she always came last in her sons' sports day events. She had promised her husband she would run a marathon; in return he would let her have another baby. She emailed both Henrietta and Suzie and didn't really expect they would reply.

Chapter Seven

Samantha arrived at the office, looking as though she were a stunt double in a movie, swimming to shore from a sinking ship. She was drenched to the skin. She had decided that there was no time like the present to start getting fit and had left the car at home and walked to work. However, what she had not taken into account was that the heavens were going to open and her umbrella would be taken away like in *Mary Poppins* minus the rosy-cheeked nanny.

Typically, the first person she bumped into when she walked through the door was The Sex God himself.

Greg looked at her with such astonishment. 'Did your car break down?' he asked in a concerned tone.

Samantha glanced up from under her hair that was stuck fast to her forehead, threw him a pragmatic look and announced proudly, 'No, I walked today.'

Greg looked her up and down, realising this woman was crazier, than he had first thought, and asked, 'Your car in the garage then?'

'Marathon training. Walking on pavements first, then progress to running on them. My personal trainer advised me to do it.' Samantha waffled on to sound convincing.

'Do you have any important clients today?' Greg sounded sincerely concerned.

'Why?' Samantha failed to understand the importance of such a question.

'Because you do not look like a respectable solicitor in your current state,' Greg replied smugly.

'I was just going to tidy up before I sat down,' Samantha remarked.

'Best of luck.' Greg turned towards his office. 'Catch up with you later.'

Samantha started to panic as she realised that Mr Smith was her first appointment of the day. Mr Smith was the snotty client whose wife had walked out on him whilst he was at work one day. Samantha needed to dry her hair and started to panic and racked her brain as to who was vain enough in the office to have a hair dryer and tongs in their desk drawer. Samantha walked over to Beth, the nineteen-year-old temp, and interrupted her painting her nails a garish red colour. Samantha coughed loudly so to make her presence known. 'I was wondering – do you have a set of hair tongs I may borrow, please?' Samantha enquired sheepishly.

Beth looked up from her nail painting and raised her eyes to show that Samantha had rudely interrupted her delicate artwork.

'I do, although I have left my ghds at home,' Beth announced, still delicately painting her nails.

Samantha did not really understand what ghd meant, but realised that it must be hugely important in the world of hair styling. 'I am not having a good hair day,' Samantha announced, hoping she had made the correct assumption of what the term ghd stood for. 'So, any hair-styling tools that you have, that I could borrow, would be much appreciated.'

Beth looked at Samantha's shrivelled hair, slapped to her forehead, and opened up her desk drawer, which Samantha thought was meant to be for stationery, but was littered with hair products, an array of make-up, and brushes of all shapes and sizes; she had no idea what some of them were used for. Beth handed the straightening tongs over to Samantha, pointing out how to adjust the temperature setting and not to have them up to hot, otherwise her hair would look like she'd had her fingers in a plug socket.

'Thank you very much,' Samantha remarked. 'I will be right back.'

Samantha ran into her office and eagerly plugged the tongs into the socket in her office and whilst they heated up, she turned on her PC. She typed into the search bar *Joggingbuddy.com*.

There to her astonishment were two emails from fellow unfit runners, wanting to meet up as they, too, had ridiculously agreed to run next year's London Marathon. Suzie who seemed very timid and scared and Sharon who was out to prove a point to her husband. 'Yesssss.' She let out a happy scream, quickly stopping herself so as not to alert her colleagues. She hastily replied to Suzie, having a few minutes before she needed to start tidying herself up before Mr Smith arrived. She rapidly typed:

So glad I am not alone. Let's meet for coffee. I suggest the Starbucks on the high street. I can make it at two o'clock on Thursday as I have my lunch break then and I hope that will be good for you, before you need to collect the children from school. Let me know either way if you can or cannot meet. Wear something pink, so I know it is you. Samantha xx.

She pressed the send button and had confirmation the email had been sent. An overwhelming panic came over her as she realised her profile name was Henrietta and she had signed the email as Samantha. She immediately sent a second email.

Sorry for the confusion over the name. Henrietta is a nickname that I use frequently, Samantha is my birth name. I will explain all when I meet you. I am not a nutcase, honest. If it is any reassurance, I am a solicitor. Xx.

She then hastily tried to tidy herself as the time was running away with her faster than she liked. Once she had burnt herself three times on the damn hair tongs, she gave them back to temp Beth and thanked her immensely. Beth did not look up from painting her nails when she replied, 'You're welcome.'

On the way back to her office she saw that Mr Smith was waiting patiently at reception. 'Mr Smith.' Samantha greeted him politely with her teeth gritted. 'I am so glad to see you. Do come through to my office and take a seat, please.' Samantha held open her office door and signalled for Mr Smith to enter.

'Thank you,' Mr Smith said, and then he cried. He cried for the duration of their meetings; things were obviously so very raw.

Samantha offered Mr Smith a cup of coffee to try to calm his nerves and started the meeting by asking, 'Do you have the list, Mr Smith?'

'I do. I did as you asked and listed everything that *she* took.' He placed emphasis on the word 'she', as if Mrs Smith was a murderer.

'Can I see it, please?' Samantha held out her hand to take the list from her client. Mr Smith handed it over to her, after straightening out the creases he'd noticed as he'd removed the list from inside his jacket pocket.

Samantha was somewhat astonished by the content of the list.

'Mr Smith, when you said your wife had left you and taken everything with her—'

'Yes.' Mr Smith sobbed. 'Everything.' 'How often did you wear your wife's make-up?'

'Never.' Mr Smith dismissed her comment as ridiculous.

'Well, then, I fail to see what relevance it is on this list.'

'You said to list everything,' Mr Smith remarked innocently.

'Yes, I did, did I not? Maybe, just maybe, you have misunderstood what I meant. I meant items that you shared and you are now without, such as furniture and electrical items.' Samantha raised her eyes in frustration.

'Aghh,' Mr Smith announced. 'If you go to item seventy-four, you will see the bread maker.'

'Aghh yes, item seventy-four, bread maker and flour, open bracket, self-raising and plain, close bracket.' Samantha looked out of the window so Mr Smith was unable to see her disgust that he was obviously from another planet. Is it any wonder his wife left him? she thought.

'Mr Smith, I think that is all I need for now. I will not take any more of your time today, as you are a busy man. I will write to Mrs Smith's solicitor and give them the list of the items here.'

Mr Smith got up, thanked her for her time and expertise, and left.

'What does he expect me to do with this list?' she muttered to herself. Was he a cross-dresser? Was he that distraught that she had taken her clothes with her when she left? Really, his wife obviously left him for being a pompous irritating twat. But Samantha had to keep those comments to herself, as he was her client and paying her wages.

Chapter Eight

Suzie had just had another disastrous driving lesson, having driven the car up the pavement, whilst reversing around the corner, and dislodged a resident's picket fence. The fence did look rather shit anyway, so she felt she'd done them a favour. However, the owner of the property did not share her observation. In fact, they were livid. The female resident threatened to take her instructor to court.

'I am going to sue you for negligence,' the little old lady shouted whilst waving her walking stick in anger.

Karen, her instructor, was always a calm, cheerful soul. 'I am sorry, madam. She lifted the clutch far too quick – before I knew it, we were mowing your fence down. I will, however, give you the name of my insurance company and they will deal with the damage.' She spoke calmly and professionally, whilst handing over her business card.

'Why do I want your card? You think I am going to recommend anyone to you for driving lessons?' The old lady was getting angrier by the minute and her walking stick was getting nearer and nearer Karen's face.

'Please, Mrs… What is your name?' Karen asked.

'Mrs Knight!' she screamed.

'Mrs Knight, please, I am sorry. My card is not so you can pop in for a cuppa when you are passing. It is so you have my details, and I have written on the reverse the number of my insurance company. I am now going to take Suzie home and suggest that she considers public transport for the rest of her life, as she really is a danger to all road users and residents,' Karen said.

'Thanks,' Suzie mumbled sarcastically. 'Thanks?' Karen asked. 'You have just torn down this lady's fence. I think you deserve to repair it yourself.' Karen waved her finger at Suzie, just to show Mrs Knight she was on her side.

'I'll get in the car.' Suzie retreated.

'Not before you say you are sorry,' Karen called.

'Sorry, miss,' Suzie muttered whilst chewing her fingers and staring at the floor as if she were talking to the headteacher after breaking a school rule.

'Mrs Knight, I am sorry once again. Take care and call me if you need anything.' Karen shook Mrs Knight's hand.

When Karen got back into the car, she looked at Suzie and said, 'Bloody horrible fence, you are right. You didn't need to smash it up, though.' Karen laughed. 'I'll drive us home, shall I? Don't think you should be in charge of the car anymore today. Quite stressful running over a fence.'

'How did you keep so calm?' Suzie asked. 'There is no point losing my rag – you did destroy her front garden. I could hardly contest that. Residents are always moaning about learners reversing around corners down this road as it is. She'd ring the police if I gave her any ammunition.' Karen tried to calm Suzie down.

Suzie started crying. 'I didn't see it honest.'

'I know, you hardly ran it over deliberately.

You didn't, did you?' Karen quizzed.
'What do you take me for?' Suzie smiled. 'I wonder sometimes, I really do.' Karen stayed silent for the rest of the journey back to Suzie's flat.

Once they arrived Karen broke the silence. 'Take care and don't worry yourself about anything. I will see you next week.'
'Cheers, I will see you soon and I am really sorry again.' Suzie exited the car with haste.

As Suzie walked into her flat the phone was ringing. It was Lucas from the college.
'Hi Suzie, how are you?' Lucas asked excitedly.
'Fine, thanks,' Suzie replied quite sheepishly. She still had visions of Mrs Knight's fence all over the ground.
'That's marvellous, Suzie. Did you get the information I sent you?'
'I certainly did.'
'So, are you keen to start?' Lucas pried.
'I am, sooner rather than later,' Suzie said. 'Wow, you are keen. That is great news, though.
Which level diploma do you wish to study for?'
'Level four, please.'
'An excellent choice. If you are going to do it, you might as well do it properly. Are you looking at evening or daytime classes?' Lucas was his enthusiastic self.
'I think daytime will be better for me. I have a youngster at nursery and I am a single mum. I am also keen to get it done as soon as possible.' Suzie pushed the switch down on the kettle to set it to boil; she needed a strong cup of tea.

'Fantastic.' Lucas seemed extremely pleased with her response. 'You just need to send back the registration form and payment. We'll get you training within a week – there is a new course starting then.'

'You are a star, Lucas, thanks for all your help.' Suzie was excited at the new adventure she was about to embark on.

After saying goodbye to Lucas, Suzie realised she was gasping for a fag. She hadn't had one for several days. But after the fence incident, she felt she needed to raid the emergency supply hidden in the bathroom. She lit the cigarette and inhaled long and hard. It felt great, but it also made her feel really dizzy and sick. She decided that she didn't need it and stubbed it out and settled just on the cup of tea she had started making instead. She fired up her PC and wondered if Henrietta had replied to her email. To her astonishment, Henrietta had replied almost immediately, suggesting they meet in Starbucks in town, on Thursday at two o'clock. How exciting. She replied to Henrietta, saying that she would be there. Then she read an email from another unfit runner, Sharon. She replied to Sharon and said how lovely it was to hear from a fellow runner and she was meeting a lady called Henrietta in Starbucks in town, and would she like to join them? Thursday this week after two o'clock was the suggestion. Henrietta had requested they wear something pink.

Chapter Nine

Sharon woke feeling revitalised and invigorated that she was changing her life and taking up a new hobby in running. She did have a small feeling of nausea when she took stock of what she was promising to do, in order for her husband to part with his sacred sperm.

She arrived into the kitchen to be greeted with the normal war zone the mornings produced. Arguments over who had eaten the last slice of bread, or who had left only two coco pops in the cereal box, and the tears over the lack of milk left in the fridge were an all too familiar affair. This fiasco that was a morning ritual made Sharon smile. She often wondered what it would be like to have a girl amongst this disorganisation. It is obviously what these soon-to-be testosterone-racing boys needed. Sadly, Gary didn't share her views and dismissed the conversation if she ever mentioned that she wanted to try for another baby. He was a man of his word, so with the bet she had just agreed to, running a mere twenty-six point two miles in return for a bouncy baby girl was now a reality.

Once the delightful little ones had fled the home for a day's learning at school, Sharon sat back as she always did with a well-deserved cup of tea and turned on the TV to watch *The Jeremy Kyle Show*. There was a middle-aged woman arguing with a teenager about the fact she wasn't allowed to see her granddaughter.

The grandma was thirty-six, just a few years younger than Sharon. She gasped at the thought of being a grandmother herself. The mother of the child was only about seventeen. How history had obviously repeated itself there. Once the drama of *Jeremy Kyle* was over it was time to watch *Morning Chat*. Gary entered the room and let out a huge tut as he was obviously worried that the show would want them to appear and discuss in public why he didn't want a seventh child when his wife did. The doorbell rang, which Gary raced to answer so to be away from the now-embarrassing television show. It was Tesco delivering their twice a week shop. With eight people in the house, the Tesco delivery driver, Eric, was on their Christmas card list. Sharon ran to the door when she heard Eric's voice.

'Hi Sharon,' Eric cheerfully called. 'I am afraid there are no chicken nuggets today. We have made a substitution of turkey drummers,' he informed them whilst handing Gary the shopping delivery report.

'Daniel will be devastated,' Sharon commented. 'If he couldn't read, I could tell him they are chicken.'

'I can take them back with me,' Eric informed her.

'Don't worry, Eric,' Sharon said. 'They will get eaten, you know they will.' She pushed Gary out of the doorway.

Sharon proceeded to bring in the fifteen crates of shopping, whilst Gary attempted to put half the Tesco store into the kitchen cupboards, fridge and freezer.

'How you doing then, Sharon? Eric enquired.

'I'm really good, thanks, Eric. Gary has promised me another baby,' Sharon informed him with such delight.

'Another one! Have you not got enough already?' Eric nearly fell off the doorstep.

'I want a girl. Living with seven males is impossible sometimes.'

'I'll need an artic to deliver your food in if you carry on anymore,' Eric joked.

'You may laugh, Eric,' Gary piped up. 'She will only get a baby when she sticks to her side of the bet,' Gary went on.

'Oh, do tell me more.' Eric's ears pricked up.

'Sharon, who cannot run ten yards at a school sports day, has agreed to run *the* London Marathon.'

Eric looked horrified. 'You are going to punish yourself by running forty-two kilometres, just so you can punish yourself with a lifetime of trouble with a little girl.'

'Forty-two kilometres, that sounds even further than twenty-six point two miles.' Sharon looked like she was about to cry, trying to conceal her horror from the men.

'You agreed, Sharon, you cannot go back on your word now.' Gary gave a satisfied smile whilst grabbing her cheeks as if she were a five-year-old.

'I am going to do it, I have told you I will,' Sharon went on.

Eric took a few steps back from the doorstep. 'I will leave you two to have your domestic. Keep me posted, Sharon, about your progress. I will give you some sponsorship money.' Eric turned and waved, happy to be leaving the clutches of a domestic crisis.

Once the shopping was put safely away, Sharon suggested a little outing to the town for her to purchase some running clothes.

Gary felt he had to humour her. 'Do they come in your size?' He laughed. 'Most runners are athletic and slim.'

'You may laugh, Gary, but I am doing something about my midlife muffin top. I don't see you trying.' Sharon chuckled back whilst brushing her hands down her waist to remove inches immediately.

Gary decided he would rather not be shopping for clothes and dismissed the idea. 'The centre will be full of Christmas shoppers and we will be lucky to find a parking space.'

'That's okay. We don't need a parking space,' Sharon said.

'I'm not getting on any bus,' Gary told Sharon firmly.

'We are not getting on a bus, or taking the car – we are walking,' Sharon replied smugly.

'Walking.' Gary almost fell over. 'Are you insane?'

'No, it's only three miles. Exercise will do you good, fatso.' Sharon laughed, smacking his midriff and creating ripples beneath his T-shirt.

'You can go on your own then, love. I'd rather stay behind and iron and that's saying something.' Gary was almost crying at the thought of walking three miles or ironing six children's clothes. If he had a choice, he'd rather put pins in his eyes.

'Get your coat on then,' Sharon told him light-heartedly, as if they had not just had the conversation.

Gary realised that he was not going to win the argument, so reluctantly he got his coat and proceeded to leave the house with Sharon.

The walk to the shopping centre was a brisk one, with the wind beating around their faces, giving them a weathered-looking glow.

Sharon's mobile phone rang which gave her a shock as the only people to phone her were from the school when one of the children was poorly. The number was one she didn't recognise, so she expected it to be a call centre asking her if she had ever thought about claiming back PPI. Sharon answered as politely as she could.

'Is that Sharon?' the happy voice asked. 'Erm, yeah,' Sharon replied cautiously. 'That's great. My name is Tarquin. I am one of the researchers from the *Morning Chat* show.'

'Oh wow.' Sharon's tone rapidly changed. She mouthed the words '*Morning Chat*' to Gary, who was looking rather bemused as to who she was talking to. Gary threw his hands into the air as he knew this was going to be bad news.

'Yes, of course we can,' Sharon replied to the caller and Gary threw a scornful look to Sharon, wondering what she had just agreed that the two of them were going to do.

'Thursday, next week? I'll have to get the children looked after. Give me a call tomorrow and I can confirm all is okay.' Sharon sounded so excited, as if she were about to explode.

'Yes, we do have six children.' Sharon laughed. 'No, you are right. We are on the right topic of show.' Obviously, the researcher felt she was mad for wanting another baby despite having six children already.

'Bye for now, speak tomorrow.' Sharon hung up and was about to burst when Gary broke her excitement with a huge, 'No. We are not going on the *Morning Chat* show next Thursday.'

'Ah, but, Gary, they are going to pick us up, chauffer drive us to Manchester.'

'Manchester!' Gary screamed. 'That's miles away.'

'Yes, but you are not driving, they are. Hear me out. They are putting us up in a hotel and giving us money towards our evening meal. It's a free holiday.' Sharon jumped up and down like a kid at Christmas.

'Some holiday – I have to sell my soul on television in return.'

'No children for one night. When did that last happen?' Sharon reminded him, throwing him a sexy look.

'Before you committed us to having six children, probably,' Gary muttered.

'You are such a cynic,' Sharon said dismissively.

'You are trying to sell me on the idea of going on television to discuss the fact that you want baby number seven. You are trying to do this by enticing me with the fact that we are going to be kid-free for a night. Something wrong there, I think,' Gary said.

'You are so funny. It's one night free of the children, not forever. Last night of freedom before our baby girl is born,' Sharon teased.

'If you can get them looked after, then I will go.'

'Oh really, Gary, I do love you.' Sharon kissed him smack on the lips. She then quickly withdrew. 'You don't think I can get them looked after, do you? That's why you are so willing. Have you not learnt anything from the marathon bet?' She went on.
Gary held up his hand as if to signal time out.

The library was in sight. 'Just need to check my emails in the library for five minutes,' Sharon explained excitedly. Gary followed her like a naughty child. When Sharon had a bee in her bonnet it didn't leave until her task was accomplished.

She logged on to *Joggingbuddy.com* and there was an email from Suzie, telling her she'd been in contact with another lady called, Henrietta and they had agreed to meet in Starbucks in town, this Thursday at two o'clock. The email went on to tell her to wear an item of pink clothing, so they could recognise each other. She emailed her back saying she will be there.

'All done.' Sharon looked over at Gary who was browsing the DIY section.

'You look pleased with yourself.' Gary gave her a worried glance.

'I have found two fellow unfit runners who have agreed to meet on Thursday in Starbucks. So exciting.' Sharon rambled on.

'Shopping it is then. Lead the way, Sally Gunnell.' Gary laughed at his own joke.

Sharon threw him a look of disgust. 'Sally Gunnell won the four-hundred-metre hurdles at the 1992 Olympics. She never ran marathons.' Gary looked as if he had just been beaten at Trivial Pursuit. 'What do I know?'

'Nothing obviously, nothing at all. That is why I love you.' Sharon kissed him on the lips.

'Wow.' Gary beamed. 'What have I done to deserve that?'

Chapter Ten

Starbucks was relatively busy for two o'clock on a Thursday afternoon. Samantha was the first to arrive out of the three girls. Or so it seemed, as there was no one else in pink. It was a miserable rainy day and most people were in brown or black. She began to wonder if this was a wake or a coffee shop. She ordered a skinny latte and informed the dreary assistant behind the counter that should two other women come into the café, each wearing an item of pink clothing, she should direct them to the table where she would be residing. The assistant looked her up and down as if to judge whether she was a tree-hugging campaigner or something. She agreed all the same.

Samantha was sipping her latte when she heard a timid young voice from behind her. 'Henrietta?' Suzie asked.
    'Yes, it is. You must be Suzie or Sharon? Not sure which.'
    'I am Suzie. Can I get you anything?' Suzie gestured towards the counter.
    'Not at all. I have a skinny latte already, thank you. That is my treat for the day,' Samantha replied.
    'I'll just get a hot chocolate, try to warm up from the awful rain.' Suzie apologised and walked towards the happy assistant behind the counter who was giving her strange looks, admiring her pink scarf. She returned to the table where Samantha was sitting. 'No Sharon yet then?'

Sharon walked into the coffee shop, looking around for two random women in pink, when she spotted Samantha with a pink hat and Suzie with a pink scarf, making small talk in the corner.

'Suzie and Henrietta, I assume?' Sharon quizzed sheepishly.

'Certainly is,' Samantha and Suzie replied in unison.

'Henrietta is a stage name, as it was,' Samantha explained.

'Are you an actress then?' Suzie asked. 'No, no. It's a long story really, but I may as well tell you.'

'I'll just get a cuppa coffee, wait until I get back.' Sharon seemed eager to hear the story, throwing her handbag onto the table, which made a loud crashing sound.

Once Sharon had returned with her cup of steaming hot coffee, Samantha started to tell the tale of Mr Sex God and how she had got herself into saying she was training to run a marathon. She found *Joggingbuddy.com* and thought she had better put a stage name on there in case The Sex God was a member and spotted her. Samantha took a sip of her latte and asked Sharon how she had come to be in this situation.

'Well, I want another baby,' Sharon started. 'My husband doesn't share the same enthusiasm.' She raised her eyes.

'Go on.' Samantha continued sipping her latte.

'He thinks we have our hands full with the six boys we've got already.'

Samantha choked on her latte. The latte she had sipped projectile launched out of her mouth, onto the coat of a neighbouring café-goer.

'Can you not afford a TV licence?' Samantha asked.

'I have not heard that comment before.' Sharon laughed.

'Catholic then?' Suzie asked.

'No, I just want another baby. In fact, we are going to be on the *Morning Chat* programme next Thursday, discussing the matter.'

'Well, young lady, you have my sincere blessing. One child is bad enough. He costs me thousands every term at university. How are you going to cope with six of them at university?' Samantha asked.

'Seven, I want another baby,' Sharon reminded her.

'Okay, seven of them,' Samantha corrected herself.

'My husband said that if I run a marathon, I would get my wish of another baby,' Sharon explained.

'You are double nuts. You are going to spend six months training, run a gruelling twenty-six miles, and then nine months being pregnant. Not to mention the lifetime of worry.' Samantha gave her motherly advice.

'Twenty-six point two. It's twenty-six point two miles, the distance of a marathon,' Sharon corrected her.

'Still a chore to get another baby.' Samantha slurped her latte.

'I have six boys and I want a girl.'

'I have one girl and she is a handful. You can borrow her anytime,' Suzie joked, slapping Sharon on the back.

'Why are you running the marathon?' Sharon asked Suzie.

'I am starting a sports science course as I thought about training as a personal trainer and accidentally told the course adviser that I enjoy running. I didn't actually realise that I needed to be fit to study the course. Just thought I'd learn all about fitness from books,' Suzie explained.

'Wow, we have a personal trainer on our team.' Samantha cheered, rubbing her hands together with glee.

'I have yet to start the course,' Suzie told her, holding up her hand to signal her objection.

'Yes, but you will be finished before the marathon surely?' Sharon enquired.

'I'll be done in January. It is a full-time course.'

'I am so excited.' Samantha rubbed her hands together as she spoke.

'This is really exciting. But where the hell do we start?' Sharon asked.

'Don't look at me,' Suzie remarked, waving her hands in the air. 'I told you I have not started the course yet.'

'I have done some research,' Samantha informed them whilst rummaging in her bag for a sheet of paper. 'We need a training plan. We need to start off walking first, then increase to intervals of running and walking, then straight running.' She showed the others the running plan she had printed off earlier.
'As easy as that?' Sharon laughed. 'You sound sceptical,' Samantha stated. 'Just a little, but I have a point to prove to my husband and a point I will prove. He thinks I will crumble at the first hurdle. I told him otherwise,' Sharon said smugly.

'Good for you.' Samantha patted her on her back.

Suzie hugged her hot chocolate and spoke between sips. 'When shall we start?'

Sharon and Samantha looked blankly at each other.

'We need someone to be in charge of the plan,' Samantha announced.

'Sharon turned to Samantha and nominated her. 'You seem to be organised. I put you in charge of the plan.'

'Flattered, I am sure. Solicitors are always organised, goes with the territory,' Samantha remarked.

Suzie added, 'Once my course starts, I can add some input, but until then, I am a little out of my depth.'

'Let us all meet by the basketball court in the local park, the same time tomorrow,' Samantha announced. 'Come dressed in trainers and warm clothes. We are going for a walk.'

Sharon looked worried. 'How far will we walk?'

'We will just go with the flow, young Sharon. We will walk for half an hour. Gentle walk, take in the sights, we don't want to look like those mad power-walkers, skiing on dry land.'

Suzie laughed. 'No, I always think they look ridiculous.'

Sharon raised her cuppa. 'Let's drink to our new adventure.'

Sharon, Suzie and Samantha clinked cups and all three of them in unison shouted, 'Girl power!' Their loud shout woke the rest of the coffee shop up and they received some strange looks from the fellow coffee-drinkers. The waitress really did look at them in disgust as if they were some strange women's group.

'If we can train and run a family at the same time, we are such multi-talented women,' Sharon remarked excitedly.

'Mum runners,' Suzie said.

'Pardon?' Samantha asked.

'Mum runners. We are all mums and we are also runners… well, we soon will be,' Suzie cheerily announced.

'Anyone who is a mum and wishes to run the London Marathon can join,' Sharon shouted out at the top of her voice.

Again, the fellow patrons thought it prudent to show their distaste at their rowdiness by throwing filthy looks in their direction.

'I have seen happier people in a hospital accident and emergency department,' Samantha remarked.

'I have to say, I have a season ticket for the local accident and emergency department, having six boys. One or the other is always falling out of a tree or riding their bike into a brick wall.' Sharon laughed.

'You're running a marathon because you want another child.' Samantha looked horrified.

'Yes, but I want a girl, they are different, they don't have their brains in their arse,' Sharon informed her.

'I have to say, that unless you have some remarkable guarantee that you are going to have a girl, I would be reluctant to even try,' Suzie advised. 'Girls can be very moody when they want to. They also have an answer to everything.'

'So do boys.' Sharon laughed. 'David was potty training and I could not get him to have a poo on the toilet. He didn't like the splashback it gave when it fell into the water. We were in B&Q and he decided to have a poo on a toilet in the showroom. He came running over shouting at the top of his voice, "Mummy, I just had a poo and my bum didn't get wet." I was horrified. I said, "Where did you have this poo?" He pointed to the white porcelain show toilet. I wanted the world to swallow me up. I started to tell him off and he retaliated with "You are always asking me to poo on the big toilet and I just have – you cannot tell me off." What could I do? Apart from leave the shop rather rapidly.'

Samantha and Suzie laughed so much they began to cry with tears of laughter.

'This marathon running is going to be such fun, I can see this right now.' Samantha hadn't laughed so much in a long time. 'We can also log our runs on *Joggingbuddy.com*.'

'Wow, that's cool.' Sharon noted. 'I didn't realise that. So, we can log our training runs and see how we are progressing?'

'Absolutely.' Samantha showed Sharon how to log her runs, using her mobile to login to *Joggingbuddy.com*.

Suzie had an excellent idea. 'Are you both on WhatsApp?'

'What's what?' Samantha seemed confused.

Sharon got all excited. 'It is a messaging service on your mobile. We can set up a group. That is what you mean, isn't it, Suzie?' Sharon showed Suzie the WhatsApp icon on her screen.

'Yes, it is. Once you send a message it goes to all the members.' Suzie was showing the app to Samantha who clearly had no idea about such things.

'My boys are on it constantly. It will make a change for me to be talking about it.'

'Excellent, I have created a group called "Mum runners". I just need both of your phone numbers and away we go.' Suzie was busy tapping away into her phone.

'Thank you, Suzie. We have such a wealth of knowledge between us, let's hope we can achieve this. I am sorry I must get back to the office as my lunch break is over and I have an appointment very soon.' Samantha was already standing, gathering up her bag and coat.

'I have to collect the boys.' Sharon heaved her enormous bag over her shoulder.

'I have to collect Chelsea from school too.' Suzie waved her phone and reminded them to WhatsApp anytime they needed to talk.

They gave each other a hug and a kiss on the cheek and left the coffee shop.

One table of fellow coffee-goers gave a loud tut in unison as the Mum Runners left the coffee shop.

Chapter Eleven

Samantha was the first to arrive at the meeting place in the local park. She looked the part in her wax jacket and waterproof trousers. She was pacing up and down, looking at her watch.

Suzie ambled up, extremely out of breath as she gasped for air; she took a long, hard drag of her fag. She coughed and spluttered before she mouthed, 'Hello Samantha.'

'You should give them up, young Suzie. You will not run twenty-six metres let alone twenty-six miles with your lungs full of poison,' Samantha advised.

'I am, Samantha. I am trying to quit and this is the first one I have had in three days.' Suzie gasped. 'I am noticing how unfit it makes me, now I am exercising.'

'Oh good, I am glad. Now where is Sharon?' Samantha looked at her watch frantically, then scanned the local area for Sharon.

'She'll be here. I posted on WhatsApp this morning. She was looking forward to it. Did you not see the message?'

'I still have not got used to the world of what's-it-called.'

'WhatsApp, it's called WhatsApp,' Suzie informed her.

'Yes, I am sure it will get easier.' Samantha looked at her watch and let out a loud tut in frustration.

At ten past two, Sharon hurriedly arrived all flustered. 'Sorry, really sorry. Child emergency, the school rang me. John lost one of his teeth at lunchtime and I had to go up and console him and give him some Calpol.' Sharon rambled on. 'They are not capable of giving a child a spoonful of medicine, this American state we live in now, for the fear of being sued.' She turned to Samantha and looked all apologetic. 'Sorry, that was not the right thing to say, was it?'

'Well, if people did not sue, I would be out of a job, would I not?' Samantha answered abruptly.

'Sorry, I really am, Samantha.' Sharon put a hand on Samantha's shoulder as she spoke. 'It is hard with six of them sometimes.'

'Contraception is free on the NHS.' Samantha laughed so loudly someone eating their sandwiches on the other side of the park looked around, quite alarmed by the outburst. Samantha returned the gesture of placing her arm on Sharon's shoulder. 'I am joking, honestly.'

'I know. It's not like I haven't heard that comment before. I am sorry for being late, honest.' Sharon looked at her watch.

Suzie was feeling very cold and unmotivated; between coughing from her recent intake of chemicals, she asked, 'What's the plan then, Samantha?'

Samantha started walking and hurried the pair of them on as if she were directing air traffic. 'We will take a brisk walk, then soon we can introduce a light jog.' Samantha sounded extremely smug.

'Why am I doing this again?' Sharon mumbled.

'For some stupid reason, only God can know the answer to, you want another baby.' Suzie laughed. 'But you have agreed to run a marathon first, then subject your body to more pain in pushing a bus through a Polo in childbirth.'

'Thanks, Suzie. If I ever want to be put off the idea of having a baby, remind me to call you.' Sharon sulked.

Samantha had raced ahead and turned to call, 'Keep up, girls.'

Suzie and Sharon increased their stride and caught Samantha up, although keeping one pace behind her.

Samantha started adding some arms into the activity, lifting imaginary weights high in the air and then bringing her arms back down to her chest. Sharon and Suzie burst into hysterical laughter and once Sharon had contained her laughter, she asked, 'Are you unwell?'

'No, I am just getting more air into my lungs,' Samantha advised. 'You should try it – it is remarkably exhilarating.'

Suzie almost choked on the amount of air she was breathing in whilst laughing so heavily. 'You are alone there, my love, carry on. I thought we were training for a marathon, not a sponsored aerobics class.'

'Okay, ladies.' Samantha admitted defeat. Sharon stopped in her tracks suddenly and
Suzie gave her a helping hand on her shoulder.
'What's the matter?' she enquired.
'I need to pee,' Sharon announced to the
girls.

'Too much information.' Samantha waved her hand to signal time out.

'Lovely. Didn't you go before you came out?' Suzie asked.

'I certainly did, but having had six children, my bladder is weaker than a paper bag filled with water.'

Samantha looked stressed that her team had to stop for a simple call of nature. 'There is a bush over there, if you need to go. We can keep guard.' She pushed Sharon in the direction of the bush.

'Don't sit down, though – you could prick your arse on a thorn. I did that once,' Suzie called out after her.

'Or sit in a pile of dog poo,' Samantha yelled.

'Very funny. Can I pee in peace, please?' Sharon rebelled. 'This is worse than trying to pee at home.'

After a few minutes, Sharon appeared from behind the bush, adjusting her trousers as she walked back towards the girls.

Samantha started firing orders once again. 'Come on, ladies, keep up. We have not even covered one mile yet.' As she said this, she turned her wrist over to show off a huge watch.

'What is that?' Suzie screamed.

'It is a Garmin Forerunner 230, GPS running watch. It tells you how far you have travelled, your heart rate, your running speed and the time of your run.' Samantha felt rather proud of her gadget.

'Wow, that is amazing. Does it make tea?' Suzie laughed.

'No, it does not, I am afraid. It does however get you back to your starting point, should you get lost.' Samantha was beginning to sound like one of those annoying QVC salespersons. 'But as we have not even travelled a mile yet, there is no chance of that happening now, is there?'

Sharon pulled Samantha's arm almost out of its socket and studied the watch. 'So what speed are we at the moment?'

'Slow. Come on, we need to cover at least two miles today.'

Sharon and Suzie looked at each other, raised their eyebrows and followed behind the leader, Samantha.

They were all walking briskly along when suddenly Samantha ran off rather rapidly into a bush. Sharon and Suzie looked at each other horrified at what she was doing. They both shouted together, 'Need a wee, do we, Samantha?'

Samantha responded by waving her arms up and down and motioning for the pair of them to join her, whilst ducking behind a bush.

'Not bloody likely. I may have had six kids, but I don't need to see anyone else peeing.' Sharon chuckled.

Samantha continued to beckon the pair of them towards her and shouted, 'Shhh'.

'We'd better go. God knows what she is up to,' Suzie said in an unwilling tone.

'Come, quick – that is him.' Samantha was crouched behind a bush as if she were on surveillance, whispering so not to be overheard.

'Who?' Suzie and Sharon whispered together.

'The Sex God himself,' Samantha said. 'I cannot let him see me. He thinks I am running this lunchtime, not walking in the park with two other unfit women.'

'Thanks,' Suzie and Sharon replied in unison.

'You know what I mean.' Samantha waved for them to duck down behind the bush with her.

Suzie looked at the sheer horror on Samantha's face and asked, 'Is this really worth it? He is going to find out the truth one day – why don't you just tell him you are not a runner?'

'Because, my dear,' Samantha's tone changed to a stern one, 'he would not look at me again.'

'He's looked at you already then?' Sharon asked.

'Yes, he came into my office. I told you.' Samantha raised her eyes as she could not believe the ignorance of the two of them.

'Suzie,' Samantha said. 'Has he gone?' 'I've no idea, as I didn't see him in the first place – you just dragged us over here.'

'Great. Now what are we going to do?' Sharon muttered.

Samantha moved her head up and down rather quickly and Suzie started to laugh. 'Someone is going to call the police on us. They will think we are weirdos.'

'He's gone. Quick – let us carry on,' Samantha commanded. She looked at her watch in disgust. 'We have only covered one mile and I need to get back to the office.'

'Such a shame,' Sharon remarked. 'I was starting to enjoy that.'

'I've got to pick Chelsea up soon anyway.' Suzie admitted defeat too.

'We should turn around and head back then,' Samantha announced whilst turning and walking in the opposite direction.

The walk back to the meeting place was in silence as all three of them were struggling to breathe.

'Tuesday? Same time, same place, everyone?' Samantha asked when they saw the basketball court.

'Yes, miss.' Suzie and Sharon both laughed.

'Are you taking this training seriously enough?' Samantha asked.

'Yes, miss.' They both laughed again.

'Great, have a good weekend the both of you.' With that Samantha was gone.

'She is seriously mad.' Suzie looked concerned.

'That is solicitors for you – more nuts than a bar of fruit and nut.'

Suzie and Sharon linked arms and made their way towards the edge of the park, laughing as they walked.

'Don't forget to log your miles on *Joggingbuddy.com*.' Samantha called.

'One mile?' Suzie added.

'I suppose it all adds up eventually.' Sharon said.

Chapter Twelve

Samantha was working her way through a huge pile of ironing as she knew that even though Garth said he would not bring any washing, he would still smuggle some home and into the washing basket.

'I really must get a housemaid,' Samantha muttered to herself. 'I am not going to have time with all this marathon training.'

Her mobile phone rang; it was Garth. 'Hi sweetheart.'

Garth replied in a rather hungover tone. 'Mum.'
'You at the station?'
'I will be in about an hour, just leaving for London now.'
'No problem, sweetheart. I'll be there.' 'Cheers, Mum.'

Before Samantha had a chance to say goodbye, Garth had hung up.

When Samantha arrived at the train station, Garth was sitting huddled in a corner amongst what looked like eleven bin liners. He looked as though he was a homeless tramp, not a law student from Cambridge.

'Garth?' Samantha called. 'Are you all right?'

'Er, yeah, sorry, just feel a little sick this morning, Mum,' he muttered before giving his mum a kiss on each cheek. 'You okay, Mum?'

'Never mind me – what have you been up to?'

'Beer and lots of it. It was a mate's birthday yesterday.'

'I did not spend thousands of pounds on your education for you to piss your university years away.'

'Yeah, yeah, Mum. I am studying bloody hard, to be precise. That is why I came home this weekend, so I can work on an essay I have to write for Monday. University is full of too many distractions.'

'Well, get in the car, old bag man. What is in all these bags for goodness' sake?' Samantha opened the boot of her car and shuffled the contents of her boot around to make room for all the bags.

'I love you, Mum.'

'Washing, I take it? I said you will bring some washing even though you promised me you would not.'

'Mum, I had every intention of doing my washing before leaving, but our machine is on the blink and I knew you would not mind.

'You are too predictable, son.' Samantha laughed.

'What's for dinner then, Mum?'

'Feeding as well as washing – anyone would think you are my only son.'

'You love me.' Garth smiled.

'Good job I do. I could not afford more than one of you.'

When they arrived home and Samantha unpacked the eleven bin liners of washing, she soon realised he had brought his three housemates' washing too.

'Since when have you worn red thongs, darling?' Samantha called from the kitchen to the living room where Garth was watching the television.
'Yeah, sorry about that, Mum, but Beth, Simon and John begged me to bring their washing too. I could not see them living in soiled clothes any longer. They pinned me down and begged me to take the washing with me. Sorry.'
'Good job I love you.'
'Have you got any Crunchy Nut cornflakes?' Garth was rummaging through the cupboards looking for them anyway.
'I am making a lasagne for lunch.' 'Yeah, but that will be ages. I am hungry now. The beer is wearing off.'
'Top cupboard on the right.' Samantha pointed to the cupboard in question. 'Leave me some, though.'
'Will do.' He poured some cereal into a mixing bowl and added, almost a pint of milk returned to the living room and perched in front of the television with his mountain of cornflakes. 'These taste so good. We can only afford shop own-brand flakes.' As he spoke cornflakes were falling from his mouth.

Garth started to flick from channel to channel, like a tribesman watching flames in a fire at the end of his busy hunting day. 'So, what you been up to then, Mum, anything exciting?' he asked, not moving his stare from the television as he spoke.
'I have as a matter of fact,' Samantha answered smugly.
Garth turned suddenly and looked interested. 'Go on,' Garth invited. 'New man?'
'No, actually I am running in next year's London Marathon.' Samantha waited with bated breath for the reply.

Garth started to choke and Crunchy Nut cornflakes flew from his mouth all over the leather sofa.

'Sorry, Mum, for a minute I thought you said you are running *the* London Marathon.'

'That is right. Me and two other women are running it for the first time. We found each other on *Joggingbuddy.com*.'

'You always said that running was archaic and that is why man invented the car so we don't need to use our legs anymore.' Garth just managed to catch his breath.

'Well, I thought it was about time I started to look after myself and take up a new hobby,' Samantha replied smugly.

'What is his name?'

'Who?' Samantha appeared shocked. 'You are obviously trying to impress a man – you certainly wouldn't do this otherwise.'

'I am not out to impress anyone. I am not interested in men since your father,' Samantha answered abruptly.

'Liar, liar, pants on fire.' Garth laughed.

'Act your age, Garth.'

'Ohh, tetchy. Definitely a man. Do you know how long a marathon is? It is miles.'

'Yes, twenty-six point two miles to be precise.'

'You are mad. I bet you a hundred quid you won't do it.' Garth turned back to watch the television.

'If you had a hundred pounds, I would gladly accept it. Thank you. However, I will not be disappointed when you do not pay up.

'I need to get on with my essay after lunch. But if you fancy a run beforehand I'll gladly come with you.'

Garth gave a smug smile as he knew his mother would not rise to the offer.

'I will get changed then,' Samantha replied whilst running upstairs to her room to get changed.
'Shit.' Garth almost fell off the sofa. Samantha arrived back downstairs in three minutes flat, dressed in jogging bottoms and a sweat top.

'Wow, Mum, you are serious. I take it all back.'

'I have only just started my training, so go easy on me.'

'Just five miles then.' Garth waited for his mother's reaction.

'You're on.' Samantha gave Garth a high five as they left the house.

'You are so embarrassing, Mum, you really are.'

'Yes, but you love me,' Samantha said and kissed Garth on the cheek.

They started jogging very, very slowly. Garth was anxious to go faster, but thought he had better not take the piss out of his old mum as she was serious about running. 'So, what's the longest you have run so far?' he asked, expecting her to say a few miles at least.

'Um, this is the first time I have run. I have been walking up until now.' Samantha was struggling to have a conversation even at this early stage of the run.
'Right, how you finding it?'
'Quite tough,' Samantha said whilst studying her Garmin watch.

'Is that one of those GPS watches?' Garth's eyes almost popped out with excitement.

'Sure thing.' Samantha was almost on the verge of collapse and really struggling to hold a conversation.

'How far have we run then?'

'We...' Samantha could not get the words out and went with holding up five fingers instead.

'Five miles? We haven't gone that far.'

'No, no.' Samantha was trying to get her breath. 'Five hundred metres. We have only made it to Barnard Park.'

'You have a long way to go before you can run a marathon, Mum. How many months have you got?'

'About six months,' Samantha mouthed. 'You should be okay if you keep at it.'

'Thank you for your input.' Samantha struggled to speak whilst clutching her chest as she came to a halt.

'You okay, Mum?'

'Yes, just need to get my breath back.' She was now sitting on the grass verge.

Garth screamed in horror. 'Mum!'

'What is it? Don't scream like that – you frightened me.' She held her hand up as if to slap him.

'No, mind where you put your hands, Mum. There is a huge pile of dog shit next to you.'

'That is the least of my worries at this stage. This is harder than I thought.' Samantha was starting to get her breath back.

'Do you want to run some more, or walk for a while?'

'We will walk,' Samantha said, using Garth as a steadying post as she stood up.

They strolled along so Samantha did not exert herself too much.

'Why are you doing this, Mum, if it is such an effort?'

'Don't ask, son.'

'But I am asking and I am your son, so you will tell me.' Garth slapped his mum on the back in jest.

'I sort of told a new member of staff that I am running the London Marathon. He believed me and I now have to carry out this silly task.'

'I told you it was a man. You said it wasn't.'

'I am not doing it to impress him.' Samantha blushed ever so slightly.

'Then why are you doing it? You are truly mad.'

'After I said it, I thought why not. So here I am,' Samantha said whilst raising her arms in the air.

'Here you are walking not running.' Garth looked at her, concerned.

'You have to walk before you can run, young man. I have been reading on how to train successfully. Too much running too soon can create injuries.'

'Let's run back to the house and have that lunch,' Garth said sympathetically.

'Race you!' Samantha yelled as she sprinted off down the road.

Garth overtook her after a few moments. Samantha arrived at the front door looking like she was about to meet the grim reaper.

'Well done, Mum. You are right, though. You need to walk first and run second. I am proud of you.'

'Well, thank you, Garth, that means a lot to me.' Samantha smiled and hugged him tightly. 'I will take a shower and then prepare lunch and upload my mileage ran, to *Joggingbuddy.com*,' she announced as she collapsed onto the floor in the hallway.

Chapter Thirteen

As Suzie entered the college room where the course was taking place, she felt everyone there turn and stare at her. She felt as though she had jam in her hair or was wearing fancy-dress clothes. She found an empty table at the back of the room and sat down quietly. Another victim walked in and everyone, including her, turned and stared. Suzie soon realised that the class was looking for their tutor, not at the bait as they entered the classroom as if they were performing in a police line-up. A few moments later a fine, handsome fellow came in wearing a football-training outfit. Suzie wondered which team he played for, not realising that some people actually wore those clothes as a fashion accessory.

'Morning, everyone.' The silence was deafening.

'I said good morning, everyone. I am Stephen and I am going to be your tutor for this course,' the trainer proudly announced.

'Morning.' A few mumbled replies were expelled.

'Okay, seeing as you are all very lethargic, I suggest a little jog around the college to remove all the cobwebs.' Stephen smirked.

'You cannot be serious?' Suzie felt herself call out.

'We are in a sports science course, are we not?' Stephen put the question to Suzie.

'Yes,' Suzie replied.

'Alas, this is a hands-on course. But you are lucky. I have another task in mind.' Stephen was looking rather pleased with himself.

Another young lad entered the room and all eyes turned to him to make a point that he was, in fact, late.

'Sorry, guys,' the young lad said, whilst waving his hand in apology. 'I couldn't find the right room. I ended up walking into the language class.' Everyone in the room laughed as the young lad walked over to the only spare seat, which was next to Suzie.

'Hi.' The young lad held out his hand to Suzie. 'Brett is the name.'

'Suzie, pleased to meet you.' She blushed slightly as she took his hand.

Stephen started handing out a small card to everyone in the room. On the cards were different words: names of pets, cars, countries, foods, sports, parents and siblings.

'Now, I can see you all looking rather confused by this. Well, don't be,' Stephen announced to the class. 'This is a fun game of bingo, to get you all up from your seats and mingling with each other. The object is to speak to everyone and find out something about him or her. You can then cross the particular word off on your bingo card. The person who crosses all the items off first is the winner.'

'What do we win?' a rather cocksure guy asked.

'You win everyone's respect, as you will know about them in a little more detail.' Stephen put the cocksure guy in his place.

'Utter bollocks,' the guy muttered under his breath.

'Well, stand up. You can't possibly talk to each other sitting behind a desk.' Stephen waved his arms to instil some enthusiasm in the class.

Brett took Suzie by the hand. 'Come with me – I've done this before.'

Suzie smiled a small smile of appreciation, but not too noticeably – she didn't want Brett to get the wrong idea. They joined the group that had gathered at the front of the room and in turn they were all telling each other about what they had eaten last night. 'Curry,' a rather large man admitted.

'I hate curry,' another burly man announced. 'I had double egg and chips last night.'

Brett showed Suzie that she had to cross off 'curry' on the bingo card and then ask another question.

'For example,' he said, 'do you have any pets?'
'Erm, no I don't,' Suzie replied.
'That's not one for me then,' Brett advised. 'Which countries have you visited on holiday? Is
that right?' Suzie asked timidly.

'Certainly is, young lady, and I have been to Greece recently. Although, it was alone and I wish I had met you before now.'
Suzie went a rather bright shade of pink. 'Sorry to make you blush,' he said.

'Oh, I blush at the slightest remark, but I am flattered, I am sure.' Suzie chewed her fingers. 'I have Italy on my card, so Greece is not required. Have you ever been to Italy?'
'No, sorry, I have been to Spain, though.' 'Thanks. I need to ask someone else.' Suzie
turned to another shy-looking girl, but before she had a chance to ask her if she had ever been to Italy, she replied that she hadn't. A young ginger-haired, glasses-wearing, shy lad shouted 'Bingo!' and was

rather proud of himself. He was the kind of kid who would have been bullied at school, for sure, for being a redhead who wore glasses.

The rest of the morning was quite relaxed, generally: going through the course structure, what work was expected and how much study needed to be undertaken at home in between sessions.

Suzie felt an awful black cloud come over her when she soon realised she was way out of her depth. She had not anticipated that the room would be full of such fitness freaks. Stephen announced that this was a tough twelve-week course from nine o'clock until five o'clock. Even though they would only meet in class on a Monday, they would still be expected to study at home. They should be prepared for some serious work.
    'What have I done?' Suzie muttered to herself, without realising that Brett had heard her.
    'You'll be fine, just fine.' Brett patted her hand to show his concern.
Suzie blushed again.

Lunch was soon upon them and the friendly young Brett asked Suzie if she would join him. 'I'd love to, thanks,' Suzie replied shyly.
    'I think we should vacate the college grounds for half an hour. I feel like I am back at school.'
'Me too.' Suzie laughed.

They found a café just along the road and ordered a coffee and a sandwich each.
    'So, what brings you to this course?' Brett asked.
    'I am a single mum and want to do something for myself and to improve my child's life, I suppose,' Suzie replied whilst stirring her coffee.

'That's pretty impressive, good for you. How old is your kid?'
'She is three. Chelsea.'
'Nice name.' Brett tried not to make it too obvious that he was pleased with her choice of name.
'What about you, Brett? Why are you here?'
'I have always wanted to be a personal trainer. I want to work with the rich and famous. Madonna has a personal trainer, that goes to her house every day. That's the kind of person I want to train.'
'Wow, you have great ambition.' 'So do you, for your daughter,' Brett replied.
'Also, I am running the London Marathon in April and have not done much training, if I'm honest. Feel a bit silly really. I'm sure it's just a pipe dream. Not really a runner, more of a watcher.' Suzie rambled on like a naughty schoolgirl between chewing her fingers.
'Don't be so hard on yourself. It's great fun, such atmosphere. You'll be fine.' Brett's eyes lit up as he spoke, remembering the experience.
'I take it you've run it then?'
'Just a couple of times!' Brett smiled back.
'Is that twice or more?' Suzie enquired gently.
'Three to be exact,' Brett mumbled through his hands to hide his enthusiasm; he didn't want to make Suzie feel inadequate.
'*Three!*' Suzie almost spat her coffee out. 'Calm down! You sound surprised.' Brett signalled time out with his hands.
'I didn't realise anyone would run it more than once.'
'Why not?' Brett quizzed.
'Because it seems such a long way.'

'It is a long way, but as long as you put the mileage in beforehand, you will get on fine.'

'That's what I am worried about. Me and two other women who have never ran in our lives have just started training.' Suzie looked embarrassed. 'We met on *Joggingbuddy.com*.'

'I'll happily come along and train with you all if you like – I enjoy a challenge. That's why I want to be a personal trainer.'

'Really? That is so kind of you.' Suzie smiled.

'You are most welcome. If the others are as unconfident as you, then it will be an awesome challenge.'

'You have not met them yet. Maybe you should meet them first, before committing to such a task,' Suzie offered.

'No, I am looking forward to it already. I go to an event on a Sunday, playing war, running around the woods. It would be great strength building for you girls, if you wanna come along? Bring your pals.'

'That sounds good. I'll ask the others. Anything to help us achieve our goal is greatly received.'

They had finished their sandwiches and coffee and so headed back to the college. The afternoon was taken up with learning all the different names and locations of the muscles in the body. Suzie was extremely overwhelmed by the barrage of information, whereas Brett thrived on the subject, and she felt as though the tutor was speaking in a foreign language. She was grateful that Brett seemed keen to help her understand the subject.

Chapter Fourteen

'Have you all emptied your bowels this morning?' Suzie asked.

Samantha and Sharon let out squeals that were a cross between a laugh and a gasp.

'What an absurd question to ask at seven o'clock on a drizzly Sunday morning,' Samantha replied.

'Brett said there are no facilities at this place,' Suzie remarked.

'Where is it then?' Sharon enquired.

'The woods. They don't have public conveniences in the woods, you know.'

Samantha started to wriggle in her driving seat. 'I did not want a number two until you mentioned it, but I think maybe I do now.'

'The next services we see, we need to drink lots of coffee and push hard, girls.' Sharon laughed.

'Deal,' Samantha and Suzie replied in unison.

However, the woods were upon them after an hour's continuous driving in the rural roads of Berkshire with not a single service station in sight.

'Sorry,' Suzie remarked, 'I wish I never mentioned the poo situation now.'

'I have a shovel in the boot.' Samantha laughed.

'You are kidding, right?' Sharon looked stunned.

'Of course, I am bloody kidding.' Samantha howled. 'Do I look an environmentalist?

As they drove into the dark abyss of the woods, they had a terrible feeling that they were lost, but it soon became apparent that they were not when all of a sudden a huge army camp sprung from nowhere. The soldiers were dressed head to toe in camouflage and carried weapons that the girls did not know existed.

'My Mercedes sticks out like a sore thumb against all these battered Land Rovers and four-by-fours.' Samantha tried to make a joke of the situation.

'There is a reason they are all four-by-fours,' Sharon replied. 'We may need a tow out of this place – look at the mud.' Sharon pointed to what looked like a bog.

'How am I going to find Brett amongst this lot? They all look the same.' Suzie felt nervous and way out of her depth.

'Isn't that the point of camouflage, to all be blended into the surroundings?' Sharon couldn't resist.
'I need a drink,' Samantha commented. It
didn't take long before a fine-looking chap came over, who looked just like the host of that American show *One Man Army*, all muscles and smiles.

'Suzie, great to see you.' Brett welcomed her with a handshake and a peck on the cheek. 'Who is who then?'

'Sharon and Samantha.' Suzie pointed to each in turn.

'Lovely to meet you both.' Brett gave each of them a peck on the cheek too. 'Let me introduce you to the owners of the game site, Chris and Tony.' The three girls followed him, unsure whether to do a military march or just stroll.
'Chris,' Brett called.

Samantha gasped. There, standing in front of her, was the butchest woman she had ever seen.

'Welcome, ladies.' Chris put out her hand. 'You look worried.' Chris looked directly at Samantha.

'Sorry, I just assumed that Chris was a man's name, but then I suppose Tony is your partner?'

'Did someone call me?' Out of the tent appeared another young lady, only this one was not butch but as thin as a pencil and carried her weight in gold on her ears; there must have been over a hundred holes. If Tony were a life raft, she would certainly sink, with all those holes in her body, Samantha thought. Maybe she had more holes elsewhere that were hidden. The thought was too much to consider.

'Meet my partner, Antoinette, but we call her Tony for short.' Chris opened her hands to gesture towards her partner.

'Chris, I assume, is short for Christina?' Sharon enquired.

'Christine actually, but I have been called worse,' Chris corrected her.

'Don't stand there with your mouths open. We must get you kitted out.' Chris handed each girl, in turn, a set of camouflage trousers and shirt. Sharon's fitted just right; however, Suzie had to roll the arms and legs up several times to ensure she could move without leaving a trail of material behind her. Samantha's set looked rather figure-hugging.

'This is the best fun you will have with your clothes on.' Chris smiled.

'Really!' Samantha choked. 'You obviously don't get out very often.'

'You wait until you have played, please, before you make assumptions like that, young lady. Stand to attention when I speak to you.'

Samantha jumped to attention and looked horrified.

Chris laughed. 'Sorry, I was only joking. I didn't mean to startle you. You'll love it, I am sure.'

'Gosh, I hope none of my clients are here and see me like this.' Samantha tried her best to smarten herself up.

'I doubt they'd recognise you anyway.' Sharon laughed. 'Camouflage, remember.'

'Very funny, Sharon,' Samantha mumbled. Chris handed each of the ladies a weapon that looked like it had been to Iraq and back. They were all then called to a safety briefing about what they could and could not do.

Chris bellowed out: 'This is the safe zone and there are a number of rules we must follow. Number one. Face protection must be worn at all times, no exceptions. Number two. All magazines must be removed whilst we are here in the safe zone.'

'That's okay,' Samantha whispered to Sharon, 'I left my *Cosmopolitan* in the car.'

'Number three. If you are hit in the field, you must shout "hit" and raise your weapon and go back to the regen point.'

'I have a really sick feeling in my stomach.' Suzie sniffled.

'If you become injured at all, raise the attention of a marshal and we will attend and call an ambulance if necessary, but thankfully this has never happened before and we don't wish there to be a first casualty. 'Number four. Cheating will not be tolerated. If you feel anyone is cheating, make a marshal aware of the player. We do not want a real-world war on our hands because of arguing.'

'You think I'm going to argue with that lot?' Sharon remarked.

'Number five. Most importantly, enjoy yourself.' Chris laughed. 'Now can I ask that you all divide yourselves up into two teams, blue and red? We will make a start immediately. The first game is going to be capturing the flag. Two teams each with a flag that needs to be captured. If you are shot, you need to return to your own flag, touch the flag and you are then back in the game. Does everyone understand the rules?' Chris looked at the girls to see how unsure they were. 'Let's go then!' Chris shouted.

They all marched up the rather steep hill into the woodland area and began the game. The three of them looked totally scared out of their wits. There came a rather sudden noise of gunfire and shouting and grenades being activated.

'Cover me, Samantha. I need a wee,' Sharon whispered.

'Okay, but be quick. I think it won't be long before the enemy is upon us.'

'Ouch, they fucking hurt!' Sharon yelled. She had been hit right in the arse with a pellet. 'Who said this was a soft game?'

'Airsoft is the name of the sport. I don't think it refers to the pain of being hit,' Suzie replied. 'Are you okay?'

'No, my fucking arse hurts. Maybe I should have put some camouflage paint on my arse as well as my face.' Sharon laughed.

'I was considering that poo. I have certainly changed my mind now – it is not safe,' Samantha joked.

There was then a loud scream a few yards away, like someone was in labour. The marshals yelled to all the players to hold their fire as they had a man down. The three girls walked towards the commotion to see a grown man on the floor. His leg was facing in the wrong direction.

Suzie threw up, shortly followed by Samantha, and then not too far behind was Sharon. The guy was obviously going into shock as he was shaking rapidly and sweating. Chris was attending to the casualty, trying to reassure him that an ambulance was on its way.

Tony was busy with other players making a stretcher out of coats and tree branches. Tony seemed to be thriving on the real army action, shouting all sorts of orders and instructions.

Some half an hour passed before an air ambulance hovered above them and the paramedics arrived. Not bad, really, considering they had to fight their way through undergrowth after landing, careful not to injure themselves in the process to add to the drama. The guy was screaming louder as they approached, like he was having a baby, shouting, 'Gas and air – give me fucking gas and air and quick.'

The paramedic had to advise him that they do not carry gas and air across hard terrain. They gave him a shot of something; Suzie had to look away again because of her severe needle phobia.

The paramedics attempted to get near to the injured guy with a pair of shears and he screamed louder than ever. 'Did I hurt you?' one of the paramedics asked.

'No, these trousers cost over two hundred pounds. You are not cutting them.'

'Gosh, I thought I'd stabbed you or something.'

'Cut them and I'll stab you,' the injured man said, holding up his good leg, modelling his expensive camouflage trousers.

'I could have bought a handbag for that price, far more practical than a pair of trousers,' Samantha said.

'I'd have gone on holiday with that amount of cash.' Sharon laughed.

'More money than sense, some people,' Suzie snarled.

Finally, the injured guy was ready to be lifted to safety towards the air ambulance, but it took the effort of six men to lift him and then carry him down the hard terrain.

Everyone stood and watched in horror as the injured man was carried into the air ambulance. Some players were covering their mouths and gasping, others were taking photos on their phones whilst moaning they had no phone signal to upload the photo onto Facebook and Twitter.

'Right, that's it, fun's over for today,' Chris bellowed. 'I think out of respect we will call it a day.'

'Why? Is he going to die?' Samantha asked.

'I hope not.' Tony laughed. 'Just think people will not play to their full potential now.'

'I'm not planning on continuing anyway,' Sharon piped up.

'We are off. Thank you and all that.' Samantha shook Tony and Chris's hands in turn.

'Right, girls, let's go. This cannot be healthy.' Sharon ran as fast as she could, without falling over, back to Samantha's car.

As the girls seated themselves in the car, Brett came over to wish them well. 'I'm really sorry about that, ladies. It has never happened before. Please let me come and train with you next time to make things up to you,' Brett mumbled, like some naughty schoolboy trying to talk his way out of detention.

'That would be lovely, Brett. Thank you. I will let Suzie have a copy of our schedule and see if you can fit in at any time.' Samantha shook his hand through the open window.

'He fancies you, girl.' Sharon chuckled. Suzie turned a rather dark purple.

'Not in this lifetime.'

'He does. What do you think, Samantha?'

'Oh definitely, absolutely definitely,' Samantha said whilst checking out Brett's captivating walk as he strolled back into the war zone.

Chapter Fifteen

'Come on, Gary. The car is due to be here by eight o'clock.' Sharon tried to hurry him along.

'It'll be fine, we've got plenty of time, stop fretting. We have no kids for the night, as you keep reminding me, and we are going on national television to tell the world that you want another one and I don't. Somewhere something is wrong with that arrangement.'

'Save it for the television. The presenter will certainly give you what for in relation to the problem in hand.' Sharon poked her tongue out.

'Really, if he has any sense, he'll be on my side. Men sticking together and all that.'

'It's my show, remember. I'm the one that instigated this TV appearance, not you.'

'You don't have to remind me. I am going to be the laughing stock of all my mates, when they find out I am on national television. It is watched by sad people with no jobs, usually.'

'So all your mates watch it then!' Sharon laughed.

'Exactly. Most of them are unemployed at present and sit and watch it with their wives.'

'Great taste then, if I do say so myself. Why don't you ever watch it with me?' Sharon asked.

'Probably because I have to work all hours to feed the six kids we have already. To make matters worse you want another one and insist that I am the one in the wrong.'

The sound of the doorbell made Sharon freeze. 'Is that the car?'

'I imagine a car cannot ring a doorbell, so maybe the driver,' Gary replied.

'Okay, clever arse, the chauffer then, is that him?'

'Unless you have inherited the ability to see through wood, you had better open the door to find out.'

Sharon opened the door to a smartly dressed man in his late sixties. 'Mrs Young?'' the smartly dressed man asked.

'Erm, yes, I am.'

'My name is Arthur and I have been asked to drive you to the television studio in Manchester.'

'That's great, Arthur, we are just coming. Gary and I will be there in just two minutes.'

'Okay, madam, I will be waiting for you, in the silver car just here.' The chauffeur pointed to the Chrysler waiting outside.

Sharon let out the loudest call of Gary's name she could manage with such urgency.

'What is it?' Gary came running down the stairs and nearly toppled over in the process.

'His name is Arthur and he is taking us to Manchester in a rather posh car.'

'Oh, is that all?' Gary breathed a sigh of relief. 'I thought you'd hurt yourself.'

'"Oh, is that all" – been chauffeured before then, have we?'

'God, woman, is this what it is going to be like all the way to Manchester? Get in the *posh* car.' Gary shoved Sharon out of the front door as he spoke, before slamming it shut behind him.

Arthur was waiting by the side of the car and took their suitcase from them and placed it into the rather large boot.

'Gosh, we could fit a lot of shopping in that boot,' Sharon remarked.

'Don't even think about it.' Gary opened the car door for Sharon and waited for her to get in before he did the same. Arthur shut the door behind them.

'Look, leather interior.' Sharon stroked the leather seats as she spoke.

'Well, if we didn't have six kids, I am sure we could afford luxuries like leather interior.' Gary smirked.

'Six?' Arthur called from the front.

'Yes, that's right. Six kids, and she wants more.'

'Blimey. Have you not heard that contraception is free on the NHS these days?' Arthur laughed.

'That is why we are going onto *Morning Chat*,' Sharon informed him.

'Why, because you cannot get free contraception?'

'No, because I want another one and *he* won't let me.' She glared at Gary as she spoke.

'Do you work, Gary?' Arthur asked to break up the domestic.

'Certainly do, Arthur, have to – to support us and also to get some sanity from the madhouse of six boys.'

'Blimey, Sharon, you want another boy, do you?'

'No, that's the thing. I want a girl and he won't let us try.'

'Probably,' Gary glared at Sharon, 'because we tried for a girl the last four times.'

'You got kids, Arthur?' Gary tried to lighten the conversation.

'Certainly have, young man.'
'Go on then.'
'Go on then, what?' Arthur smiled.
'How many?'
'Nine.'

'See,' Sharon said, jumping up and down on her seat. 'There are people madder than me.'
'Catholic, you see.'
'Who is?' Gary enquired.

'The wife and I. We do not agree with contraception, even though it is free on the NHS.'

'No television licence either, I suspect. That's what we are always being accused of,' Sharon joked.

'How long is it going to be before we arrive in Manchester?' Gary asked.

'Oh, I say sometime between four and five hours, depending on traffic. Relax, folks, and take a rest. Sounds like you need one.'

Sharon and Gary both closed their eyes and for the first time in a long while, they did not have to worry about anyone else but themselves.

Arthur shook Sharon and Gary awake. 'We're here, guys,' he announced.

Gary stretched and rubbed his eyes to see Arthur smiling at him.

'You certainly had a nice sleep, the pair of you. Maybe you can go and make a baby girl after all.' Arthur gave Gary a nudge and a wink.

'What a great idea!' Sharon exclaimed. 'How long were we asleep for? It seemed like a lifetime.' Sharon stretched herself awake then jumped excitedly out of the car.

'Careful, love,' Arthur called to Sharon, but it was too late. She was flat, face first, on the pavement, screaming in pain.

'It's broken.' Sharon sobbed.

'What's broken?' Gary asked, concerned. 'Your shoe?'

'No, my bloody foot, you fool.' The screaming started to attract the attention from passers-by.

'Shush, people are looking at me as if I am a violent husband or something.' Gary started hugging Sharon to try to calm her down.

'Where's the nearest hospital, Arthur?' Sharon continued to sob, clutching her foot as if it were about to fall off.

'It's about five minutes by car. Do you want me to drop you there?'
'Ah, would you?' Sharon sobbed harder. 'Please, let us get checked in first – are you sure you can wait?' Gary asked.

'Go and get yourself sorted in your room and I'll be here waiting for you.' Arthur gave them both a reassuring pat on the shoulder. 'I'll help you with your bags. You are in no fit state to be carrying bags, young lady.' Arthur grabbed the suitcase from the car boot and they all walked into the rather plush hotel, which was aptly named 'The Grand', and took a moment to take in the ambience of the place.

'A Travelodge would have done.' Gary laughed.

'Shush. People are staring at us as if we don't belong here.' Sharon snuffled.

'We don't. We have six kids. When was the last time we stayed in a hotel?'
'Soon to be seven,' Arthur added with a wink.
Gary shuffled off to get them checked in. 'Room 101,' he said on his return. 'This way.' Gary ushered Sharon towards the lift. 'Room one, zero, one – do you know the significance of that? We are doomed.

My foot is going to be broken in more than one place I can tell!'

'Come on, we are away from home, let's not get too upset.'

'It's a little difficult with a foot that throbs like hell.' Sharon sniffled.

'Room 101 – here we are.' Gary put the key card into the lock to allow the green light on the door to illuminate, before removing the key and then opening the door.

'Wow, it's dark in here,' Sharon whispered. 'Where is the light switch?' She fumbled around on the walls for a switch.

'You are a nightmare.' Gary placed the door key into a slot on the wall and the lights came on.

'Wow, that is amazing!' Sharon had never seen anything like that before.

It was a fresh double room, with a lounge area. 'Like I said before, a Travelodge would have done.' Gary remarked, embarrassed.

'This is a suite. They've given us a suite – how kind. Shame it's only for one night, I could spend a few days here. Anyway, I need to get this foot looked at.'

They removed the key card from the slot on the wall and went back down to the lobby to meet Arthur who was waiting patiently.

The waiting time at the accident and emergency department was stated as five hours. Which in Sharon's experience of having a season ticket to accident and emergency normally meant six or seven hours. 'We are going to be here all night. We have a lovely hotel room to sleep in and we are not going to sleep in it at all,' Gary joked.

'I am sorry. I didn't intend on breaking my foot.' Sharon sobbed.

Gary gave Sharon a hug and a kiss. 'I was only joking, as long as you get seen and sorted, that's the main thing.'

'Sharon Young,' a friendly voice called out from a triage room.

Sharon shot up like a rat out of an aqueduct and the pain shot through her foot as she did so, causing her to scream, 'Yes!' Sharon explained that she had fallen out of a car. The nurse asked questions such as was the car moving, did she intend to leave the car and where was the car parked at the time.

'Can I have some pain relief, please?' Sharon was getting angry now after all the questions.

'Yes, you can. Are you allergic to anything?'

'Nothing, absolutely nothing, apart from being in pain and it's hurting.' The nurse realised that Sharon was obviously in some discomfort and gave her a cup of water and another cup with two tablets in.

'Sorry, the wait is around five hours – we are really busy at the moment.'

'That's fine, I'm used to waiting, I've got six boys.' Gary and Sharon took a seat back in the waiting room.

The nurse called after them, 'Contraception is free on the NHS.'

After almost six hours of waiting, which felt much more like ten, a rather young doctor called out her name. He didn't look old enough to be living alone, never mind practising medicine on the general public. After lots of poking, prodding and questions that Sharon had already answered with the triage nurse, the doctor gave his diagnosis.

'It looks as though you have just badly sprained it, no break or fractures.' The young doctor smiled.

'Only sprained it! I've only been here for almost six hours. If I had known that I would not have bothered.' Sharon was angry and almost disappointed.

'I would have thought you would be pleased there is no break?' The doctor was startled that this woman seemed to wish she had broken her foot.

'Thank you, doctor. Sorry, I am very tired.' Sharon redeemed herself.

'You take care and don't go falling out of any cars again.' He smiled to himself.

'I'll try not to.'

Sharon and Gary went outside and waited for a taxi to take them back to the hotel.

'Only you, really,' Gary teased.

Chapter Sixteen

Brett and Suzie were just going through a warm-up routine when Samantha appeared, all stressed out for being late.

'Gosh, Samantha, what on earth happened to you? You look like you have been abducted by aliens.' Suzie giggled.

'I almost was, Suzie, absolutely bloody almost. There is a demonstration in town – I got caught up in it on the walk here. Turned out of my road into a demonstration of thousands of kids shouting all sorts. Police thought I was involved. I said, "Do I really look like I am involved with this lot? Look at how I am dressed."'

'Did they leave you alone then?'

'No, they accused me of being obstructive. I told them, "I am a solicitor and I am on my way to meet some friends for a run, so please let me go."'

'They obviously did, then. Don't worry, we are just warming up,' Suzie reassured Samantha.

'Where's Sharon?' Samantha turned around, realising the other part of the trio was missing.

'She's on the *Morning Chat* show tomorrow. Her and Gary went up to Manchester today.' Suzie's phone made a sound to indicate a new WhatsApp message. 'Talk of the devil.' Suzie took a moment to read the message. 'Oh my gosh, she has been in accident and emergency for six hours. She thought she'd broken her foot falling out of the car, but thank God it was just a sprain.'

'It is a long story, Brett. Only a woman would understand. Six boys and longing for a girl. She's agreed to run the London Marathon to prove to her husband she would do anything for another baby.' Samantha gave her motherly advice.

'I've sent her our love and said best of luck for tomorrow. Come on, let's get a move on. We won't run the marathon standing here chatting.' Suzie ran off into the distance.

'Brett, come on, you are the trainer, let us get training.' Samantha was soon off in the distance too. Brett followed and overtook them.

After they ran to and around Regent's Park, Brett said enthusiastically, 'Ladies, this is mile four. How are we feeling?'
Both Samantha and Suzie looked as though they had run a full marathon already, not four miles.

Samantha managed to mumble a few words, which sounded along the lines of 'Can we stop?'

'Okay, ladies, walk it out. Don't stop, though – you must keep moving.'

Samantha and Suzie both stopped, bent over and exhaled, 'Thank you.'
'Squats, ladies?' Brett shouted.

'Who has?' Samantha looked around to see who was in need of the toilet.

'Squats, they are an exercise. Shall we do some now?'

'Not if they are going to hurt and they sound like they are.'
'Come on, Samantha, they aren't that bad.'

'Maybe for slim, supple little you, but not for sixteen-stone and rather rotund me.'

'This will help to shape you a little then, Samantha, as Suzie said they are not too bad.'

'Okay, you show me what I need to do.' Samantha sighed.

Brett performed the squats with such ease and grace.

'Mine will not be so elegant, I can tell you that now,' Samantha informed him.

'One, two, three, four, come on, keep up, Samantha, five, six, seven, eight and relax. How was that, Samantha?'

'Sore, very sore.'

'Good, again, one, two, three, four, five, six, seven, eight and relax.' Brett clapped to show his appreciation.

'I am not in primary school, Brett, but thank you. How's your arse feeling, Suzie?'

'Not bad. Shall we run back towards home now?'

'Good idea. Come on, ladies.' Brett was off.

'Trust Sharon to get out of this one.' Samantha sneered. She was talking to herself as Suzie was trying to catch Brett up.

'Bretttttt!' Suzie asked as if she were five years old and asking for the biscuit tin.

'Yes, what is it now?'

'I need to poo,' Suzie shouted, clutching her stomach.

'Ah, that could be difficult.' Brett started to blush.

'What am I going to do?' Suzie looked as if she needed to use the toilet within the next five seconds.

'There is a bush over there.' Samantha pointed to a dishevelled plant.

'There is no covering – how can I pull my pants down and poo over there?' Suzie was miming the actions of pulling down her pants and squatting.

'Right now, I do not see you have any other option, Suzie.' Samantha sniggered.

'It's not funny. I'm busting my guts here.' 'Can you hold out for two more minutes? There is a public toilet up ahead in the park,' Brett informed her.

'I'll run ahead.' Eager Suzie sprinted off. 'Gosh.' Brett gasped. 'Maybe she should need the toilet every run. I've never seen her run so fast.'

'When you have got to go, you have got to go.' Samantha laughed.

They finally caught up with Suzie who had obviously been to the toilet as she was waiting outside and looking rather relieved.

'Better?' Brett enquired.

'Much. I do not want to feel like that ever again. How many more miles do we need to run today?'

Brett looked at his watch. 'Well, we've run five miles so far. Have you had enough, ladies?'

'Yes!' they both shouted out in unison. 'I'll take that as a yes then. My car is just over in the car park. I'll race you both there.' Brett sprinted off as fast as Mo Farah.

'Shall we stroll, Suzie?' With that, they linked arms and strolled to the car, where Brett was waiting rather anxiously and looking rather annoyed. 'You said we had finished running – why exert ourselves even more?'

'Yes, I did, Samantha, you are right. I have some protein powder in my car. Maybe you girls could start using it, build up those muscles.' Brett removed a tin of protein powder from his car boot.

Samantha looked horrified. 'Why do we need to use this?'

Suzie took the tin from Brett and read the label. 'It's to build up muscle mass,' Suzie informed her.

'I have enough mass of my own. Look at me – sixteen stone of it. Besides, I have used it before and nothing happened.'

'Gosh, that's unusual. How often were you using it?' Brett looked flummoxed.

'I was using a scoop twice a day and rubbing onto my upper arms and nothing happened.' Samantha was very matter-of-fact.

'You rubbed it where?' Brett was struggling to contain his surprise.

'My upper arms and nothing happened.' Suzie broke down into fits of laughter.

'You're meant to drink it, not rub it on your body.' Suzie was almost choking as she spoke.

'How can you drink it? It's a powder. I thought you rubbed it on your muscles?'

'You mix it with water, you silly woman,' Brett explained. 'Look at the instructions: mix one scoop with two hundred and fifty millilitres of water, and drink. No wonder you had no results using it as if it was talcum powder.' Brett was almost on the floor with Suzie now; both were screaming with laughter.

'Okay, so I made an error. It still will not work.'

'Try it, Samantha, please, just try it. I am guaranteeing if you use it correctly you will see results, or your money back.' Brett handed Samantha the tin.

'If there is a money-back guarantee, I will try it.' Samantha grabbed the tin of powder from Brett and started to read the instructions intently.

'Did you take the last lot back to the shop you bought it from?' Suzie giggled.

'No, I was too embarrassed it did not work, remember.'

'Good job you didn't, Samantha. They may have locked you up with no sharp instruments or protein powder.' Suzie was still unable to control herself. 'Oh gosh, I need a wee now I've laughed so much.'

'I am so glad my story has been so amusing for the both of you. Do not repeat this to anyone. Now I feel a stupid arse for using it as an all-over body powder rather than a food.'

'You ladies want a lift home?' Brett asked, getting into his car and starting the engine.

'Please, if you don't mind.' Suzie jumped in. 'You coming, Samantha?'

'Please. Only if you promise not to mention protein powder in any conversation.' Samantha started towards the rear door.

'How much did you say you *whey* again?' Suzie laughed.

'Okay, children, that is quite enough. The fun is over.'

Brett drove Samantha home with a smile on his face. Samantha had a look of embarrassment. 'Don't forget to log your miles run, on *Joggingbuddy.com*, when you get home.'

Chapter Seventeen

Samantha sat on her own at the Spanish restaurant awaiting her best pal, Georgina. She thought she had been stood up for half an hour, until Georgina came bounding through the door with a crashing of designer carrier bags full of shopping.

'Sam, lovely to see you, honey, so sorry I'm late.' Georgina was the only person who called Samantha Sam and she never objected.

'I can see you have been busy.' Samantha eyed all the bags Georgina was struggling to carry. Georgina let go of them, unconcerned as they all crashed to the floor.

'Sorry, there were these divine shoes in a new boutique around on George Street. Couldn't resist them.'

'Evidently. Show me them, then.' Samantha pointed to the mass of bags. Georgina placed the bags onto the table. 'No!' Samantha screamed.
'For God's sake, girl, what?'

'Have you never heard of it being unlucky to place new shoes on a table?'
'No, I haven't, sorry.'

'That is obvious. Just take them out of the box and hand them to me.' Georgina removed the box from the bag, opened it, unwrapped the tissue paper and removed the scented pouch. She looked at the shoes longingly before handing them, rather sheepishly, to Sam. 'I am not going to steal them –

besides, they are not my size. They are gorgeous. How much?'

'Half price, two hundred pounds.' Georgina was excited at her bargain purchase.

'Bargain, I say.' Samantha rolled her eyes. 'Anyway, enough of my shoes, what have you been up to?' Georgina always loved a gossip. It was the only reason she agreed to meet, fitting Sam in with her busy retail therapy sessions.

'Nothing much, just agreed to run next year's London Marathon.'

'Fucking hell, did you say run next year's London marathon?' Georgina was making a good impression of a guppy fish, mouth open wide.

'Yes, why not? It is not that hard,' Samantha advised.

'Hard? Gosh, do you remember that hunk of a personal trainer I was shagging recently?'

'Vaguely, there has been more than one.' Samantha raised her eyes to the ceiling. Another of Georgina's pastimes was shagging anything that had a pulse, it seemed.

'Very funny.' Georgina smirked. 'I'm talking about Richard, the one with six kids. The really, really fit one, that had a tattoo on his…'

'Enough.' Samantha raised her hand and her voice to stop Georgina in her tracks. 'I remember now, yes. Anyway, what about him?'

'He ran the London Marathon once. Hated every minute of it.'

'Probably never managed a shag on the way around.'

'No, he said he was shagged at the end of it, though. Absolutely bollixed is what he said.'

'So, what are you implying then, Georgina?' Samantha was gesturing for Georgina to come forwards.

'You are unfit. In fact, you have not exercised since we were in senior school. How are you going to manage this?'

'Training, Georgina, I am training.'

'I can pass you Richard's number if you like?' She reached for her phone.

'No, no, no.' Samantha shook her head whilst raising her hand again. 'I have got two new friends and we train together. One of them is at college studying fitness and she has a colleague who is a wannabe personal trainer. He is helping us also.'

'Is he fit, this wannabe personal trainer?' Georgina's eyes widened at the thought of a new conquest.

'Yes, no, he is not your type. He is helping us girls achieve a goal. If he met you, he would never personal train again.'

'Don't think I like the sound of him.' Georgina shook her head in disapproval.

'Why? Because he will not be interested in you? You are so shallow.'

'Why the London Marathon then? There must be a reason, God only knows what it is.'

'It was an accident really.'

'An accident is falling down the stairs, or breaking a nail, not agreeing to run *the* London Marathon.'

'There is this new guy in our office—' 'Knew there was a valid reason.'

'It was not intentional. We were chatting about fitness, because he is fit, and I said that I run too and said I was running London next year. He thought I

was joking and offered me afternoon tea at the Ritz if I complete it.'
'Smitten then?'
'No, just have a point to prove now.'
'To Mr Fit, or to yourself?'
'Both really. Garth is really pleased for me.'
    'I am too, honey, if it's what you want. I'll give you a few quid in sponsorship.'
    'The cost of them shoes would be a great start to my sponsorship pot.'
'Babe, if you do it, I will give you a grand.'
Samantha's eyes lit up. 'I will definitely do it now for that amount of sponsorship.' 'Mmmm, we will see. Surely you don't have time to train?'
    'I will make time. I have already started looking for a cleaner to take some pressure off at home. Has your cleaner got any spaces for a new client?'
    'Ah, I don't think so. Jen has – she is a friend of Beth's, my cleaner. Shall I pass her your number?'
    'That would be great. Especially if Garth comes home from university with the whole halls of residents' washing again. My house looks like a laundrette at the moment.'
    'I'll text her now. I'll ask her to call you as soon as possible.' She took her phone from her back pocket and eagerly ran her fingers over the screen. 'You sound like you need all the help you can get.'
'Thank you, love. I appreciate it.'
    'Got to go, Sam. There is a dress to die for in the boutique next door – they are holding it for me for an hour.' Georgina was already halfway out the door and she waved and blew a kiss.
    'See you later, Georgina,' Samantha called, but it fell on deaf ears.

Samantha's phone rang; the call was from a number she did not recognise.

'Hello, Samantha Lloyd speaking.' She answered in her best telephone voice.

'Hi, my name is Jen, Georgina just text me and said you needed a cleaner.' Jen gave off a sense of excitement.

'Gosh, that was quick. I only left her a few moments ago.'

'Yes, she said you are a lady in need, and I am a lady that can help. Shall I pop over and see you and your house?' Jen pushed for an answer.

'Well, yes, that would be fantastic,' Samantha replied cagily.

'Excellent, how about now? Are you home?'

'No, not today. I will text you when I am going to be home, just got a lot on at the moment, which is why I need a cleaner.'

'Yeah, Georgie said you were busy.' Jen sounded eager.

'I will text you on this number the address before we meet up. I am in a public place – I do not really want to tell everyone where I live.' Hopefully, I will be in touch in the next couple of days. Is that okay?'

'Fantastic. When you are ready, just let me know, Sam.'

'Thanks, Jen, will do.' With that Jen had hung up and Samantha was not sure if Jen had heard the final part of the conversation.

Samantha thought to herself that Jen was certainly desperate to clean her house. She was a little unsure as she'd never had a cleaner before, but if Georgina had recommended her, she must be good at her job – Georgina had amazingly high expectations.

Chapter Eighteen

Suzie was driving along the high street quite well on her nineteenth driving lesson.

'How's the college course going?' Karen enquired.

Suzie smiled. 'Okay.'

'Just okay?'

'It's great, if I am honest.' Suzie smiled again.

'What's his name then?'

'Who?' Suzie sounded shocked.

'The guy that's making you smile all the time.' Karen delved deeper.

'What on earth makes you think there is a guy?'

'I've been teaching ladies to drive for more than a decade – I know when a girl is in love.'

'I'm not in love,' Suzie bit back.

'There is a guy, though, isn't there?'

'Yes, Karen, there is a guy, but he's far too out of my league,' Suzie mumbled.

'Who says he's out of your league?' Karen screeched.

'Me.'

'You silly girl. You are lovely, caring, determined and a pleasure to be in the company of. Why would any guy be out of your league?'

'Well, I wish I had your confidence, Karen.' 'Attention back to the job in hand. There is a pedestrian crossing up ahead, Suzie. Which type is it?'

'Ahh, I know.' Suzie was excited at the thought of getting it right. 'It's a penguin,' Suzie blurted out.

Karen started laughing so hard tears were streaming down her face.

'Karen, did I say something wrong?'

'Just slightly the wrong name for the crossing – it's a pelican crossing.'

'Oh, I knew it was a bird of some sort. Pelican, penguin, what's in a name? Sorry I made you laugh so much.'

'It's okay. See, you are an amazing girl. Very funny also. I forgot that on the list of traits you have. Why not go for this guy?'

'Maybe when I have achieved the London Marathon?'

'Good aim, definitely. How's the training going?'

'Little slow, but Brett, the guy, he's started to come training with us.'

'Go, girl. He must like you then, Suzie.'

'Why do you say that? You've not even seen him.'

'Why else would he come and train with you, if he didn't like you?'

'No idea, Karen, but maybe you are right. The other Mum Runners, they met him at the weekend and they both said he liked me.'

'There you go then. Get yourself trained, complete the marathon and have Brett come to your rescue at the finishing line to give you the kiss of life – you are certainly going to need it at the end.'

After a cyclist overtook Suzie, Karen asked, 'What is the speed limit on this road?'

'Why? Am I speeding?' Suzie turned red with embarrassment and eased off the gas pedal.

'No. Why are you so negative all the time?' Karen coaxed.

'Oh, you had me worried for a minute. It's thirty miles per hour, isn't it?'

'Yes, it is. I was just testing your confidence, or lack of it. You need to have more trust in yourself, the same goes with men.'

'Phew, I thought I was about to get a speeding ticket.' Suzie wiped her brow in relief.

'We have just been overtaken by a MAMIL.' Karen pointed to the cyclist who was now far in the distance.

'What is a MAMIL?'

'It's a Middle-Aged Man In Lycra. That is what happens to lots of middle-aged men. They decide to take up cycling and wear Lycra, which is not the most fetching look on a middle-aged man.'

'Oh my gosh, that is funny.'

'Why is this road thirty miles per hour? Do you have any idea?'

Suzie contemplated her answer for a few seconds. 'Because that is the speed at which pedestrians like to be hit at?'

'Wow, you weren't a transport minister in a previous life were you?' Karen laughed.

'Not that I know of. Why? Am I right?'

'No, pedestrians would rather not be hit at any speed. But legend has it that the minister in charge of transport who introduced the thirty-mile-per-hour limit had a colleague who was hit by a galloping horse and survived, so he chose thirty miles per hour as horses could only gallop just below that. Leslie Hore-Belisha was the man who introduced the thirty-mile-per-hour limit and the zebra crossings – that's why the flashing lights on the poles on top of the zebra crossings are called Belisha beacons. The first zebra crossings were just studs across the road and he almost got run over as car drivers didn't see them, so he created the flashing beacons.'

'Wow, that is interesting. How did people cross the road safely before the zebra crossing?'

'They didn't. That's why almost eight thousand people were killed in the early 1930s, which is why Belisha had to do something.'

'Maybe I should have been the minister in charge of transport. I would certainly have called it a penguin crossing, much more entertaining than a zebra.' Suzie laughed.

'Can you do me a favour, Suzie?' 'Depends what it is?'

'Read *The Highway Code* on the different types of pedestrian crossings before next lesson.'

'Deal, Karen, deal. Are any of your other pupils as much fun as me?' Suzie enquired.

'Well, it depends what you mean by fun? I have had some strange people in my car previously.'

'Oh, sounds interesting. You'll have to fill me in now.'

'Where do I start? Well, okay, one rather elderly gentleman, very sweet. On the first lesson, he told me that he was a naturist.'

'What's one of them?' Suzie looked confused.

'Someone that walks around naked.'

'Shit, what did you say?' Suzie sat open-mouthed.

'I said it is none of my concern what he does in his private life. Just as long as he keeps his clothes on during the lessons, we won't have a problem.' Karen smiled.

'Oh my gosh. What did he say?'

'I take it by the fact that I never saw him again, that he was not impressed.' Karen laughed.
'Wow, that is funny.' Suzie laughed.
'There are more.'
'Really? Worse than a naked man?' Suzie looked horrified.
'There was a young girl, gets in my car and says, "Hi, pleased to meet you. I have my clit pierced."'
'No way?'
'Yes way. Told her as long as it doesn't affect her control of the clutch pedal, it won't be a problem.'
'Are all your pupils nutty?'
'Mostly. I seem to attract the nutcase on the train, if I ever travel on one. To be fair, I try and avoid public transport for that reason.'
'I don't blame you. I can't wait until I don't have to travel by bus anymore.'
'Here you go.' Karen confirmed they were back at Suzie's flat.
'Blimey, I had no idea we had arrived back already.'
'Maybe it's a good thing you don't drive just yet if you are unsure of how to get here.' Karen smiled.
'Thanks, I will see you next week.' Suzie got out of the car and ran towards her flat.

Chapter Nineteen

Sharon and Gary were driven to a disused warehouse on a rather grotty industrial estate, which was not what Sharon was expecting, but when inside, the building was totally transformed into the *Morning Chat* TV show. Sharon gasped in amazement whilst hobbling along on her sprained foot.

The audience were waiting with bated breath for the guests to come up on stage. Sharon and Gary were taken into the dressing room where they both had make-up applied, much to Gary's disgust.

'I don't want to look like Lily Savage,' Gary yelled.

'Of course you won't, sir. It's just to reduce the shine from your face reflecting off the cameras,' the make-up artist explained.

'You saying I've got a shiny face?' Gary replied angrily.

'No, it's what happens in front of the camera. You'll be fine. I won't put much on. In fact, no one will know you have make-up on, unless, of course, you tell anyone.' The young girl laughed.

'Sharon, your turn now.' She pointed to the chair for her to sit in.

'I've never had my make-up done by anyone else before.' Sharon was grinning from ear to ear.

'You don't wear make-up for me.' Gary grunted.

'When do I get time with six boys?' Sharon argued.

'I rest my case. What are you wanting another baby for, then?'

'Gary, save it for the television show.' 'Don't worry, I will.' Gary left the room and went to find the tea and coffee machine. He needed a double shot right away. They also had more than an hour to wait until the show went live, so they had plenty of time to kill.

After almost an hour, the presenter, Archie, came to the waiting room to speak to Sharon and Gary. 'Hi, pleased to meet you both. How are you feeling?' He offered his hand.

'Nervous,' Gary mumbled whilst shaking his hand.

'It's normal,' he remarked.

'Let's get this over with.' Gary ambled on behind him.

The floor crew sat Gary in his seat and told him how to sit and not to cross his legs and to face the presenter and not the camera and to look as relaxed as possible.

'Ladies and gentlemen,' Archie began. 'This is Gary and Sharon Young. They have six boys. Sharon is desperate for another baby as she wants a baby girl. Gary here won't let her have one.'

'All I've ever wanted is a baby girl and Gary won't agree to one.' Sharon strained to put on fake tears.

'Because you said that after baby number two, and here we are after six kids and you are still saying the same thing,' Gary replied sternly.

'Surely if I want a baby girl, I shouldn't have that right taken from me, should I?'

'Six does seem like a handful to me, but if you want another one, you obviously have your reasons,' came the diplomatic reply.

'Yes, I live with seven men – all I want is a girl to dress up in pretty clothes, plait her hair and go shopping with when she's older.' Sharon had tears welling up in her eyes.

'Yes, but who has to work all hours God sends to pay for another baby? Not her. It's down to me all the time.'

'I can imagine that washing, ironing and cleaning is a full-time job where Sharon is concerned, is it not?'

'Yes, it is, which is why one more is not going to make a huge difference,' Sharon snarled.

'Are you not aware that you are being selfish, Sharon?' Archie asked.

'Selfish? How? All I want is a girl.'

'There are so many children in our country that are unwanted, sick or unparented and you are asking for another one just because you don't have a girl. Surely you should be grateful you have six healthy children and carry on with your life.'

'Well said, mate,' Gary sneered.

'Are you saying you don't love your boys, Sharon?' Archie quizzed.

'Of course I do. That's the most ridiculous comment I have ever heard.' Sharon looked angry, as if Gary had won. 'It is natural for a woman to want a baby girl.

'I would walk to the end of the earth and back to have a girl of my own.' Sharon tried talking whilst fighting back the tears.

'Sharon, what are you going to do to convince Gary that you are serious about wanting another baby?'

'Well, this is the thing. Gary said if I run the London Marathon, I can have another baby.' Sharon looked rather pleased with herself.

'Never in a million years are you going to achieve that, that's why I said it.' Gary laughed loudly.

'That's where you are wrong. I am running the London Marathon. I am in training right now, so you will have to eat your words when I have run it.'

'That is amazing, Sharon, if you are going to run the marathon.' The presenter looked surprised. 'I think that is commitment from Sharon that she is serious, don't you think, Gary?'

'Yes, I do, but I cannot see her running for a bus, let alone twenty-six miles.'
'Point two,' Sharon butted in.

'Well, Gary, I think if Sharon is going to run the length of a marathon for another baby, you have to admire her commitment.'

The presenter changed tack. 'Gary,' he asked, 'what is so worrying for you that you don't want to give in to Sharon's plea?'

'Many reasons. We are too old to be up all night feeding and changing nappies. Our kids now are at school and have commitments such as homework and football training – it would be impossible to run the house and look after a young baby.'

'You're out at work all day,' Sharon retaliated.

'Yes, to pay for the six boys we have already.' Gary was getting angrier and angrier.

'Exactly, B-O-Y-S.' Sharon spelt it out. 'All I want is a girl.'

'Okay, guys, let's not turn this into a domestic argument. If Sharon runs the marathon, Gary, would you be prepared to give Sharon one last attempt at conceiving a girl?' Archie asked kindly.
'Do I have a choice?' Gary grunted.
'Divorce?' Sharon suggested humorously.
'I'm not going to divorce you over a silly disagreement,' Gary remarked. 'I'll stick to my word. If you run the London Marathon, I will let you have another baby – just one more try, though,' Gary announced firmly, whilst holding up his hand.

Sharon jumped from her seat and kissed Gary so hard. 'I won't let you down, I promise, and I love you.' She then screamed out in pain as she had forgotten she had sprained her foot the night before. 'Sorry, I sprained my foot last night.' Sharon held up her bandaged foot.

'Well, come back after the marathon with your medal and we will discuss the updated situation,' the presenter informed them. 'I do hope the foot heals for you.' The audience clapped loudly and cheered the couple as they left the stage. They were escorted into the green room and given more coffee and cake while they watched the rest of the programme on the television in there.

Once the programme was finished, Archie came out. 'Was that okay?'
'Suppose.' Gary grunted.
'Excellent, thanks.' Sharon shook his hand.

'My producers want to know if they can follow you through your training and the race day. Would you be happy to do that?'

'Oh my gosh, how exciting, wait until I tell the other two.' Sharon was almost crying tears of happiness.

'There are more of you?'

'Yes, two others. All three of us have never run in our lives and we are training together. We call ourselves the Mum Runners. We met on *Joggingbuddy.com.*'

'Oh my, this is amazing. I'll get the producer to call you – sounds like we have a great programme to be made out of this.'

'Oh dear,' Gary muttered and walked off in the direction of the coffee machine.

Sharon gave Archie a kiss on the cheek and hobbled off to find Gary, whilst sending a WhatsApp message to the Mum Runners to tell them of the good news.

Chapter Twenty

Brett was eagerly waiting on the side of the Finsbury Park athletics running track for the ladies to arrive. First was Samantha, organised as ever.
'Hi Brett,' Samantha called out.
'Hi, Samantha. You are the first to arrive.' 'I always am – blame it on being a solicitor. You need to be organised in that game.'
'I can only imagine, Samantha.'
'Ah, here they are.' Samantha waved to Suzie and Sharon as they ambled along; Sharon was struggling with her sprained ankle.
'Hi,' they both said in unison, looking at Brett and Samantha in turn.
'Sorry I am late,' Suzie announced shyly.
'Yes, sorry, it was my fault. This ankle is really hurting me.' Sharon lifted her foot up to display the bandage.
'Ladies, don't panic. We have the track for an hour, so plenty of time.' Brett glanced at his watch. 'Sharon, I only want you to do what you can. We don't want any serious injuries. We need to warm up first, just some gentle movements to warm the muscles before we begin our training. Follow me and my movements, please, ladies.' Brett started to lift his legs up and down to walk on the spot. 'Higher knees. Come on, you lot – you'll end up with an injury if you don't warm up properly.'

'Knackered already and we have not even started,' Samantha panted after a few minutes.

Brett blew his whistle. 'We are going to start with the hundred metres sprint. If you all can line up and I'll blow the whistle when I want you to start.' The ladies ambled up to the start line. 'Quicker, ladies, please, quicker.' The ladies quickened their pace, but not by much. 'On my whistle, I want you to sprint to the cone that I have placed down the track. On your marks, get set, go.' Brett blew his whistle with some aggression.

Samantha was ahead, but only for a moment. Sharon overtook her and she was in the lead, until the last second when Suzie steamed past her and beat them both to the finish line.

'Yes!' Suzie jumped in the air, punching her fist as if she had just broken a new world record. 'That was amazing.'

'Glad you enjoyed it. Samantha, Sharon, are you both okay?' Brett looked at each of them in turn; they each turned to display their red faces. 'Only another nine times of that.'

'Nine!' Samantha squawked. 'Resistance building. It's only on a flat surface – you wait until we start doing this up hills.'

'Shit,' Sharon muttered. 'Childbirth is a piece of piss in comparison to this.'

'Yes, darling, but you have got to go through this first, before your husband will even entertain the idea of you being pregnant *again*,' Samantha said.

'Don't remind me. Which is why I am doing this, as I will not be beaten by any man. I will run this bloody marathon if it kills me, even with this bloody ankle, and take whatever it takes to complete it.' Sharon gave a high five to Suzie, Samantha and Brett in turn.

'Excellent. Ladies, can we get back to the start line, please?' Brett asked, whilst pointing to the start line and ushering them along.

Nine more hundred-metre sprints required more endurance than they had both imagined. Sharon only managed three sprints before her ankle gave up. She sat on the grass and watched the other two ladies struggle.

'I could murder a curry,; Samantha gasped.

'A curry will murder all your training you have just completed,' Brett explained, with a little disappointment in his voice.

'I am only saying I could murder a curry. I am not going to eat one, Brett.'
'Thank God for that.'

'I will stop at the chip shop instead,' Samantha muttered as she ran away from Brett so he could not inflict pain on her. Holding up her hand to surrender, she said, 'I am joking, Brett, honestly. Thank you for all your help this evening – you have been amazing. Why you would want to train a bunch of very unfit women to run a marathon, God only knows.'

'It is a challenge and what is life without challenges?' Brett proclaimed.

'Thanks, Brett,' Sharon said whilst giving him another high five. 'I had better get back to my madhouse and put some ice on this ankle. I've also got six-packed lunches to make and school uniform to iron before bed.'

'Yeah, thanks, Brett.' Suzie gave a timid look at Brett. 'I'd better go and pick Chelsea up from my mate's house. I'll see you at college Monday.'

'You're all very welcome and well done, ladies, very well done. I'll see you on Sunday for a run.'
'Guys' Sharon announced sheepishly.
'Yes,' they all answered rather

concurringly.

'So, are you ladies excited about *Morning Chat* following our training progress and the race day itself?' Sharon asked.

'Mind?' Samantha shouted. 'What about Mr Sex God? When was this agreed?'
'I sent a WhatsApp after the show.'

'Oh, that bloody what's-it-thing. I must get on board with this. What other important news have I missed?' Samantha muttered. 'I can log my runs on *Joggingbuddy.com* with ease, but other technology, I am not so good at.

'Never mind Sex God.' Suzie brushed off her comment. 'We are going to be famous. Of course, I don't mind. When are they coming?'

'Sunday,' Sharon informed them whilst looking at the ground.

'Awesome.' Brett jumped up and down.
'Bang
goes my afternoon tea at the Ritz then,' Samantha whined. 'And my credibility.'

'Stop whinging, woman. We are going to be on TV.' Suzie could hardly contain her excitement.

Chapter Twenty-One

Samantha was in the middle of writing to Mr Smith's wife's solicitor, thinking what a waste of time and money this was, asking for a bread maker back that cost twenty pounds and two bags of flour that probably cost little over a pound each. This letter was costing Mr Smith a staggering two hundred and fifty pounds, so why would he not just replace the bread maker and flour, open brackets, plain and self-raising, close brackets, and save himself her fees? She did, of course, point this out to Mr Smith at their last meeting, that her writing this letter was not commercially viable, but he was not willing to budge on the matter. Samantha was deep in concentration, which was rudely interrupted by her secretary calling her. 'Yes, Liz?'

'I've got the cleaning company on the phone for you.'

'Oh, okay, put them through.' Samantha was rather confused; why would Jen be calling her at work? She could not even remember giving Jen her office number.

A northern accent asked, 'Hi is that Mrs Lloyd?'

'It is *Ms* Lloyd, yes.'

'We here at Bogs and Brushes understand that divorce is on the increase,' the northern lady commented. Samantha very quickly twigged that this was indeed a sales call.

'How very observant of you,' Samantha replied with a hint of sarcasm in her voice.

'I am calling today as we have a great deal on a bulk purchase of tissues.' The line went silent. 'Mrs Lloyd?'

'Yes, I am here, what did you say?'

'We have a great deal on a bulk purchase of tissues.'

'I thought that is what you said. What is the significance between divorce rates on the rise and me purchasing a bulk load of tissues?'

'I am sure you have many clients in your office in tears – just thought it would be more cost-effective for you to purchase them in bulk?'

'How much bulk are you suggesting I purchase, Mrs Bog and Brushes?'

'Elizabeth, please call me Elizabeth. Only a hundred.' Elizabeth began her best-negotiating attempt.

'Only a hundred?' Samantha was beginning to question this lady's ethics. 'Are you out on day release?'

'Cases, one hundred cases.' Elizabeth sounded excited.

'You are insane – where would I keep a pallet load of tissues? My office has barely room to swing a cat.' Samantha was raising her voice.

'Most solicitors charge their clients for the use of their tissues, so it is no cost to you, only profit.'

'I will ask them to bring their own hankies, thanks. I cannot add to their bill a list of charges stating "tissues a pound a sniff", that is absurd.'

'Can I not interest you in one case?' Elizabeth was getting rather persistent.

'No, sorry, I do not want to purchase any tissues. If I do need any, I will pop down to Costco and purchase a few boxes. I will have just enough room to store them in my desk drawer, rather than your unfathomable suggestion of hiring a storage locker to keep them in,' Samantha snapped. 'The cost of storage will obviously outweigh the cost of your cheap tissues.'

'We are cheaper than Costco.' Elizabeth was trying her hardest.

'You do not say!' Samantha screamed into the handset and slammed it on the receiver.
Liz knocked cagily and entered Samantha's office. 'You okay, Samantha?'

'Nothing a large bar of fruit and nut cannot rectify, thank you, Liz. If anyone asks, I have popped out for a moment.' Samantha got up from her chair and immediately fell back down.

'Gosh, Samantha, are you okay?' Liz sounded concerned.

'Yes, thank you, Liz, just overdid training last night. I will be fine once I get moving. Do you want anything from the shops, Liz? Can I tempt you with some chocolate?'

'Oh, go on then, you know my usual, thanks.'

Samantha walked down the corridor as if she had just shit herself and attempted the painful descent of the stairs as if she were recovering from a hip replacement operation. The deranged woman on the phone call with the tissue proposal reminded her she had not yet met Jen. She sent Jen a text, giving her, the home address and telling her she would meet her at nine o'clock Sunday morning, if that was okay. Hopefully, she thought to herself, she was normal and not a raving lunatic like everyone else she seemed to have come into contact with that day.

On her return to the office, she noticed Greg standing at the top of the stairs and he had obviously been watching her for some time, as she struggled to climb the steep stairs.

'Wow, are you in pain?' Greg asked.

'Yes, I am. I did some sprinting on a racetrack last night.' Samantha grunted as she climbed the last stair and used Greg to steady herself.

'Fruit and nut, my favourite.' Greg licked his lips.

'Caught red-handed. That does not look good, sorry.' Samantha blushed.

'Oh, Samantha, don't beat yourself up. We all need a little guilty pleasure occasionally.' Greg patted his six-pack stomach. 'Although, looking at the state of you it is not looking promising for your trip to the Ritz for afternoon tea.' Greg smiled.

Samantha winced from the pain. 'Mr Horsforth, I shall go to the ball. I am extremely determined, more than anything else I have ever endured in my life.'

'Glad to hear it.'

'Anyway, enough about me, how are you today?'

Greg shook his tie. 'I wish I could say okay, but it never is in the building game.'

'Another building changing designs part way through a project with a nod from the owner?' Samantha enquired.

'No, it is an employee this time.'

'Oh, what have they done?'

'There was a fire on a building site and the employee just stood there and watched several buildings burn to the ground.' Greg shook his head in disapproval.

'Wow, that is awful. Did the employee not have a mobile phone on him?' Samantha asked.

'Yes, he did. He said he didn't know the correct number to call for help. He claimed he was never given instructions on what to do in the event of a fire in his joining instructions.' Greg twirled his fingers around the side of his head to signify stupidity.

'Well, best of luck with that one is all I can say. I thought I had a hard time fighting for a bread maker and some flour, open brackets, self-raising and plain, close brackets.' She demonstrated opening and closing of brackets with her spare hand.

'Well, I would love to hear about this bread maker, but I am sorry, I have a fight on my hands.'

'Not a problem. I must go and get some coffee to go with my chocolate. I will see you later and best of luck.' Samantha entered her office, slammed the door shut and rummaged through her small cupboard for her fan as she needed to cool down; the conversation with Greg had given her a hot flush.

Chapter Twenty-Two

Sharon was relaxing with a well-earned cup of tea after the usual morning chaos was over and the kids were safely in school. She was planning a walk into town. She didn't really need anything – she just fancied a walk to help build her stamina, as she was determined not to be beaten by this gruelling training. She hadn't mentioned to Gary how tough things were; she didn't want to give him the satisfaction of knowing she was struggling with it, as he would not leave her alone. Her thoughts were interrupted by her phoning ringing. She answered it.

'Sharon, how are you? It's Tarquin.' The chirpy voice trilled down the phone as if he were calling from the other side of the Atlantic, not the other side of the country. 'Did you enjoy the show?' Tarquin went on to ask.

'Yes, great thanks, and yes, it was fantastic.' Sharon was trying to match Tarquin's enthusiasm.

'I've been asked to call and arrange for a camera team to follow you on your training.

'When is your next training session?'

'Oh shit. Sorry, I didn't mean to swear. We are training Sunday at ten o'clock, is that okay?'

'Perfect, just send me an email with the address and everyone's contact numbers and a camera team will meet you there. Looking forward to seeing how you get on.' His enthusiasm was almost wearing her out.

'Yes, will do, thanks.' Before she'd finished her sentence, he'd hung up.
Sharon immediately composed a WhatsApp message to the other girls to tell them that a camera crew was going to be with them for Sunday morning's training. 'They'll love it I am sure,' she muttered reassuringly to herself as she pressed send.

The postman arrived with a mountain of post and she sat and opened it all whilst finishing her tea. Her BT phone bill was astonishingly high. One of the friends and family numbers was her local GP surgery. Did she really call them that many times last month? It showed how long she had to wait on hold before she got a reply from the growling receptionist if she spent an average of forty-two minutes per call to the surgery. 'Too depressing. Surely a girl would not cause so much drama in her life,' she muttered to herself again, whilst gathering her coat and making her way out of the door, heading towards the town centre.

The wind whipped around her ears and she sure felt as though she was starting to suffer from frostbite. The wind chill factor made it feel as though it was minus twenty. Trying to run in this weather would be interesting. With the film crew attending on Sunday for the first time, she had better not show herself up; Gary would almost certainly divorce her. Rain started driving against her skin. She made a quick dash into the library, where the new-age librarian was busy putting some books away on the shelf nearest to the door.
'Hi, how are you today?' She smiled as if she were a long-lost friend.
'Cold and wet.' Sharon shivered.
'How's the training going?' the librarian quizzed.

'Good, thanks.' The librarian's jaw almost fell to the floor. 'I've got a film crew following my progress actually,' Sharon retaliated smugly. It was evident this woman did not expect she would run or indeed finish the Marathon.

'That's amazing,' she said, through gritted teeth and showing a resentful expression. 'You must keep us posted. We like to recognise local achievements.' She busied herself putting books away on the shelf.

'Really?' Sharon was sure this woman was winding her up. 'I must get on, sorry. I'll see you soon, no doubt.' Sharon made a quick march towards the computers to send the email to Tarquin with the details he required. She urged him, in her email, not to reply via email and only via phone, due to her not having an internet connection at home. On looking around the library whilst the email was sending, she could see the new-age woman whispering to her colleague and sensed she was talking about her. Sharon got up with her head held high and made a beeline for the door back into the heavy rain and wind. It was a kinder option than being made fun of by a woman who dressed as a 1960s throwback.

As she passed the baby shop, she couldn't contain herself and peeked through the window to idealise the new baby clothes, all pretty and pink. 'Soon, very soon,' she muttered under her breath so not to be noticed by any passers-by. 'I will get my girl.' Smiling, she walked off looking like she had just won first prize on the National Lottery.

Chapter Twenty-Three

Samantha drove back from the shops and onto her driveway, where she noticed a woman sitting on her step. 'You must be Jen?' Samantha called from the car as she was shutting the door and pressing the central locking button.

'Yes, I am, and you must be Sam. Pleased to meet you.' Jen was holding out her immaculately manicured nails.

'Samantha, please call me Samantha. Only my mother called me Sam and it drives me insane when anyone does. Sorry, nothing personal,' Samantha apologised.

'No offence taken, honest.' Jen was unruffled by the comment. 'Nice gaff, Samantha. You must have a pretty decent job to afford a place like this – it is absolutely gorgeous. Is it four floors? How much did this place set you back? A small fortune, I should imagine. George said you were a woman in need. I can see why. Is it just you at home, or is there a man around?' Jen gabbled on, ten to the dozen.

Samantha finally managed to answer a question without being interrupted. 'No, just me, with a son at university,' Samantha responded, with an air of caution. Was this woman always this nosey with someone she had just met, or did she have an alternative agenda? She had been a solicitor for too many years to even contemplate trusting someone during the first meeting.

'Oh, I am so jel. This is amazing.' Jen took in the house with a large breath.

Samantha brushed her fingers frantically through her hair. 'I have not, have I?' she quizzed Jen.

'Haven't what?' Jen looked puzzled.

'You said I had gel?'

Jen laughed hysterically. 'No, I said, "I am so jel." It's short for jealous – I am so jealous of this place. Oh, you can tell you don't have small children.' Jen gave Samantha a poke in the ribs. 'I can see we are going to hit it off.' Jen slapped Samantha on the back, a little too hard for Samantha's liking.

Through gritted teeth Samantha snarled, 'Thankfully, I will be out while you are cleaning,' whilst opening the front door and disarming the alarm. 'Come in, please. Do you want to walk around and take a look at each room to see the size of the job before you agree to take it on?' Samantha immediately regretted saying this as Jen looked like a kid in a sweet shop. She was obviously going to be nosey rather than practical in her viewing.

'Love to, thanks.' Jen's eyes were on the verge of bulging out of their sockets.

'Great, I will stick the kettle on. Just come through to the kitchen when you are finished.' Samantha wasted no more time and marched towards the kitchen with haste to escape this *TOWIE*-type star who was now making her way around her house, nosing in every drawer and cupboard. From the kitchen, over the sound of the kettle boiling, she could hear Jen squealing with delight after she had entered every room and climbed every floor. What had Georgina sent her?

'Sam.' Samantha looked up from the kettle. 'Oh, sorry, I mean Samantha. This house is delightful. You keep it nice. When do you want me to start? I have a job on Monday and probably the next day. I can start Wednesday if you like? What time would you like me to be here? Will you be home or will you leave a spare key somewhere? Or perhaps you can have one cut?' Jen didn't seem to come up for air in between questions.

'That will be lovely. Wednesday it is. I have a spare key and I need to show you how to disarm and activate the alarm.' Samantha spoke whilst filling the teapot, so she did not have to make eye contact with Jen. 'I will be at work. I do work long hours, which is why I am "in need" as you so put it.' Her sarcastic tone went straight over Jen's head.

'What do you do then, *Samantha*?' Jen exaggerated the word, Samantha, so not to get it wrong again.

'Just a boring solicitor, been one for over twenty years. Nothing exciting.'

'Are you kidding me?' Jen sla[[ed Samantha on the back as she spoke, almost knocking her over. 'That's amazing.'

'Is it?' Samantha was feeling really uncomfortable with this conversation already.

'Yeah, you must earn a fortune? Well, you obviously do, judging by this house. I had to have a solicitor once, almost had to remortgage my house to pay the fees. Probably so the stuck-up solicitor could buy another house.' Jen then stopped in her tracks. 'Sorry, that wasn't very kind was it?'

'Not really, but I know what you mean. But if you realised what we had to go through on a daily basis, you would understand why our fees are so high.' Samantha raised her eyes and looked out towards the birds feeding on stale bread in the garden.

'Oh, do tell, I love a bit of a gossip.' Jen was eagerly waiting like a dog waiting for his stick to be thrown.

'You do not say? I am afraid I am not able to comment on my clients' cases. Confidentiality.' She hoped to close this conversation down straight away. Samantha placed a cup of tea in front of Jen, which she started drinking, despite the temperature.

'Oh, I see, like the SAS? I knew someone in the SAS once. They used to go to work every morning in a suit and commute to London. Even his wife didn't know he was in the SAS – she thought he was in IT.' Jen started laughing hysterically. 'What a basis for marriage that is, not even knowing what your husband is up to on a daily basis. Grounds for divorce, I say. What area of expertise are you in, Samantha?'

'Divorce.' Samantha tried to dismiss the comment.

'No way, fancy that, there I am going on about divorce and you are a divorce lawyer. I'd love to be a lawyer. Must be so interesting.' Jen was gazing into thin air as if she was daydreaming of a big house, smart suit and gossip.

'Are you able to start Wednesday, then?' Samantha tried to turn the conversation back to a more constructive one. 'What is your hourly charge and how long do you think it will take you to clean?'

'Drop in the ocean to your hourly rate, I should imagine?'

'How much?' Samantha was getting slightly annoyed now.

'Call it a tenner.'

'For the whole house?' Samantha was startled.

'No, silly. A tenner an hour and it'll take me about five hours, so forty quid then.' Jen was starting to count her fingers. 'Sorry, silly me, fifty quid. Yeah, fifty quid. If you can just leave the money in the kitchen, that'll be lovely. Any ironing you need doing? I love ironing, so therapeutic.'

'That is great. I will leave the money out each week and if there is any ironing it will be in the utility room. I really am sorry I must be rude – I need to get showered and changed.' Samantha opened the kitchen door and showed Jen the front door once again, handing her the spare key and explaining how to work the alarm.

'That's fine, sorry, I didn't mean to take up too much of your time. Just once I get talking, I don't stop.'

'Thank you, Jen.' Samantha spoke whilst pushing Jen out of the door. 'If you have any problems whilst you are cleaning, please give me a call at work. Here is my card.' She shoved a business card into Jen's hands and closed the door, before realising that it was probably the worst thing she had ever said to someone, to ring her at work. At least she wouldn't have to see her very much, being as Jen would be here whilst she was at the office. Samantha's mobile rang. It was Jen. 'Hi Jen, did you forget something?'

'Sure did. Can you get me some rubber gloves? Don't want to break a nail. Thanks again. Bye and see you soon.'

Samantha shook her head as she headed upstairs to shower and change into her running clothes. For the first time she was actually looking forward to running, with the hope it would de-stress her after meeting such a melodramatic woman.

Chapter Twenty-Four

There in the distance, across the field, Samantha could see a cameraman, sound engineer and someone else without any equipment. 'Wow.' She let out a little screech. 'The film crew are here already. They are keen.' As usual, Brett was there already, star-jumping and squatting, which she had come to learn was the safest way to warm the body up. 'Hi Brett,' Samantha called from behind a tree before walking towards the film crew. She smiled and introduced herself, and then went to stand next to Brett.

'Hi, you okay?' he asked. 'You look like you have seen a ghost.'

'You have no idea, young Brett, but I won't bore you with my troubles. Thank you for asking. The others not here yet?'

Samantha studied her watch to realise that she was already five minutes late.

'No, why break a habit of a lifetime.' Brett smiled. 'It must be hard training and running a house and family, don't you think?'

'Yes, it must be. I should not be so rude. I have no children at home and just got myself a cleaner, so I suppose I am lucky in that respect.'
'A cleaner? Wow, that's great.'

'You have not met her.' Samantha spoke through gritted teeth.

'You can put extra running hours in then.' Brett nudged Samantha as he spoke. Samantha just smiled warmly.

'In another life, maybe. I have enough trouble doing what we are doing already. Thank you anyway for the offer.' Samantha was really unsure if he was joking or not.

'Hi guys.' A loud stressed call came from the other side of the field. Suzie was running over towards Brett and Samantha.

'Sorry, babysitter was running late.' Suzie was almost out of breath from the short jog. 'Hi, you must be the poor TV crew that have the job of following us three extremely unfit women to the London Marathon?' Suzie enquired.

'Yes, I am George, in charge of the camera.' He pointed to the camera. 'This is Linda, in charge of sound, and that is Elvis the director.' He pointed to each in turn as Suzie shook their hands.

'Elvis, aye? Can't guess what your parents were into.'

'Not many people can guess.' Elvis stroked his hair.

'I am just as bad. My daughter is called Chelsea.'

'Brett and I were just talking, saying how hard it must be for you and Sharon with the children and house to run. There is one benefit to having a son at university. At least I do not have to look after him on a day-to-day basis.' Samantha's mobile gave off a new-text-message-received tone. 'I speak too soon – that has to be Garth. No one else would send me a text apart from you guys and you are here.' -The message was from Garth.

Mum, can you send me some money please. A grand should cover it, need some books. Love you. XXXX

'This is what you have to look forward to, Suzie, messages asking for money. He knows I won't refuse.' Samantha stood stroking the phone as if Garth were actually there and not just the picture on her screen saver. 'Here comes Sharon. Gosh, she looks stressed. Should call ourselves the Mum Stressors, not Mum Runners.' Samantha called out to Sharon as she strolled over to the others. She, too, introduced herself to the film crew.

'Defo stressed. Men – why do I have to live with so many of them?' Sharon was about to explode with rage. 'All I want is a girl.'

'Or a nanny.' Samantha smirked, whilst starting her warming up routine and joining in with Brett and the squat jumps.

'You can borrow Chelsea anytime you wish. She could do with an auntie and you make excellent auntie material.' Suzie was now starting to join in with the squatting.

'I'd love to, anytime you need a babysitter. Only you may struggle to get her back off me, you do realise that, don't you?' Sharon winked at Suzie.

'Ladies.' Brett cleared his throat. 'We need to get running now, please. I would suggest we are out for around two hours today.'

A trio of grumbles came from the girls. 'Do you want to run the London Marathon or not?' Brett was very insistent.

Suzie put her arm around Brett's shoulder. 'Of course we do. we are just busy with our lives and this is a struggle. With your determination and motivation, we will do it, won't we, girls?' She turned to give a high five to Samantha and Sharon in turn.

'Girl power!' they all shouted in unison. 'This is great footage.' Elvis beamed.

'Great, let's begin, now.' Brett ran on ahead, leaving the girls to pick up their pace slowly. The film crew did their best to keep up with the runners. They were running on ahead to get forward shots and then lagging behind to get shots of them from behind and also running past.

After about thirty minutes, Sharon shouted, 'Stop, I need a wee.'

Suzie and Samantha didn't need to be asked twice to take a breather.

'I've got a Shewee.'

A flabbergasted Samantha looked in astonishment at this tube contraption Sharon was holding. 'A she-what?'

'Shewee. It allows you to wee whilst standing up. No more pricking my arse on a bush.' She turned the contraption in all directions as she spoke. 'Don't get that on camera, please.' Sharon looked straight into the camera as she spoke.

'You could have done with that at that Airsoft game – could've prevented you from being shot in the arse.' Suzie slapped Sharon on the bottom as she spoke.

'Sounds like we missed a good weekend, Linda.' George looked rather bemused at what Airsoft was or why indeed Sharon was shot in the behind.

'Well, I don't really want a QVC demonstration,' Brett urged. 'Just go and do your wee-wees and catch us up when you've finished.' Brett was increasing his stride once again.

'He's demanding, isn't he?' Samantha enquired of Suzie as if she would know.

'He is determined to make a good personal trainer and wants to train celebrities in their homes. I am pleased he has a goal. It has to certainly be an easier occupation than training us three to run the London Marathon.' Sharon came running up at speed behind Samantha and Suzie with the camera crew following.

'Works wonders – no mess and no prickly thistles to sit on. You should get one.'

Samantha looked horrified. 'I'm okay, thank you, Sharon. I have only had one child, so my bladder is nowhere near as sensitive as yours. I am pleased for you, that you have found such an amazing contraption.'

Samantha spoke whilst moving her eyes up and down the Shewee. 'Did you get it on camera, her using that thing?' Samantha asked, looking repulsed.

'No, it's daytime viewing, you know.' George spoke unemotionally.

After almost two hours of running, they arrived at Kilburn Park Station. 'Well done, ladies, that was amazing. I am so proud of you all.' Brett spoke with ease as if he'd just been for a casual stroll in the park, not a six-mile run. 'I think we should get a train from here. We can change at Oxford Circus and get the Tube back to Angel and Islington.'

All three of the girls were panting and having trouble making any sound from their mouths. They each held their hand up whilst bending over and breathing heavily.

The film crew were unaffected by the morning's events. They all climbed the stairs onto the platform and waited for a train to take them back towards home.

Everyone sat in silence on the train, lost in their own thoughts, when out of nowhere Brett asked, 'Fancy dinner tonight, Suzie?'

Suzie blushed and didn't know where to put her eyes, as the question took her by such surprise. The film crew smiled subtly to each other.

'That's really kind of you, Brett, but I don't have a babysitter.'

'I'll have her.' Sharon jumped in before she was even asked.

Suzie glared at Sharon as if that was the wrong thing to say at that moment.

'I'll have her overnight. You don't have to worry about what time you get back.' Sharon gave Suzie a wink when Brett wasn't looking.

'Perfect. Thanks, Sharon.' Brett kissed Sharon on both cheeks.

'Yeah, thanks, Sharon.' Suzie didn't sound as excited.

'I'll pick you up from Sharon's this evening at about eight o'clock then.' Brett was animated. 'Oxford Circus, we need to change here.' He jumped up.

They returned to silence for the rest of the journey back to Angel and Islington and Suzie occasionally gave Brett a casual smile.

'Here we are,' Brett announced. 'I have to rush. I will meet you at Sharon's house.' Brett turned and walked away.

Suzie was left open-mouthed. 'I am shocked. What does Brett want with me?' Suzie whispered to Sharon.

'Everything,' Sharon whispered back.

'I am a single mum with no prospects. I can't drive, run or anything.' Suzie sobbed.

'You will get there, young lady.' Samantha gave Suzie a reassuring hug. 'We are all in this together, remember?'

'He's invited you out to dinner. Does that not tell you something?' Sharon quizzed.

'I suppose. Just feeling rather overwhelmed with everything – college, Chelsea and this training.' Suzie searched for a smile.

'Girl power.' All three girls gave a high five in turn. The film crew confirmed the day and time of the next training session and walked back towards their cars.

'That's another five miles to add to the *Joggingbuddy.com* log.' Samantha was chuffed.

Chapter Twenty-Five

Suzie knocked loudly on Sharon's door so it could be heard over the roar from inside the house. Chelsea looked worried. 'How many boys does she have, Mummy?'

'Six, darling, and they are looking forward to playing with you.' Suzie tried to reassure her.

Chelsea screwed her face up to show her disgust at there being no girls. 'Boys. Yuck.'

The door flew open and Sharon had a young boy dressed only in underpants and wellington boots behind her. 'Hi Suzie, welcome to the jungle, please come in.' Sharon waved her arm in the direction of the hallway and bent down to Chelsea's eye level. 'You must be Chelsea. Your mummy said you were a pretty girl and she was not lying. Do come in. This is Dennis.' Sharon pointed to Dennis. 'Come and meet the others.'

Dennis shoved the toy dinosaur he was holding into Chelsea's face. 'Grrrrr.'

Suzie held Chelsea's hand and walked into the hallway.

'Michael and Roger are upstairs playing on their Xbox or whatever it is. Daniel and John are attempting to complete some complex math homework and I have no idea where David is. He wants to be a magician when he grows up. He doesn't need much practice, as I can never find him when I need him.' She gestured with her hands as if he had disappeared in a puff of smoke. 'David?' Sharon shouted at the top of her voice, but no other child appeared.

Gary emerged from the kitchen with a greasy spatula in his hand. 'Hi, you must be Suzie. I have heard so much about you and the other lady. I haven't seen Sharon so dedicated and keen on anything before – this running lark is really keeping her focused… Sorry, the bacon is burning.' Gary ran back into the kitchen.

Sharon looked Suzie up and down, admiring her dress. 'You look stunning, Suzie. I am sure Brett will be very pleased. What time is he picking you up?'

'About eight,' Suzie remarked sceptically. 'Why are you looking so worried? He's a lovely guy and he thinks the world of you.'

'I know. I just don't see why. I don't think I am worthy of anyone as lovely as him. He's fit, good looking and such a gentleman.'

'You shouldn't be so hard on yourself, Suzie. You are a fantastic girl. There is someone out there for all of us.'

There was a loud knock at the door. Suzie went as white as a sheet. 'That'll be Brett, I suppose.'

Sharon opened the door to the most gorgeous-looking Brett. 'Hi, Brett. You look lovely. Wish I was a few years younger myself.'

From the kitchen, over the sound of sizzling bacon, came the voice of a rather disgruntled Gary. 'I heard that.'

'I'm old enough to be this guy's mother. Besides, I have six boys already. I don't want any more, remember.' Sharon laughed.

Brett eyed Suzie up and down and took in all her beauty. 'Wow, you look stunning.'

Suzie went a bright shade of red. 'I've gone red, haven't I?' Suzie looked horrified.

'You still look lovely.' Brett smiled. 'Are you ready then?'

'Chelsea?' Suzie called. 'Mummy is going now. Please be a good girl for Auntie Sharon.' Suzie gave Chelsea a huge hug and a kiss.

'Let's go then.' Brett opened the door for Suzie. 'After you, young lady.'

Suzie turned to see Sharon give her a wink.

Brett's car was warm from the drive to Sharon's house, which was a blessing as the air was very cold outside and Suzie was not wearing many clothes. 'Are you cold?' Brett quizzed.

'Just a little,' Suzie admitted.

'Would you like my coat?' Brett handed over his coat before Suzie could answer.

'Such a gentleman, thank you.' Suzie was shocked.

'Where do you fancy to eat tonight? Any preference?'

'Don't mind. I can eat anything. Depends if you approve of the menu, not being too fattening to interrupt our training regime. Pizza is always a safe bet, can't go wrong with pizza. I've had some dodgy curries and Chinese food in my time.' Suzie nervously rambled on.

'Pizza it is then, young lady. Do you have any preference to a particular restaurant? We can go to either Pizza Hut or Pizza Express.'

'Pizza Express will be just lovely.' Suzie didn't dare to admit she had never been to a Pizza Express, but she had heard from some of her friends that the pizza was the best in the business. The drive to the restaurant was silent as Suzie was too nervous to talk. Brett could see this and thought he would wait until they were in the restaurant before trying to open Suzie up about herself.

The restaurant was almost empty, which suited Suzie just fine. Brett asked for the table in the corner of the restaurant so they were not in view of everyone else. Holding out a chair at the table for her to sit on, Brett asked if she was okay.

Suzie smiled. 'I'm great thanks, just I've never left Chelsea overnight before. I will miss her and worry for her all night.'

'Sharon will look after her, you don't doubt that, surely?'

'Of course, I don't doubt that. She's probably had her nails painted, hair plaited and is being spoilt rotten. I do feel sorry for her not having a girl. Having six boys must be such a chore – well, even six kids must be a chore. She's running the marathon so she can have another baby. That lady is an inspiration to anyone.' Suzie babbled like a toddler. Brett just searched into Suzie's eyes as she spoke. 'I am really nervous. Sorry, Brett. I've not done this sort of thing before. I am sure you have women falling at your feet and do this every week?'

'I have never met anyone as amazing as you and no, I don't have women falling at my feet, not that I notice anyway. Yes, I have been on a few dates, but to be fair I'd rather forget them.'

'That bad then.' Suzie smirked.

'You could say that. But that is not why we are here, to discuss my previous dates.'

The waiter came over and introduced himself as Marcus and said he would be looking after them that evening. He took their drinks order and said he would be back shortly to take their food order.

'What do you fancy to eat then, young lady?' Brett asked, reading the menu as he spoke.

'Not sure. There certainly is a huge selection.'

'What do you usually have when you come here?'

'To be honest, I have never eaten here, but thought it a change from Pizza Hut, which will no doubt be full of screaming kids and it's my night off.'

'You are a very wise woman. Shall I order for us?'

The waiter returned and took their order. A couple at the table on the far side of the restaurant were having a rather heated debate about whose turn it was to wash the dishes. The girl was saying it was his turn and how it was a cheap shot to bring them out so he got out of washing up.

'Why are some people really that selfish?' Suzie whispered to Brett, so she was not overheard.

'I'd make her pay if that were me, ungrateful cow,' Brett mocked.

The girl stood up and threw her napkin at the man and stormed out of the restaurant. The man looked rather embarrassed and asked for the bill, threw some cash on the table and ran out after the girl, calling her name.

'Just like watching *Jeremy Kyle*,' Suzie remarked.

'Food. Thank God, I am starving,' Brett said whilst smelling the hot pizza as the waiter placed it on the table and then brought over the Parmesan cheese and pepper mill. 'Looks amazing. I hope you are hungry.' They tucked into the pizza and there was a long silence before Brett broke it. 'So, tell me about yourself.'

'What is there to tell? Not much really. I'm single

mum to a three-year-old girl. Struggling and trying to improve my prospects by going to college.' Suzie didn't look up from her food whilst talking.

    'I am not concerned with you being a single mum to one child or ten children. You are perfect to me.'

    'You do say the nicest things.' Suzie slapped Brett on the back of his hand with her fork.
'I mean every word of it.'

After they had finished, Brett offered to drive her home. Again, they sat in silence in the car. Suzie had not felt like this since she was a teenager and had a crush on Brian McFadden from Westlife, thinking about what it would be like to be his girl.

    'Thank you, Brett, for such a lovely evening.' Suzie opened the car door to leave. Brett grabbed her hand and gave her a long-lasting kiss and cuddle. 'Thank you again, you are wonderful.'

    'So are you. Good night, sleep tight and I will see you at college Monday.'

    Suzie stayed in the passenger seat and chewed her nails. 'Would it be wrong to ask if you would like a coffee?'
'Wrong?' Brett quizzed.

    'You know, wrong. In all the movies the girl always invites the boy back for a coffee and well,' Suzie stumbled, 'things happen.'
Brett raised his eyebrows. 'What things?'
Suzie blushed again. 'You know, things.'
Suzie looked Brett up and down.
'Oh, those things.' Brett smiled.
'Do you want a coffee?' Suzie asked sternly.
'I would love one.'

    'Great. Go and park up in the car park around the back. Come up when you are ready. It is flat number eighteen.' Suzie pointed towards the car park entrance, left the car and ran towards the block of flats.

Once inside she burst into tears; she had not felt this happy for a long time. She began to imagine things going wrong. She filled the kettle and fumbled in the cupboard for two clean cups and the jar of coffee. She sent a text message to Sharon to check on Chelsea. Sharon replied almost immediately.

Chelsea is fast asleep, she has been worn out by six boys all fighting for her attention. She is a lovely girl, you should be very proud. How did your evening go? XXXX

Suzie smiled to herself as she realised that she was now surrounded by a lovely, caring bunch of friends. She replied to Sharon.

Thanks Auntie Sharon. The evening went marvellously well, Brett is just having a cup of coffee at mine now. XXXX

She was just pouring the water into the cups when there was another, almost immediate reply.

Lovely, glad it went well. Can't wait to hear all about it tomorrow. Be a good girl ☺. XXXX

Brett pushed open the front door and called out, 'Hello.'
'Hi, come in, I am in the kitchen.' Suzie was already holding two cups of steaming hot coffee.
'What a lovely flat you have,' Brett said.
'It always shocks people, as from the outside

it looks rough, which is why I try to keep it clean and tidy.' Suzie handed Brett a cup of coffee. 'This does seem weird,' Suzie confessed.

'Weird?' Brett quizzed.

'Yes, weird. Here I am with a hunk of a man in my flat and I have not got Chelsea home for the night.' Suzie blushed.

'There is nothing weird about that. I would say exceptional.' Brett raised his eyebrows.

'Are you thinking what I am thinking?' Suzie questioned.

'If it involves *things*. Then yes, I am thinking what you are thinking.'

'As you can see, I am not used to inviting gorgeous men back to my flat.' Suzie cuddled her cup of coffee.

'Well, there is only one way we can stop this feeling weird.' Brett threw his gaze towards another room. 'We can make it real.'

Suzie took Brett's hand and guided him across the hall into her bedroom.

Chapter Twenty-Six

Suzie woke to find Brett not in her bed any longer. She jumped out of bed and panicked, thinking the worst: that she had upset him and he had left. She ran around the rest of the flat but could not find him. Looking out of the window into the car park she could see that his car was no longer there. She went back into the kitchen to make a cup of tea and saw a note stuck to the fridge with her many magnets that hung there.

Hi Darling, please don't panic, I have just popped to the local shop as you are out of milk. XXXX

'Phew.' Suzie sighed. Her mobile phone signalled a new message.

Hi Darling, I will be five minutes. Xxx

Suzie filled and boiled the kettle and waited for Brett to arrive back. She saw his car pull into the car park. She stood waiting at the open door, to save him from knocking. She was greeted by Brett hidden behind a huge bouquet of flowers.
'Oh my gosh, they are amazing and huge.' Thankfully, Brett couldn't see her blushes behind the huge bouquet. She took them from Brett and gave him a huge kiss. 'Thank you.'
'Come on. I will help you put them in water and arrange them lovingly.' Brett walked towards the

kitchen and opened and closed several cupboards whilst Suzie just watched. 'Do you have a vase?' Brett asked whilst continuing to rummage in cupboards.

'No, sorry, I have never needed one until now. No one has ever bought me flowers before,' Suzie apologised. 'There is a measuring jug in the cupboard by the cooker – that will have to do, I suppose.'

Brett looked horrified. 'For now, yes, but I will have to buy you a vase to put them in. You can't keep them in a measuring jug forever.'

'It is turning out to be an expensive bouquet of flowers if you are having to buy me a vase also.' Suzie chewed her fingers.

'You are worth every penny.' Brett admired Suzie longingly, even with her bad hair, running make-up and pyjamas. 'Get yourself ready and we can pop to the shops before we collect Chelsea from Sharon's.'

Suzie ran to the shower and was back in the kitchen in less than ten minutes, dressed and with a new face of make-up.

'Gosh, that was quick,' Brett commented. 'I don't want to leave Chelsea at Sharon's any longer than I need to as I may not get her back.' Suzie laughed.

Brett drove to the homeware shop in silence, just turning occasionally to Suzie and grinning like a cat that had got the cream.

'Wow,' Suzie exclaimed. 'A pound shop would have sufficed. You don't need to spend a fortune on a vase also.'

'Like I said before, you are worth every penny. Why spend a fortune on a huge bouquet of flowers and put them in a vase that cost a pound?' Brett looked lovingly at Suzie.

'Thank you. You are so sweet. I have no idea what I have done to deserve you.' Suzie averted her eyes in embarrassment.

'Likewise.' Brett held her face.

'Likewise.' Brett kissed her longingly on the lips. 'Come on, let's take a look before we pick Chelsea up.' Brett got out of the car so he could open the door for Suzie.

They searched the shop and it wasn't long before Brett found the most beautiful vase. It was red, with 'LOVE' written on it. 'Here you go, what about this one?' Brett held up the vase so Suzie could get a good look.

'Is it expensive?' Suzie asked.

'Nothing too expensive for such a lovely lady.' Brett walked towards the checkout, paid for the vase and handed the bag to Suzie.

'Thank you.' Suzie showed her appreciation with a huge hug. 'Can we stop at the local shop on the way, please?'

'Sure.' Brett smiled.

Suzie had seen an advert in the shop window that said they were looking for part-time staff. She wanted to apply to show Brett she wasn't useless. She left Brett waiting outside and returned with an application form.

'Oh, what's that?' Brett enquired.

'An application form. They have vacancies,' Suzie announced. 'I am not confident I will get the job, it's only part-time, but I need to do something.'

'You are doing enough already, but I wish you luck all the same.' Brett gave Suzie a huge kiss and they continued the journey to collect Chelsea from Sharon's house.

Chapter Twenty-Seven

Samantha was drafting an important letter into her Dictaphone when Liz called to say that someone called Jen was on the phone, sounding rather distressed.

'Put her through.' Samantha held her breath waiting for Jen to dive into a manic conversation.

'Samantha, it's Jen. You know, your new cleaner. I've just got to your house and your fridge is not well. When I say not well, I mean it's not working. It's all gone kind of wrong. Well, when I mean kind of gone wrong, I mean totally wrong. The freezer thinks it is a fridge and everything in the fridge is frozen. Sorry, I wasn't snooping, just opened it to see if it needed cleaning.' Jen didn't stop for air.
'What are you talking about, Jen?'

'It's all wrong. Surely the fridge is meant to be cold and the freezer frozen, but it's not. It's what you call a psycho fridge.'

'Schizophrenic, is that what you mean?' Samantha replied whilst rolling her eyes and thankful that this woman was only on the end of the phone.

'Yes, that also, it's not working. What shall I do? There is water all over the kitchen floor where the freezer has defrosted. Good job I came in when I did.'

'Just turn the fridge freezer off at the socket and I will sort the mess out when I get home,' Samantha said.

Jen let out an almighty laugh. 'I'm here to clean, Samantha. I am your cleaner, remember. I can't expect you to clean up. Do you want me to throw all the food away? I can then give it a thorough clean for you.'

'Jen.' She paused for a breath. 'That would be lovely, if it is not too much trouble.' Samantha was desperately trying to get rid of Jen off the phone, so she could concentrate on some real work.
'Super, consider it done...'

Samantha hung up whilst Jen was still talking. The idea of having a cleaner was to take away the stress of cleaning the house herself; she could sense that this woman Jen was going to be more trouble than it was worth. She was interrupted again by a loud knock on the door. 'Yes!' she shouted with some venom.

'Sorry, I hope I am not disturbing you?' The Sex God was standing there in all his glory.

'Sorry, please, I must apologise for my outburst. It is just my cleaner is causing me more stress than cleaning my house myself. I thought it would help.' Samantha looked rather embarrassed.

'It is fine, honestly. The life of a solicitor is a stressful one at the best of times.' Greg smiled. 'I was just wondering if you fancied a run sometime?' Greg smirked, knowing this woman was still deranged and couldn't run for a bus.

'That will be lovely. When are you thinking?'

Greg was taken aback by the comment; it was not what he had expected at all.

'You can come out with us girls anytime. We have a TV crew following our training up to and including the big day,' Samantha announced, looking rather pleased with herself that she had at last found fame.

'TV crew.' Greg stumbled. 'How on earth did that happen?'

'Not sure really, but it is exciting all the same. The programme will be on ITV in the summer. I just hope none of my clients see me in all my running gear – it does not look that fetching.'

'No, I can only imagine.' Greg had the most awful thought of this rotund lady wearing her Lycra running stockings and a fitted sweat top. 'When is your next training run then?'

Samantha looked at her running schedule pinned to her noticeboard. 'Tonight, actually. Six o'clock sharp at the local park, by the basketball court. Are you sure you are free? You are obviously a very busy man.' Samantha hoped the answer was no.

'Great, I will see you tonight. I am looking forward to it already.' Greg turned and attempted to punch the wall on the way out, wishing he had just asked how the training was going, not if he could join her on a run.

Samantha sunk down into her chair immediately. Could this really be happening? The most gorgeous man had asked to come out and train with her on a run. Was she reading the signals correctly? Did this amazingly fit man really fancy her? She sent a WhatsApp message to Sharon and Suzie, telling them that Mr Sex God himself would be joining them that evening for a run. She asked that they did not mention too much about the fact she created the Mum Runners club, as she did not want Sex God getting the wrong idea about her previous fitness level.

Samantha arrived home after a hectic, but exciting, day in the office to find the house immaculate. Jen had left her a note saying she hoped that everything was okay with the cleaning and giving a list of a few cleaning items she needed for next time. Samantha ate her Waitrose microwave meal for one of beef wellington, which she did not enjoy very much. After she had showered and changed, she studied herself in the mirror and realised she would have to apply some make-up as Mr Sex God may find her repulsive. She did not feel that comfortable displaying her naked skin to him yet. After a quick application of foundation and mascara, she made her way to the local park to meet the others. On arrival, she received a text message from the man himself.

Sorry Samantha, something has come up this evening, I will join you for a run some other time.

Samantha was more than relieved.

Chapter Twenty-Eight

Samantha arrived at the meeting place and was delighted to see everyone else there already. Brett and Suzie were arm in arm, Sharon was warming up and the film crew were setting up their equipment.

'Hi Samantha, where is your running buddy? We haven't noticed a sexy man alone yet.' Sharon waved her arms around to signal that she had not seen anyone.

'Something has come up – I had a text message earlier. He said he will join us another time.' Samantha sounded disappointed.

'Ah, that's a shame, you sounded so excited.'

'Well, things happen. I am not going to lose any sleep over the situation.' Samantha dismissed the subject. 'I have an early start in the morning, so if we can get going... Sorry to be a party pooper, I just do not want to be out all night.'

Brett and Suzie gave each other a long, loving kiss before starting to run.

'The date went well then,' Samantha noted.
'Yes, I suppose it did,' Suzie remarked.
'Only suppose,' Brett retaliated.
'You know what I mean.' Suzie apologised.

'There is no need to apologise. I had a great time.' Brett raised his eyebrows and eyed Suzie up and down.

'Get a room please.' Samantha waved her hand to signal time out.

'I am really pleased for you both.' Sharon patted Suzie on the back to show her approval.

'Thanks, it means a lot and so does Brett.' Suzie smiled at him.

'Sorry to break up the party,' Samantha announced, 'but are we running tonight or discussing your love life?'

'Yes, Samantha, we are. Is ten miles okay?' Brett asked.

'We will see,' Sharon remarked. 'Besides, you two sounded like you have been getting plenty of exercise. You both must be knackered.' She winked.

'Do we get a wedding invite?' Elvis asked. 'Bloody hell, we've only been out together on
one date,' Suzie said.

'Come on, ladies,' Brett ordered. 'We need to get a move on otherwise we won't get any running in tonight.'

After five miles the girls were struggling.

'I need to stop,' Sharon yelled.

'Wee?' Suzie asked.

'No, not this time. I have a stitch.' Sharon slowed down to a stop.

'Breathe through it,' Brett advised.

'I am not in bloody labour,' Sharon yelled.

'I hope not, but you need to breathe through the pain. Imagine you are in labour. You are obviously an expert in it having been through it six times already.' Brett smiled.

'Thanks, Brett. I am sorry. It is just so frustrating, this training. I was all up for ten miles tonight and then I go and get a stitch and let the side down.' Sharon sobbed. 'How far have we run?'

'Five miles, so not that bad.' Samantha tried to calm Sharon's hysteria. 'Richmond station is just over the road. We can get the Tube back home if you want to stop?'

'I'm so sorry.' Sharon pulled a face whilst holding her side.

'Think of it as a learning curve, Sharon. No one is born running. We have to train and condition our bodies to cope,' Brett informed her.

'I realise that right now and I am not coping very well.' Sharon flopped onto the ground.

'What did you eat before training tonight and how long before you came out did you eat?' Brett asked.

'I had some reheated pasta from yesterday just before I came out.' Sharon was rubbing the side of her stomach where the pain was.

'Lesson one, do not eat less than an hour before exercise otherwise you can get a stitch.' Brett sounded as though he was reading from a textbook.

'As I have.' Sharon cried in pain.

'If it won't go away, then you need to stop for the evening,' Brett said.

'Sorry, ladies,' Sharon said. 'Sorry, film crew.'

'Don't mind us. We are always having our filming schedule change. Just keep us posted with your next training date and time and we will be here,' George assured her.

'Thank you.' Sharon apologised.

'No need to apologise, Sharon.' Samantha gave Sharon a hug to comfort her, and then carried her like a wounded soldier towards the Tube station.

'We can talk on WhatsApp,' Suzie suggested. 'Looks like you have your early night, Samantha.'

'I must log my run on *Joggingbuddy.com* first'. Samantha advised.

Chapter Twenty-Nine

Sharon was in the middle of refereeing the usual breakfast rows when there was a loud knock on the door. She turned to look for Gary to answer the door, then realised he was in the shower still. The knock came again, only louder this time. She placed her second cup of tea on the table; she now expected it would go as cold and undrinkable as the first one. On opening the door, she found the TV film crew, eager to start filming.

'Sorry, guys, you are a little early for today's training run.' Sharon looked herself up and down to display to the crew that she was still in her pyjamas.

'I'm John and this is Gerald with the microphone.' John carefully placed his camera on the doorstep and held out his hand.

Sharon shook their hands in turn. 'It's like World War Three here in the mornings. You are welcome to come and see, but it is never a pretty sight.'

'That's exactly why we are here. We wanted to get some pre-school antics, if we can?' John smiled.

'You should have warned me.' Sharon looked as though she had won the lottery but lost the ticket.

'If we had've warned you, we wouldn't have got a true reflection of your mornings with the boys, would we?'

'Good point,' Sharon mumbled.
'We are looking for the true drama of running a home of six young boys whilst you are training to run the London Marathon,' John said soothingly.

Sharon opened the door wider, so to invite them in. There were screams coming from the kitchen about who had stolen the voucher from the box of cereals and who had eaten all the jam.

'Gentlemen, welcome to my world. It really is like a scene from World War Three in there at the moment, as I am sure you can hear.' Sharon directed them into the bedlam that was breakfast in the Young household.

Gary emerged with just a towel wrapped around his middle, leaving behind a trail of water as he walked into the kitchen and was met by the film crew. 'Whoa! You should have told me we were expecting filming today.' He clutched his towel tighter to save it from falling down.

'I'm as shocked as you are, Gary. They have made a surprise visit.' Sharon waved him out of the kitchen, which he ignored.

The film crew looked embarrassed, not knowing where to put their faces with Gary standing there half-naked.

'We can go and come back at a prearranged date and time if you wish, Sharon? We didn't think it would be this inconvenient.' Gerald was holding the microphone and spoke whilst trying to avert his eyes from Gary.

'No, you are here now. Let me put the kettle on and you can tell me what it is you want to film. Gary, please go and put some clothes on.' Sharon picked up the kettle and walked to the sink to refill it with water for the third time. Gary excused himself and went upstairs to get dressed.

'Just a normal morning in the Young household, really.' John moved his camera into several different angles to get a better view.

'This is a typical morning, so film away. Tea or coffee?'

'Tea, please. Milk, no sugar. For both of us, please,' John called out from behind his equipment.

The boys continued to scream and shout at each other as if nothing strange was going on. The microphone was shoved in Sharon's face.

'How do you deal with this every morning?' Gerald asked as if Sharon were a celebrity being interviewed.

'I have absolutely no idea. I just know that by half-past eight they will all have left for the day and I can relax with a cup of tea and sit down and wait to watch *Morning Chat* on TV. It's the only thing that keeps me going. Then I can go for my training run later, relaxed, knowing that soon after it will start all over again for teatime.'

John stuck his thumb up to signal that she was doing great.

When Gary returned to the kitchen, the boys were taking it in turns to be interviewed regarding their mum and the training she was doing for the run.

'It's time for school now, boys. Please go and wash your hands and get your school bags, and I will see you all later.' She kissed each one in turn and told them she loved them. All the boys let out a loud groan as they could see that being filmed was much more exciting than schoolwork would ever be. Gary ushered the boys out of the door after lots of fighting from each of them as to where their shoes and coats were.

'Wow, that was manic. I can see why you want a girl – she would certainly bring some order to the

breakfast table.' Gerald wiped his brow and had to sit down, avoiding the soggy Rice Krispies left all over the table, chairs and floor. 'You could do with a dog.' Sharon looked horrified by this statement.
'He could eat up all the leftover food and it would make clearing up easier. That is why my wife and I got a dog.'

'A girl in the house would do just fine, if I ever get there.' Sharon sighed.

Gerald started firing questions, whilst John held the camera. How was the training going? Had she encountered any injuries? How was she managing to fit training in around a family of six young boys?

Sharon sat there with her hair a mess, and still in her pyjamas, saying how it was the best thing she had ever done, next to having the boys and marrying Gary.

'You are an inspiration, Sharon.' Gerald smiled. 'Many other people, I am sure, will be spurred on by your determination. A credit to you.'

Sharon blushed. 'Can I go and get showered and dressed now? Please make yourself at home and make another tea if you wish. I will be back in ten minutes.' Sharon showed John and Gerald where the tea bags were kept.

'I feel human again now,' Sharon announced as she entered the kitchen to find John and Gerald had made a start clearing the breakfast dishes away. 'Wow, you can come around every morning if you are going to help with the dishes.' Sharon laughed.

'Sorry, we felt so bad just landing on your doorstep, it was the least we could do,' John apologised.
'I loved it, you are very welcome, anytime.' John and Gerald made their way towards the front door.

'We got some excellent footage. Thank you.' Gerald shook Sharon's hand as he was leaving the house.

'Bye, guys, and thanks again.' Sharon stayed on the doorstep and waved them off in their car.

Sharon made a cup of tea and sat down for peace and quiet to watch her daily fix of daytime television, including *Morning Chat*.

Chapter Thirty

Brett and Suzie entered the college room arm in arm, and everyone cheered. Suzie was blushing more than she had ever blushed before. 'How does anyone know about us?'

'I have no idea. Maybe they guessed, or even saw us together in the restaurant the other night. Come on, let's sit down.' Brett directed her to the desk at the back of the class. Everyone was looking and whispering.

'I feel like I am a monkey in a zoo,' Suzie whispered.

'They are jealous because I have the most beautiful girl by my side.' Brett leant over and kissed her cheek.

'And I have the most gorgeous man by my side.' Suzie gave him a kiss back, only this time it was a long, loving kiss on the lips. The whole class just watched, stunned for a moment, before there was a roar of cheers and clapping from the other students.

'When's the wedding?' one of the students called.

'Get a room, man, that is gross,' another yelled.

The banter was soon rudely interrupted by Stephen entering the room, wondering what all the fuss was about. He soon realised and smiled at Brett and Suzie.

'Today, class, we are going to be looking at nutrition. Nutrition is a very important part of sports science. You are what you eat. I would like everyone to list the foods and drinks they consumed over the weekend and that includes Friday night.' Stephen winked at Brett. 'We will look and discuss with the class how balanced each of your diets are.' Stephen gave his instructions.

'It will be obvious we were out on Friday sharing a pizza.' Suzie laughed.

'Yes, but I am sure all the others ate far worse food than us. Especially double egg and chips man over there,' Brett whispered whilst casually pointing to one of the other students on the other side of the room.

Stephen read out each student's meal list in turn. Most had salad, jacket potatoes, crisps, cakes, sandwiches and even McDonald's.

Stephen's face was a picture. 'You all need to take a good look at your food intake. How can you possibly train others to be fit, when you are all stuffing your faces on rubbish and chemicals?' He slammed his fist on the table. The class went deathly quiet.

Brett broke the silence. 'We are here to learn, sir. I for one will take on everything you say.'

'Thank you, Brett, I appreciate that. I will ask that everyone keeps a food diary for an entire week and we will review the situation next week. Keep an eye on not having too many carbohydrates. No McDonald's and certainly no fizzy drinks, diet or otherwise. In fact, diet drinks are even more of a sin.' Stephen looked around at the class to be sure everyone was listening. Everyone was scared to even murmur. 'Okay, we will move on now. If you can all open your textbooks at page ninety-eight and start memorising the muscles as there will be a test at the end of the day.' Stephen was not going to take any prisoners now, not after such an abysmal attempt at a lesson on nutrition.

'Someone is in a bad mood today,' Suzie muttered under her breath.

'Obviously didn't have such a wonderful weekend as I did.'

Finally, after a very long morning, it was lunchtime.

'Salad for us then?' Suzie laughed.

'We need to go off campus, if that's okay with you?' Brett took Suzie's arm. 'I am not interested in childhood banter all lunchtime also. It is bad enough in class. I know just the place.' Brett literally dragged Suzie out of the classroom.

In the little teashop on the high street, they both devoured a feta salad without the dressing, to keep the calories to the lowest. They ate in silence, just admiring each other as they ate.

Brett looked at his watch. 'Shit, we had better be going. We dare not be late for more of a grilling from the sergeant major.'

'Such a shame. I was enjoying our lunch break together.'

'I will pay the bill. You get yourself sorted.' Brett picked up the bill and walked towards the till.

'You are too generous, Brett.' Suzie blushed.

'You are worth every penny and every effort, young lady,' Brett informed her.

'I have no idea what I have done to deserve you, but I like it.' Suzie kissed Brett on the cheek.

'Please, stop putting yourself down. I know things must have been hard for you in the past, but now you have so much to look forward to. A diploma in sports science and your first marathon run, which I am sure will be the first of many.' Brett gave Suzie a reassuring kiss on the cheek.

'Thanks. I don't mean to go on – you must be sick of me going on?'

'There you go again. You are lovely as you are and I wouldn't want to change a thing.' Brett smiled.

'Honestly?' Suzie quizzed.

'Yes,' Brett replied sternly.

They left arm in arm and walked back towards the college.

Back in college, Brett and Suzie were the last two to arrive back in class, just before Stephen walked in.

'Okay, class, now this afternoon we are going to look at vitamins – which ones are needed for each part of the body to function correctly. Does anyone know any vitamin names and their uses?'

Cocksure put his hand up. 'My mum takes evening primrose oil to stop her being a moody bitch around her monthlies.' He laughed.

Everyone in the class turned to look at him as if he had just committed cold-blooded murder and he soon realised he was laughing alone.

'Thanks for that.' Stephen tried to not look astonished. 'Evening primrose oil is great for hormone balance, but it is not a vitamin that is needed for everyday body function and also it is not a vitamin but an oil, hence the name evening primrose *oil*.'

Cocksure put his head in his hands to try to shield his reddening face from his colleagues.

Suzie was becoming restless at the time it took the afternoon session to finish, when Stephen announced the homework he expected to be handed in next week. 'I would like you all to read the labels on the foods you have in your house and write down all the vitamins and minerals that are in them and what quantity and we can then analyse them next week, and don't forget your food diary. Have a good evening and see you all next week.'

With that all the pupils practically ran out of the classroom as if there were a fire alarm sounding.

'Shall I give you a lift home, young lady?' Brett squeezed Suzie's hand.

'If it's not too much trouble, thanks.' Suzie winked back.

Chapter Thirty-One

Samantha studied her diary in dismay that she had all of the most annoying clients booked in on the same day. She was relieved she had a run to look forward to in the evening. Soon Samantha's happy thoughts were interrupted by Liz calling her.
'Samantha, your cleaner is on the line.' Samantha rolled her eyes and let out a huge
sigh. 'Put her through.'
'Hi Sam, it's Jen.'
Samantha rolled her eyes. 'It is Samantha, my name is Samantha. What can I do for you this morning?'
'Did you get the cleaning products I asked for?'
'Yes, I did get everything on your list.' Samantha really worried about Jen's intelligence.
'I cannot find the Jif cleaner. I have found the bleach, cloths and rubber gloves.' Jen rambled on as always.
'Jif is lemon juice. You asked me to get Jif lemon juice. It is in the fridge.' Samantha heard Jen open the fridge and then an awful scream. 'Jen, are you okay? Are you hurt?'
Jen was laughing so hard she struggled to get her breath. 'How am I supposed to clean the bathroom with this?'
'You asked for it – I have no idea what you planned to do with it.' Samantha was anxiously looking

at her watch, realising she had a client arriving in less than ten minutes.

'Jif lemon cleaner, not a Jif lemon you put on your pancakes.' Jen was still laughing like a hyena.

'Well, maybe if you had been specific and asked for the correct product, I would not have bought the wrong one. Anyway, I believe it is now called *Cif*.'

'Is it? When did they change that, then?' Jen spoke like a five-year-old who had made an error in a simple spelling test.

'Can you just clean the best you can, Jen? I have got a client in less than ten minutes. I will buy some *Cif* on the way home today.' Samantha took great pleasure in over pronouncing Cif.

'Sorry, Samantha, I will crack on. Thanks, bye for now.' The line went dead.

Samantha was amazed that a cleaner did not know Jif changed its name to Cif. She asked Liz to bring her a coffee and when Mr Smith arrived to send him straight in to see her. She started reading her emails and there was one from the charity Guide Dogs for the Blind informing her that there was a seminar in February and inviting her to attend. It was an information day for new marathon runners with talks from athletes and sports providers giving help and advice on the race day. Samantha replied saying she would be delighted to attend. She entered the date in her diary so not to forget the event and sent a WhatsApp message to Sharon and Suzie to share the good news. Samantha quickly hid her mobile phone away like a naughty schoolgirl when she heard her door open. Mr Smith was standing there like a lost child, crying again.

'Please do come and sit down, Mr Smith. How are you this morning?' Samantha realised that was the wrong question to ask as Mr Smith let out a huge fake-sounding cry.

'Awful, Mrs Lloyd, awful.' Mr Smith made himself comfortable and asked for a cup of coffee.

Samantha telephoned Liz and asked her to bring Mr Smith a strong black coffee.

'She won't even talk to me,' Mr Smith whinged. 'Why won't she talk to me?'

'That is what I am here for. What do you want to ask her?' Samantha held her breath and awaited Mr Smith's reply.

The crying was unbearable for Samantha. 'Did she ever love me or was the whole marriage a fake? That's all I want to know.'

Samantha rolled her eyes and began to wish she had never asked. 'It is not really a question for a divorce solicitor to ask. Can you ask a friend for you?' Samantha could see this was going to be a very long and drawn-out meeting.

'I have no friends. They were all her friends.' Mr Smith blew his nose into a rather soggy tissue. Samantha offered him a fresh one.

'I am sorry. What is the purpose of this meeting, as I am conscious this is going to be costing you an awful lot of money to be sitting there crying, is it not?' This comment made the situation worse and Mr Smith let out an awful scream followed by a wail that she had never heard a human being make before. 'Mr Smith, can I recommend a counsellor for you to talk through your concerns and issues with your marriage? I know a very good one, just local to here. I am not trained to counsel, only to act as a solicitor.' She rummaged hastily in her desk drawer for the card of the counsellor and handed it to Mr Smith. He took it reluctantly and said his goodbyes and left. Samantha sat open-mouthed for at least three minutes, until she was interrupted by Liz bringing in a fresh coffee.

'You look like you have seen a ghost, Samantha. Is everything okay?'

'No, not a ghost, Liz. I think Mr Smith is an alien. Some clients think I can get answers to every part of their marriage. He wanted me to ask his ex-wife if she ever loved him.' Samantha shook her head violently. 'If anyone asks, I am just popping next door. If there was ever a chocolate emergency, it is now.' Samantha grabbed her handbag and fled the office.

'Get me one can you, please, Samantha?' Liz called after her, but she wasn't sure if she heard her.

On her return to the office, Samantha was given another message. 'Your cleaner has called again. I told her you were out of the office.'

Samantha raised her eyes. 'Oh gosh, that woman puts the fear of God into me. I wonder what I have done now. Probably purchased the wrong brand of rubber gloves.' Samantha stuffed the entire bar of chocolate into her mouth and made heavenly noises as she did. Once she was able to talk enough with chocolate still dripping around her mouth, she dialled Jen's mobile number.

'Hi Jen. Is everything okay?' Samantha sounded concerned.

'Yes, everything is fine here. I just need some advice.'

Before Samantha had a chance to reply that she was due a client any minute, Jen babbled on ten to the dozen. 'You see, he told me that it was all a misunderstanding and that he was never convicted of having sex with a kid, but I have since found out from his ex-wife that he actually did.'

Samantha was not paying much attention as she was watching the clock, being conscious that her next client would be arriving at any moment.

'What should I do, Samantha? I do love him, but I am not sure I can trust him. If he's lied to me once, then surely he can lie again.' Jen barely came up for air.

'Sorry, yes, my secretary has just buzzed to let me know my next client has arrived,' Can we talk about this later?'

'You are a star, thank you so much. What time will you be home? I can wait until you get back.'

Samantha was horrified that Jen could possibly be waiting for her when she got home. 'Not tonight, Jen, sorry. I am off out as soon as I get home. If you give me a call tomorrow, I can give you a more definite date and time.' Samantha gritted her teeth as she hung up. 'Mrs Braitwaite, how lovely to see you.' Samantha signalled for her client to sit down, but she already had. 'How are you today?'

'I am going to kill him, really I am.' She clenched her fists as she spoke.

'That good then.' Samantha was considering a life of shelf stacking in the local supermarket at this point.

Chapter Thirty-Two

Suzie's knuckles were turning white as she gripped the steering wheel hard, bracing herself for the signal from Karen to carry out an emergency stop. Karen gave the signal with a prompt 'Stop' whilst holding her hand forwards. Suzie brought the car to a stop but was too frightened to press the brake pedal sharply for the fear of skidding out of control.

'That was a great reaction,' Karen advised. 'However, it wasn't prompt enough. You would have killed the pedestrian.'

Suzie looked horrified. 'I am sorry. Can I try it again?'

'Of course we will, until we get it right. Why does the area we are driving in have a thirty miles per hour speed limit, do you think?'

'There are lots of houses and a school. Is it because of what you said before with the man with the horse who survived being hit at thirty miles per hour?'

'There is less chance of a pedestrian being killed if they are hit at thirty miles per hour as opposed to forty miles per hour, but since Lord Belisha introduced thirty miles per hour we now have twenty miles per hour, at which there is more chance of survival'

They practised the task four more times and each time Suzie became more competent, until Karen announced, 'That's all for today. We won't be practising the emergency stop again today.'

'Thank God for that,' Suzie said. 'It was really scary.'

'It does cause panic for most students. Shall we drive back towards your flat then?'

'Yes, please.'

'Are you confident you can navigate your own way home from here?' Karen asked.

'I think so. If we get lost, you can direct us.' Suzie smiled

'Great, over to you then. If you are going wrong anywhere I will let you know.'

They got onto the dual carriageway when Karen broke the silence. 'How is your love life going then?'

'Great, thanks.' Suzie blushed. 'I've just got a part-time job in the local shop.'

'That's great news. How is it?'

'Awful, if I am honest, but I need some cash to fund my college course if nothing else.' Suzie didn't take her eyes off the road.

'I worked in a local shop when I was many years younger. Bloody hated it. I got called into the manager's office once, saying that my till was twenty quid short and I must have stolen it.' Karen made a loud tut sound as she relived the story.

'Shit, did they sack you?' Suzie turned in horror.

'No, they fired the assistant manager. Turns out he was helping himself to booze, fags and making everyone's till twenty quid short, so they looked at the CCTV. Not everyone can have a till that is twenty quid down.'

'What an arse. What happened to him?' 'No idea, hopefully, rotted in prison, bloody twat. All of us that worked on the tills were in tears at the thought that we had been accused of stealing money and all the

time it was the assistant boss.' Karen pointed out of the windscreen. 'What colour are the traffic lights?'
'Red, thanks, I did see them.'
'What about the running? You are looking much fitter, so it must be doing some good,' Karen complimented her.
'Thanks for that. Yes, it is great fun. Also helps that I've managed to pack the fags in. It was killing me trying to run with lungs full of that shit.'
'What distance have you run so far?' Karen quizzed.
'Oh, about ten miles I think, maybe just over. We are going for twelve miles this Sunday, with a few intermediate runs during the week.' Suzie had such excitement in her voice.
'What about next week?' Karen asked.
'What about it?'
'Well, it's Christmas, surely you are having a few days off from running?'
'Absolutely not. We are all going out Boxing Day for a long run. We would like to go Christmas Day, but it wouldn't be fair on the kids. Samantha's Garth is all grown up and at university, but my Chelsea and Sharon's six are all still young.'
'How long is a long run?' Karen was intrigued.
'We have agreed between us to run at least twelve miles, maybe more. It all depends on how much Christmas pudding we all eat.' Suzie laughed.
'I suppose it beats being stuck in traffic with everyone else, going to the sales.'
'Well, this time last year I would have said the sales were more appealing than a twelve-mile run. It's amazing how much can change in a year,' Suzie reflected.
'Shit!' Karen screamed out.

Before Suzie had a chance to ask what was wrong, there was a massive crash into the rear of the car.

'Bloody hell. Are you okay?' Karen asked, worried.

'I am not sure. What the fuck just happened?' Suzie was rubbing her head to soothe the pain from hitting the side window in the shunt.

'Can you turn the ignition off, please?' Karen ordered as she selected neutral, put the handbrake on and stumbled out of the car to meet the driver of the car that was now attached to the rear of her car.

'Sorry, I didn't see the traffic lights,' the rather embarrassed young girl admitted.

'Obviously. Let's just exchange details and we can be on our way. Let me get my phone and I will take a photo of the scene.' Karen ran back to her car. 'You okay?' Karen asked Suzie.
'Yes, what happened?'

'Young lady didn't see the traffic lights, she said.' Karen pointed to the lights. 'Jump over to the passenger seat. I will drive us back once I have exchanged details with the young girl.'

Other motorists started to sound their horns to show their disgust that Karen and another motorist were blocking the lane of traffic.
'Oh no, everyone is getting angry,' Suzie cried.

'Ignore them. Like they've never had a crash before.' Karen ran back to the girl behind who was now busy tapping away on her phone.

'All done,' Karen advised when she got into the driver's seat. 'Are you feeling okay?'

'I am so sorry. Was it my fault?' Suzie was holding back the tears.

'How can it be your fault? The driver went into the back of us. It happens, don't worry. As long as you are okay.' Karen comforted her.

Suzie sat in the passenger seat and held her wrist. 'Ouch, this fucking hurts.' Suzie was crying in pain.

'Okay, I will take you straight to A & E, no drama. I need to be sure you are okay.' Karen pulled back into the traffic.

The handwritten sign in the A & E waiting area stated there was a waiting time of six hours.

'I need to call Brett.' Suzie panicked. 'I have to tell him where I am. He is expecting me back.'

'No problem. What is his number? I will call him – you just sit there and keep still,' Karen ordered. Suzie gave her the number.

'I will go outside and call him.' Karen left the waiting room.

A short time later Karen re-entered the waiting room and told Suzie it was all sorted. 'Brett said he will come up once he has collected Chelsea from school. I can then leave you and get my car sorted.'
'I am so sorry.' Suzie looked in such pain.
'Stop it.' Karen closed her eyes to ease the headache she was starting to get.

An hour later Brett and Chelsea came running into the A & E department. Brett was holding a huge box of chocolates.

'That's lovely, Brett. Just what I need.' Suzie kissed Brett long and hard.

'Mummy.' Chelsea ran towards Suzie and jumped to give her a hug. Suzie let out a huge howl in pain. 'I am sorry, Mummy.' Chelsea retracted back.

'It's okay, honey, just I think I have broken my wrist. It is painful. You were not to know.' Suzie wiped Chelsea's hair from her face.

'I am going to get off now.' Karen stood up and hugged everyone. 'Let me know how you get on, please,' Karen insisted.

'Thank you, Karen.' Brett handed Karen the smaller box of chocolates he had been concealing under his jumper.

'That is very kind, Brett. I will certainly feel better once I have eaten them. Take care, everyone.'

After four hours a young doctor called Suzie through. He looked at her wrist and said it needed an X-ray. He asked lots of questions relating to the car crash. 'I will call you back to see me once I have the X-ray results,' the doctor informed her.

Another hour passed after the X-ray and the doctor called her back and told her it was broken and that it would need a plaster cast.

'Oh no, can I still run?' Suzie sounded panicked.

'Well, I should say so, young lady. It is not your foot that is broken,' the doctor reassured her.

'We are in training for the London Marathon. We have got so far we don't want to give up now,' Brett informed him.

'I am very glad to hear it, best of luck. Running may irritate the bones for a few weeks, so take it easy. If there is pain then please stop,' the doctor advised.

'Of course, Doctor.' Suzie nodded.

The plaster cast was heavy on the wrist. Suzie stroked it as if that was going to make the bone heal quicker.

'The car is just over in the main car park. Looks like you are going to get waited on hand and foot for a while.' Brett nudged Suzie in the ribs.

'That is fine by me.'

'When we get home, I need you to go straight into the kitchen as I have your Christmas present in the living room. Chelsea and I were going to wrap it up before you got home this evening.'

Suzie was ushered into the kitchen where Brett made her a cup of tea and sat her down at the table. Then he and Chelsea went into the living room to wrap the present. All Suzie could hear was lots of paper and laughter. She panicked over the thought she needed to prepare for Christmas dinner and started making a shopping list.

Chelsea calling interrupted her thoughts. 'You can come in now, Mummy.'

'Okay, baby, just coming.' Suzie rushed into the living room to find Brett beaming from ear to ear and Chelsea was patting a huge box wrapped in gold paper with several bows delicately placed on it.

Suzie stood open-mouthed, stunned at the enormity of the box. 'Wow, it is huge!' Suzie blushed.

'Wait until you see what is inside it,' Brett tempted.

'Well, I have no idea and I don't want to know. I love surprises, thank you.' Suzie then started to panic again as she realised that she had not even thought about what she could get Brett as a present. Maybe aftershave and pants would be an insult after the box that was almost the size of a small car sitting in her living room.

Chapter Thirty-Three

Garth spent over an hour in the bathroom attempting to smarten himself up so he didn't look like a shabby university student, preparing for a heavy night of drinking in town with some old school mates. Samantha was busting to use the toilet and wished she had used the bathroom when Garth had asked her before he disappeared into the abyss.

'Garth!' Samantha screamed. 'How much longer are you going to be in there? I am so in need of a wee.' Samantha was banging on the bathroom door frantically now, paranoid she was going to wet herself.

'Almost done, sorry, Mum,' Garth mumbled from behind a toothbrush. 'Why don't you use one of the other three bathrooms in the house?'

When Garth emerged from the bathroom smelling of an aftershave counter in a department store, Samantha was taken aback by his appearance. 'Oh my gosh, you do scrub up well. Why do you let yourself go so frequently?' Samantha remarked.

'Why do I need to spend hours getting myself ready for a university lecture? I would have to get up at six o'clock in the morning! Sleep is very important in the world of a university student,' Garth stated.

'Okay, out of the way, quickly before I pee myself. You do look lovely. Enjoy yourself. What time can I expect you home?' Samantha knew this was an absurd question as where Garth and alcohol were concerned there were no time limits.

'All I can say is don't wait up. Love you, Mum.' He kissed her on the cheek and flew down the stairs like a rat out of an aqueduct.

'On a promise, are we?' Samantha called out after him whilst sitting on the toilet having a very rewarding wee, but he was already out of the door.

Samantha scooped up a bottle of wine, a wine glass, a large box of Thorntons chocolates and the television magazine and made herself comfortable on the sofa for a night watching rubbish television with her wine and chocolates as her only companions. After half a bottle of wine, too many chocolates and several repeated episodes of *Only Fools and Horses*, Samantha emerged from the sofa feeling rather guilty at her gluttonous actions. She picked up the latest copy of *Runner's World* that she had purchased a few days ago and was yet to read. She opened the magazine up at the page displaying a series of exercises to improve on runners' stamina. She decided to give them a go, standing up and then falling back on the sofa as the wine had gone to her head. 'Bugger!' she yelled. 'That puts that idea out of the window.' She was annoyed with herself that she had not seen the exercises before the consumption of wine and chocolates.

Samantha almost jumped off the sofa when she heard her phone make a strange Christmas jingle she had never heard before. It was showing that she had a new WhatsApp message. 'Bugger you, Garth,' she muttered through gritted teeth. He had obviously set up her phone to make this annoying noise every time she received a message after she had told him earlier that day she did not understand fully how it worked. The message was from Sharon.

Hi Ladies, I hope you are enjoying your Christmas Eve? It is the usual bedlam here at the Young household. The kids running riot and bouncing off the walls XXXXX.

Samantha replied:

Hi Ladies, just me and a box of Thorntons and a bottle of wine. Garth is out on the town, no idea what state he will be in when he finally returns home.

Suzie replied:

Hi Ladies, Chelsea is fast asleep, we took her to the local soft play today to tire her out and then had a pizza on the way home, she is exhausted and so am I. Just having a few guilty glasses of wine and a cuddle with my beloved at the moment. Have a great day tomorrow and I will see you both on Boxing Day XXXX.

Samantha must have fallen asleep on the sofa as her mobile phone ringing woke her up with a start and she saw that it was a call from Garth.

'Mum, please help me.' Garth sounded troubled.

'What is it?' Samantha was standing up now in emergency mode.

'I've lost my shoes and I need to walk home,' Garth mumbled through his drunken state.

'Oh, for God's sake, I thought you had been hurt.' Samantha sat back down and realised she needed not to panic. 'Can you not get a taxi?' She couldn't believe that this Cambridge student had the brains of a goldfish sometimes.

'I would but I have spent all my cash. Can you not come and pick me up? Please, Mum,' Garth pleaded.

'No, sorry, darling. I have drunk a bottle of wine this evening. Get a taxi and I will pay for it when you get home.' She looked up at the clock and realised it was two o'clock in the morning. 'Please hurry as I have just realised the time.'

'Thanks, Mum, love you. I'll hail one now.' Garth blew a kiss down the phone. 'Taxi!' Garth shouted down the phone.

'Thanks for that, son.' Samantha ended the call. 'I am almost deaf now.'

Ten minutes later Samantha could hear the sound of an engine idling outside the house. She put on her shoes and coat and made her way to the taxi driver who was waiting to be paid.

'Twenty-two pounds, please, love,' the taxi driver informed her.

'Bloody hell, where have you been?' Samantha quizzed.

'It's Christmas Day now, love. Double time,' the taxi driver announced.

'Yes, sorry, I forgot. Thank you for getting him back here in one piece anyway.' Samantha handed the taxi driver a twenty-pound note and a five-pound note. 'Keep the change and Merry Christmas.' She dragged Garth out of the taxi as if he were five years old again.

'Thank you, miss.' The taxi driver looked delighted with his tip. 'And a merry Christmas to you, too. Have a lovely day.' The taxi driver sped off, possibly to his next overinflated fare.

Garth stumbled up the driveway holding on to his mother's arm as if he had been wounded in gunfire. He slurred something that sounded like, 'Shit, I can hardly stand up.'

'Where have you been? Why do you not have any shoes? Why are your clothes all covered in mud?' Samantha asked angrily.

'Please, Mum, I have a headache,' Garth slurred.

'You will have an even bigger one in the morning. Mind the step and get yourself into bed and I will see you sometime in the morning.' Samantha struggled to steady him whilst he climbed the stairs.

Garth pushed open the bedroom door but it was already open and he fell face-first on the floor. 'Night, Mum, love you and thanks.' Garth lifted his right hand slightly from the floor to show his appreciation. Samantha left him there as he was in the recovery position, so if he did throw up, he would not choke on his own vomit. She then got herself into bed, setting her alarm for ten o'clock as she needed to get up and prepare dinner.

Chapter Thirty-Four

David was running from the kitchen to the Christmas tree with food and drink ready to leave out for Father Christmas. He had already placed one glass of milk, two mince pies, three cookies, four cakes and eight carrots. He then put the rather large bowl that is used as the sick bowl next to the food and drink.
'What's that for?' Sharon was startled.

'If Father Christmas eats all the food, then he will be sick, so I have left the sick bowl for him,' David informed her as a matter of fact.

Sharon and Gary fell around laughing. 'That is so thoughtful, son.' Sharon patted him on the head. 'Why are there eight carrots?'

'One for each reindeer, stupid,' David replied smugly whilst folding his arms.

'So thoughtful. Father Christmas will certainly appreciate this and leave you lots of presents.' Sharon smiled to herself, so grateful for the way David had grown up. He was still the baby in the family, but hopefully not for much longer if Sharon managed to achieve the twenty-six-mile run ahead of her in April.

'Well done, son. It is time to get yourself off to bed now. Father Christmas will only deliver presents if you are asleep – you know that, don't you?' Sharon held out her hand to take David's.

'Come on, I will take you up and tuck you in.' Sharon climbed the stairs slowly at David's pace, tucked him into bed and gave him a huge kiss on the

forehead. 'Night, son. I am so excited to see what Father Christmas brings for us all in the morning. Sleep well.' She turned off the bedside lamp and crept downstairs.
'That's all of them in bed now, Gary.' 'Thank goodness for that. I was thinking we were going to be kept awake all night.' Gary sighed.

'Well, it is not over yet. We have all the presents to get out of the garage, sort into piles under the tree and put their stockings into each of their rooms.' Sharon was chirpy considering the mammoth task that lay ahead of her.

'I'll go and pour us a drink and start bringing the presents in from the garage and you can sort them into piles.' Gary was pulling bottles of drink out of the cupboard. 'Gin or vodka?' Gary called from inside the cupboard.

'Gin, please, and you had better make it a large one,' Sharon yelled back.

Gary returned with two large glasses of gin and tonic, placed them on the coffee table and disappeared into the garage. After he had made seven trips to and from the garage with black bags full of presents, the fun began as they started sorting all of the gifts into piles; the piles were extremely high for each of the boys.

Gary started rattling and shaking all of his presents to try to guess what was inside each of them.

'Stop it, you could break the contents,' Sharon screamed.

'Oh, I see it is fragile. I wonder what is in this one, then?' Gary rattled the present some more.

'Not necessarily, but that doesn't mean I can tell you what is in there.' Sharon put her hand over her mouth. 'Can you hear that?' She flew out of the living room and ran upstairs to see who had woken up. Dennis was running across the hallway, having been to the bathroom. 'You okay, sweetheart?' Sharon whispered.

'I thought I heard Father Christmas in the bathroom,' Dennis explained.

'Oh really? I didn't hear anything. I don't think he will use our bathroom – he has his own.' Sharon smiled.

'Is he still coming tonight?' Dennis looked disappointed.

'Yes, but you know you have to be asleep first before he can deliver presents.' Sharon kissed him on the cheek and walked him back to his bed, tucked him in and gave him another kiss on the cheek. 'Love you, son.'

When Sharon returned to the living room, Gary was tucking into the tub of chocolates. 'All okay?' Gary mumbled whilst eating the chocolate and most of it dribbled down his chin.
'Yes, Dennis was up for a wee.'

'Is it safe to put their stockings in their rooms now, then?' Gary asked, stuffing more chocolate into his mouth.

'I'd leave it a few minutes. It should be okay then.' Sharon removed the tub of chocolates from Gary's lap. 'You will make yourself sick eating that amount of chocolate before bed.'

It was three o'clock when they had finally finished and fell into bed.

'Merry Christmas, Gary.' Sharon kissed him on the lips.

'Merry Christmas, Sharon.' Gary gave her a hug.

They were both asleep within a few seconds.

Chapter Thirty-Five

'Ouch!' Suzie yelled out, which startled Brett.
'Where is the fire?' Brett murmured groggily.
Chelsea was jumping up and down on the bed. 'Santa has been, Mummy! Please come and see.' She jumped off the bed with such excitement she landed head first on the bedside cabinet. Blood exploded from her head. The screams filled the bedroom and the whole flat.
'Brett!' Suzie screamed. 'Get up! Chelsea has hurt herself.' Suzie scooped Chelsea up in her arms and carried her to the bathroom. She found a towel and wrapped it around Chelsea's head, but the blood was soaking through extremely fast. 'Phone an ambulance, Brett, please, now!' Suzie shouted. Brett appeared in the doorway of the bathroom, standing there in just his boxer shorts, horrified by what greeted him. It was like something from a *Psycho* movie. 'Suzie, please don't panic. We can take her in the car, it will be quicker. Get yourself dressed. I will keep Chelsea calm and then I can get dressed.' Brett held Chelsea close and tried to comfort her, but she was extremely distressed and wailing loudly.
'Blood, there is blood!' Chelsea cried out. '
It's okay. Mummy's here, darling.' Suzie took over holding the towel and Brett ran to get changed.
'Right, let's go,' Brett ordered after throwing on a few clothes from the washing pile.

The drive to the Whittington Hospital was a short journey – it being Christmas morning there was hardly any traffic on the roads apart from the odd taxi driver. On arrival at the hospital, Brett dropped Suzie and Chelsea at the entrance and then went to find a parking space. Suzie carried Chelsea in screaming and pouring blood. 'Help, someone, please help me!' Suzie yelled as soon as she was in the door.

A nurse stopped looking at the paperwork in her hand, ran over to Suzie and ushered her into an empty cubicle. 'Oh, sweetheart, what have you done to yourself?' the nurse asked Chelsea.

Chelsea was sobbing trying to get her words out. 'I... fell... off... the... bed.'

'Well, don't worry, sweetheart. We will get this looked at by a wonderful doctor. Can I have a look under the towel, please?' The nurse carefully removed the bloodstained towel from Chelsea's head.

'Ouch, that hurts.' Chelsea hugged her mummy.

'It will need a few stitches,' the nurse whispered to Suzie. 'I will get a doctor to have a look. When I return, you can book the little one in with the desk.' She pulled the curtain closed as she left, to give Suzie and Chelsea some privacy. Brett opened the curtains and looked ill when he saw the size of the cut above Chelsea's eye.

'How is my little soldier doing?' Brett asked.

'It hurts a lot,' Chelsea replied, still sobbing.

The nurse returned with some painkiller for Chelsea. 'Here you go, sweetheart. Can you take this medicine for me? This will help to take the pain away for you.' The nurse fed a spoonful of medicine to Chelsea. 'Well done, you little brave lady. The doctor won't be very long and he will make your head stop bleeding for you.'

Chelsea was just starting to doze in Suzie's arms, as the medicine was starting to take effect, when the doctor pulled the curtains back and smiled as he came in. 'Do I have a little girl in here with a little cut on her head?'

'That's me,' Chelsea mumbled. 'Are you going to make it better?'

'Of course I am. Can I have a look, please, little one?' The doctor prepared himself by washing his hands and putting on a fresh pair of rubber gloves. 'What were you doing to hurt your head?' the doctor asked.

'I was jumping on the bed and fell off.' Chelsea sobbed.

'Oh dear, if I had a pound for every time I heard this I would be a millionaire by now.' The doctor looked closely at the cut above Chelsea's eye. 'It is not that bad, poppet. I can put a few butterfly stitches on it and it will stop bleeding and you can get back to your Christmas.' The doctor turned to the nurse who was holding a tray of butterfly stitches. He carefully peeled them from the wrapper and placed them gently on Chelsea's head. 'There you go, poppet. All fixed.' The doctor stood back to admire his work.

'Thank you so much and sorry for being hysterical,' Suzie apologised.

'You are welcome, and please don't apologise. It looked worse than it was. Children bounce back very quickly. Please speak to the nurse, who will give you some advice on what to keep an eye out for once you are home. Merry Christmas to you all. Enjoy your day and no more jumping off beds, young lady.' The doctor gave Chelsea a high five. 'Can you give the parents advice on concussion, please, Nurse?' the doctor asked and left the cubicle.

'How are you feeling, sweetheart?' the nurse enquired.

'Can I open my presents from Santa now?' Chelsea asked.

The three adults laughed together. 'I say that you are feeling much better now.' The nurse smiled. 'Please keep an eye on her for concussion, as the doctor said, and take this leaflet as it has some information on it with regards to what signs to look for.'

Brett took the leaflet from the nurse and then Suzie's free arm; she carried Chelsea with the other. 'Thank you, nurse, for all of your help and have a merry Christmas.'

'Merry Christmas to you too.' The nurse smiled and showed them the way out.

'Thank you, Brett.' Suzie gave him a kiss on the cheek once they were in the car.

'You don't need to say thank you. I am just glad Chelsea is okay.' Brett looked in the rear-view mirror, to see Chelsea huddled up in the back seat. 'Shall we start Christmas again?' Brett smiled.

'Absolutely. Although I am sorry that dinner may be delayed slightly,' Suzie apologised.

'It doesn't matter if we don't get Christmas dinner until next week, as long as we spend the whole day together.' Brett kissed Suzie lovingly on the lips.

On arrival home, they realised Chelsea had fallen asleep in the car. Brett carried her up the stairs to the flat and through to the living room, where he placed her carefully onto the sofa. He covered her with a blanket and kissed her delicately on the wound on her head.

'Cup of tea?' Suzie whispered.

'Oh, yes, please, and put some brandy in it,' Brett whispered back.

'I'll make it a double.' Suzie put the kettle on to boil and rummaged in the cupboards for the brandy.

'How often do we need to check on Chelsea?' Suzie panicked.

'She is breathing just fine. It looked worse than it was.' Brett hugged Suzie.

Chapter Thirty-Six

Samantha was busy preparing the vegetables for dinner and singing along to 'White Christmas' when Garth appeared in the doorway of the kitchen, looking as though he had been dragged through a hedge backwards. 'What time is it?' he whispered.

'Why are you whispering?' Samantha joked.

'Because my head hurts really bad and so does my body. Would you believe me if I said I woke up fully clothed on the floor of my bedroom with no shoes on and covered in mud? Did you not hear me come in?' Garth questioned.

'You do not remember, do you?' Samantha was starting to enjoy this.

'Obviously not, no.' Garth was shocked by the smug grin on his mother's face.

'Please do not worry yourself. It was nothing really. Grab yourself some painkillers and I will have dinner ready in around an hour.' Samantha handed Garth two tablets and poured some water into a glass.

'Do you have any stomach-settling medicine? I think I'm gonna puke.' Garth rummaged in the cupboard.

'Delightful. Yes, it is possibly at the back as I cannot remember the last time I used it.' Samantha waved her spatula around towards the rear of the cupboard.

'Thanks, Mum. I am just going to lie on the sofa. Do you know where I took my shoes off? I can't find them anywhere.' Garth walked towards the living room, searching the corners of the house as he went.

Samantha smiled to herself as he did. He was so drunk last night he had no idea what state he was in when he got home or indeed how he got home. 'Would you like white or red wine with your dinner?' Samantha called out to him.

'I am never drinking again,' Garth shouted back.

'That is what they all say.'

Samantha watched the Queen's speech with a glass of red wine and then gave Garth a little shake. 'Garth, honey, lunch is ready.'

Garth rolled onto the floor with a thud. 'Never again am I going to touch alcohol.' Garth rubbed his head.

They sat down at the dinner table and tucked into the feast that Samantha had prepared.

'So, Mum, when are you going running next?' Garth mumbled whilst shovelling food into his mouth as if he hadn't eaten for a whole week.

Samantha put her glass of wine down in astonishment. 'Tomorrow, actually. Hopefully twelve miles, or maybe more after the amount of food we have eaten today.'

'Sounds great. I may join you, if that's okay?'

Samantha smiled. 'That will be lovely, the more the merrier.'

Garth rubbed his temples to relieve his headache. 'I think a run will do me the world of good to clear this hangover.'

'You are young, Garth. You will bounce back quickly enough. It is when you get to my age a hangover lasts for days or even weeks.'

'Can I go upstairs and get your present, please?' Garth asked to leave the table as if he were six years old.

Samantha walked towards the Christmas tree and retrieved Garth's presents. 'That will be lovely.'

Garth came down with two presents and handed them to Samantha, who handed over a huge pile of presents in return.

The first of Samantha's presents was a workout DVD called *Insanity*. Samantha didn't like the sound of the title. 'Sounds interesting or bloody painful.'

'It's the best on the market – I have done my research like a true university student.' Garth winked.

Samantha unwrapped the second present. It was a year's subscription to *Runner's World* magazine. 'How thoughtful,' Samantha exclaimed.

'I have seen several copies lying around the house. Please don't tell me you have a subscription already?' Garth looked horrified.

'No, I do not. I was considering it, though. Please open yours.'

After unwrapping several packages, Garth showed his appreciation with a hug. 'Thank you, Mum.'

'You are always so difficult to buy for, sorry it is only clothes, but I can see the shoes coming in handy sooner than expected.' Samantha smiled. 'Where are my shoes, Mum?'

'No idea, son, no idea, and it seems you have no idea either. Merry Christmas.' Samantha hugged and kissed Garth.

'Maybe it is best I don't know. Merry Christmas.'

Chapter Thirty-Seven

'Father Christmas has been,' Dennis screamed as excitement rang through the whole house.

There was a thunder of feet running down the stairs, which sounded more like a herd of elephants than six boys.

'What time is it?' Sharon opened her eyes but couldn't see the time on the clock.

'Five o'clock,' Gary murmured.

'We have been asleep for two hours. We had better get up otherwise we will miss them opening their presents.' Sharon threw herself out of bed and descended the stairs with Gary following slowly behind.

'Look, Mum, Dad!' David screamed excitedly. 'Father Christmas has brought us loads of presents.' David was dangling his stocking whilst jumping up and down to show his excitement.

'Wow, you must have been good boys this year, then.' Gary smiled.

'Wow, there are more.' David ran towards the huge pile of presents in the living room.

The tidy pile of presents and the clean living room was soon turned into what looked like a war zone. 'That has to be a record. Thirty-two minutes,' Gary said whilst fighting his way through wrapping paper and boxes before sitting down. He had several toys thrown onto his lap. 'I take it I am going to be busy this afternoon making all these toys up?' Gary laughed.

'Mine first, please, Daddy?' Dennis asked. 'No, mine first, please, Daddy,' David pleaded.

'Please don't argue. I will build them both after dinner.' Gary signalled time out with his hands.

Gary handed a present to Sharon. 'Here you go, gorgeous.'

Sharon ripped the paper off with excitement and squealed in delight when she saw it was an iPod. 'Thank you, just what I wanted.' Sharon turned and gave Gary a huge hug.

'I'll go and put the turkey in the oven.' Sharon shuffled her way to the kitchen. With a family of eight to feed, the turkey would only fit in the oven if all the shelves were removed, and it took several hours to cook. Once the turkey was done she could then start cooking all the other items: pigs in blankets, stuffing, roast potatoes, roast parsnips and Yorkshire puddings. Every year she told herself she would cook the turkey the night before, but this had never happened, as Christmas Eve was always so busy and full of such excitement. It obviously wasn't going to matter this year with the kids all rising at five o'clock. They may get to eat just after the Queen's speech this year. It was a tradition of her late mother's that dinner could only be eaten after the Queen had spoken. She never did share her mother's enthusiasm for this tradition when she was growing up, although now she was older, with her own family, she could see the importance.

After several hours of bedlam, arguing and excitement, Sharon appeared from the kitchen holding a huge turkey and placed it proudly on the table. The boys all stopped what they were doing and ran to the table, as if they had not eaten for weeks. They each pulled their crackers, fought over the useless plastic toys inside, and placed their paper hats on their heads waiting for the rest of the festive food to arrive. Dinner was the usual fighting over the last Yorkshire pudding and pig in blanket, but they were all well fed and happy.

'Anyone for pudding?' Sharon asked the seven stuffed-looking faces before her whilst clearing the table.

'Is it chocolate cake?' Michael quizzed.

'Yes, I have chocolate cake, Christmas pudding, mince pies and a huge trifle. So there is something that everyone likes.' Sharon smiled.

'Roger, what would you like?' Sharon called whilst walking from the kitchen.

'Some of everything, please Mum.' Roger's eyes were almost popping out.

'Gosh, you will be sick. Have you not eaten enough already?' Sharon looked concerned.

'Yes, but it is only Christmas once a year,' Roger retaliated.

'Thank God, I couldn't cope with two hours' of sleep every night.'

'You had better get used to it, love.' Gary smirked. 'That is all you are going to get when you have a baby to look after,' Gary teased.

'Next year will be even more manic, boys,' Sharon told them.

Daniel pulled a disgusted-looking face. 'Please stop all this baby talk. It is making me sick.'

'That will be your mother's cooking,' Gary joked.

'She's got to run the marathon first though, *stupidly*,' Michael said.

Daniel got down from the table and picked up his iPad from the sofa.

Gary ordered him to get back to the table. 'You can play with that once we have finished dinner.' Gary pointed to the seat where Daniel had been sitting.

Daniel threw his new iPad back onto the sofa and shuffled over to the table once again. 'Trifle for me, Mum, please.'

Sharon served each one of the boys their pudding and then retrieved the cream and ice cream from the kitchen.

After all the puddings were demolished, everyone crashed onto the sofa and watched a rerun of *The Snowman*. Gary stood up rather sharply, ran upstairs and returned with another present for Sharon. 'Here you go. This is a present from all of us.' Gary handed Sharon the delicately wrapped gift.

'Oh, wow, thank you. It looks too lovely to open.' Sharon had a tear in her eye. On opening it she discovered a Fitbit watch. 'Amazing, thank you. It is great, just what I wanted.' Sharon was delighted and immediately put it on.

'You are going to have to charge it up first, love,' Gary advised. 'You can also download an app on your phone – I did my research on it before I bought it.' Gary was pleased with himself.

'Thank you. I will use it tomorrow when we go for our long run.' Sharon kissed each of the boys in turn and then Gary.

It was just after six o'clock in the afternoon and the entire house crashed out on the sofa. They were soon soundly asleep.

Chapter Thirty-Eight

Chelsea woke after sleeping for an hour. 'Hey, sweetheart.' Suzie stroked her head as she came round. 'Santa has been. Would you like to see what he has brought you?'

'Oh yes, Mummy, but you have to open your huge box first.' Chelsea jumped up and led Suzie to the hallway where the box was sitting. 'Do you want a hand opening it, Mummy? It is huge.' Chelsea started to peel the paper off.

'Whatever can it be?' Suzie was starting to feel rather embarrassed by the size of the box. It soon became clear that inside was a state-of-the-art treadmill. 'Wow!' Suzie squealed. 'Thank you, thank you, that is amazing.' She turned to kiss and hug Chelsea and Brett in turn. 'This is the most amazing Christmas present anyone has ever bought for me.' Suzie wiped tears of joy from her eyes.

'You are welcome, darling.' Brett kissed her in return. 'You are the most amazing woman I have ever met.' Brett reached for another present from his pocket, only this one was amazingly small and delicately wrapped.

'You have bought me more? Why on earth is the treadmill not enough?' Suzie covered her face with her hands to shield her embarrassment.

'Please, this one is from me. The treadmill is from Chelsea and I.' Brett handed her the perfectly wrapped parcel. 'Well, it won't open itself.'

'I'll open it for you, Mummy,' Chelsea cried.

'Okay, darling, but please be careful – it is so beautifully wrapped.' She gave Chelsea the parcel.

The paper was torn off at the speed of light and inside was a velvet jewellery box. The colour started to drain from Suzie's face. 'Wow, could it be jewellery?' Suzie took the box from Chelsea and opened it slowly. Her breath was taken away when she saw the most exquisite drop pearl earrings she had ever seen. 'Oh, Brett, they are amazing, you really shouldn't have.' Suzie removed them from the box and tried to put them in her ears, fumbling for the tiny holes in her lobes.

'Only the best for my best girl.' Brett smiled. 'Now, young lady,' Brett turned to Chelsea, 'what has Santa brought you?'

Chelsea ran into the living room. 'Slow down,' Suzie called after her.

Chelsea was squealing as she removed the paper from all the presents that were wrapped and placed under the tree. 'Oh, look, Mummy. This one is for Brett.' She handed Brett the parcel.

'I am embarrassed now, as it is nothing as elaborate as a treadmill or pearl earrings.' Suzie turned red.

'It is not a competition. I bought you those items as I care about you, more than you can possibly imagine.' Brett tore the paper from the present and was made up with the contents: the latest Chelsea football shirt. Brett kissed Suzie and Chelsea in return.

'Here is another.' Chelsea handed a present to Brett that Suzie had not seen before. 'I made it at school, just for you,' Chelsea informed him.

'Oh wow, that is a lovely thought.' After opening it he sat staring into the box that was beneath the paper for several minutes and shed a tear.

'Why are you crying?' Chelsea asked. 'Do you not like it?' Chelsea looked horrified.

'Absolutely not. This is the most fantastic present I have ever been given.' Brett was beaming from ear to ear.

'Well, what is it?' Suzie was anxious to see.

Brett proudly held up a handmade mug with the words 'Worlds best Dad' written on it, in Chelsea's own handwriting. 'Come here, little one, and give me a cuddle. If you want me to be your daddy, I will be most proud.' Brett hugged Chelsea tightly.

'Does that mean you will marry Mummy?' Suzie and Brett looked at each other but didn't say anything; they could read each other's minds.

'One day I hope so,' Brett informed Chelsea. 'Merry Christmas to my two special ladies.'

'I suppose I had better go and cook the dinner, as it won't cook itself. I hope you are hungry, I have enough to feed an army.'

Brett and Chelsea laughed so hard they started to cry.

Chapter Thirty-Nine

Sharon and Suzie were waiting at the meeting place in the park for Samantha to arrive, jumping up and down trying to keep warm under the falling snow. The film crew were busy wrapping themselves in several hats and scarfs, as they knew they were going to get very cold being out for several hours. A rather large person dressed in a Santa suit came towards them, waving frantically. They all looked at each other in turn, thinking a homeless person was coming to talk to them – only when the person got closer did Sharon and Suzie realise it was Samantha.

'I know it's Christmas, Samantha, but you didn't need to dress for the occasion.' Sharon laughed.

'Bah humbug to you as well, Sharon,' Samantha snapped.

'At least you won't get cold,' Suzie remarked.

'Neither will you two, as I brought you a Santa hat each.' Samantha passed the hats to Suzie and Sharon in turn. 'I did not forget the camera crew either.' Samantha handed over hats to the camera and sound crew. 'How did you two get the short straw, filming on Boxing Day?' Samantha enquired.

'We are married and have no children at home, so it suits us. I'm Christine and this is John.' She shook Samantha's hand as she spoke.

Samantha shook John's hand next. 'I am pleased to meet you both. Sorry it's going to be a cold one today. No one thought about the possibility of training in the snow. Rain is one thing, but this white stuff is a different kettle of fish altogether.'

Suzie, Sharon, Christine and John put their hats on and felt ridiculous, but not as ridiculous as Samantha.

'Twelve miles today, then, girls?' Suzie enquired.

'I have no objection to doing twenty, after the amount of food I ate yesterday,' Sharon informed her.

'Me too,' Samantha added. 'I've calculated twelve miles if we run around Richmond Park and then on to Ladbroke Grove.'

'I've brought the grippers for us to put on the bottom of our trainers – these are to prevent us from slipping and causing ourselves harm.' Sharon handed out a pair to Suzie and Samantha in turn. 'I am not sure how easy it is going to be running with these on the bottom of our trainers, but I suppose it's better than ending up in A & E on Boxing Day.'

'I don't want to go there two days in a row.' Suzie sighed.

'Why are you planning to go there tomorrow?' Samantha asked.

'No, we were there yesterday. Chelsea jumped off the bed and smacked her head on the corner of the bedside cabinet.' Suzie demonstrated the jumping and flying motion that Chelsea had made for her to become injured.

'Gosh, is she okay?' Sharon was concerned.
'Fine, just a few butterfly stitches.'

'I thought it was only boys that did things like that?' Sharon looked horrified at the thought of a girl doing such a thing.

'Maybe your girl, if you get her, will be more girly than my tomboy Chelsea.' Suzie rested her arm on Sharon's to give her reassurance.

The girls started jogging slowly to warm up before breaking into a more strenuous run.

'So, Suzie,' Samantha said, 'what was in the huge box that Brett got you for Christmas? I am dying to know.'

'It is a state-of-the-art treadmill!' Suzie blushed.

'Wow, that is amazing. Around yours to train in future then?' Sharon continued, 'I got an iPod, a Fitbit watch and a new pair of running leggings, for which I am eternally grateful, as my others were falling off me seeing as I have lost so much weight since starting this training.' Sharon made a modelling pose in her new running leggings. 'What did Garth get you, Samantha?'

'He bought me a DVD of the most gruelling exercise workout called "Insane".'

Suzie laughed. 'It's called "Insanity" not "Insane".'

'Whatever it is called, it looks bloody scary. If he had bought me it this time last year, it would have gone straight to the charity shop in the new year, but now I am reluctantly looking forward to giving it a go.'

'We can all come around and be insanely worked out,' Sharon stated. 'We are in this together, remember.'

'Amazing idea. At least I will not feel so stupid prancing around my own living room if there is more than just me. Definitely, we will set up a date and time. Samantha was soon out of breath and rather warm in her suit. 'What do you normally do on Boxing Day, ladies?'

'Usually building Lego in my house. I've left it all to Gary this year,' Sharon replied smugly. 'Having six boys, who all get Lego for Christmas, it's a mini Lego world in our house.'

'I usually hit the sales. I've spent many a Boxing Day standing outside Next at five o'clock in the morning, queuing for the bargains. I buy all of Chelsea's clothes for next summer and winter. You know how much they are going to grow in a year, being children. Sometimes I pick up a bargain for me while I am there, but my main reason for going is to buy clothes for Chelsea. Being a single mum, you have to take advantage of these sales, otherwise, she would be dressed in Primarni clothes.'

'What is Primarni?' Samantha asked, stunned, as she had never heard of this brand of clothing before.

'It's Primark, but people call it Primarni to make it sound more glamorous than it really is,' Sharon informed her. 'I have to say, having six boys who ruin clothes so easily, Primarni is a must in my house.'

'Are their clothes good quality then?' Samantha quizzed

Suzie laughed. 'They are just so cheap, you can afford to throw them away when they are ruined.

Samantha was horrified at the thought of throwing clothes away.

'Gosh, I have never thrown any of my clothes away.'

'What? Never?' Sharon almost choked on the thought.

'No, that is why I live in a four-bedroom house, as every room is full of clothes. Most of them do not fit me as I have developed a middle-age spread, but after all this training I hope to get back into some of them again.'

'You should have a boot sale to raise some cash for the Guide Dogs charity, to add to your marathon funds,' Suzie suggested.

'Now that is a fine idea, young Suzie.' Samantha pondered the suggestion.

After they had run three miles, they stopped at a petrol station to purchase a bottle of water each. They disposed of the bottles and continued to run. The snow was settling and it made running more difficult, as if they were running on sand, having to get their knees up higher. The grippers on their feet were helping them stay upright; however, the motion of running was more strenuous.

'I'm going to need to wee very shortly,' Sharon announced.

'Have you got your peeing contraption?' Samantha asked.

'Of course. I never go anywhere without it.' 'What? Even in a Tesco toilet? You do not need it in there, surely?' Samantha was concerned.

'You do if you don't want to sit on the loo seat,' Sharon announced.

Suzie joined in. 'I just hover.'

'I place paper on the seat before I sit on it,' Samantha advised.

'Can we please stop talking about peeing? I need to wee right now.' Sharon ran towards a bush.

'Cover me, ladies,' Sharon yelled from behind the bush. 'And no filming me pissing in a bush, please, Christine and John.'

'There is no one around, only us saddos out for a run on Boxing Day,' Suzie shouted after her.

After five miles Samantha tripped over a loose paving slab and fell straight onto her knees in a huge, freezing cold, muddy puddle. Just as she was getting up, fell backwards as three young lads rode past and stopped on their nice new shining pushbikes and one shouted, something rude. He laughed to himself. Another started chanting, 'Who ate all the pies? Who ate all the pies? You fat bastard, you fat bastard, you ate all the pies.' He completed his chant with a middle finger as the lads rode away.

'The youth of today,' Samantha muttered to herself whilst brushing herself down as if it were going to make any difference to the mess she was in.

Suzie started laughing hysterically. 'You look like you have shit yourself, Samantha.'

'Well, thanks for the observation,' Samantha retaliated.

'Don't blame her, Suzie. She didn't intend to fall in the puddle.' Sharon tried to calm Samantha.

'My arse is very wet and freezing cold and not through sweat. Come on, let's not give up.' Samantha ran on, displaying her brown arse.

After seven miles it was Suzie's turn to stop. 'Shit, stop, I've got cramp.' She fell to the floor, extending her legs in the air.

'You look like you are in labour too.' Sharon laughed.
'Please rub my legs,' Suzie pleaded.
'Yes, sounds like you are in labour.' Sharon rubbed Suzie's legs to ease the cramp. 'Gosh, we are going to be great entertainment for spectators on race day,' Samantha fretted.

'We have four months yet and we are still in training. We will be fine as long as we stick together.' Sharon calmed Samantha's fears.

'It's gone now.' Suzie got up and ran ahead. 'Come on, just a few more miles and we can get back to the kids.'

'Not sure I want to get back to the madness of my house,' Sharon remarked. 'Can we prolong this run any longer?'

'You can come back to mine for a cuppa, if you want? Tell Gary we did fifteen miles,' Suzie said.

'Deal. Come on, let's step it up a notch.' Sharon ran ahead and was eager to get her cup of tea and peace and quiet at Suzie's flat before heading back to the Lego wars in her house.

Once they arrived at Ladbroke Grove Tube station, they were just relieved that they had achieved the twelve-mile run that they had set out to complete.

'How is everyone feeling?' Samantha enquired.

Sharon was struggling for breath but managed to squeeze out, 'Okay, you?'

'Amazing. Well, I do not feel amazing in body, but mentally that was amazing. Why did I not take up running sooner in my life?' Samantha quizzed herself. 'I cannot feel my fingers or my toes, but my body is warm as toast in this suit.'

'I agree,' Suzie added. 'It's better than standing outside Next at five o'clock. I am so glad I decided to do this, and of course the best part is I have met you two wonderful ladies.'

'Hopefully the Tube train is warmer. Thankfully, there won't be many people on it, as we do look a sight.' Sharon laughed.

'Come on, let us go. Garth is probably still in bed. He probably will not believe me when he gets up and I tell him I have been for a twelve-mile run this morning. He was going to join us, but he has a hangover from hell, as he calls it.'

'Don't forget – if Gary asks it was fifteen,' Sharon said.

'Of course. Your secret is safe with me.' Samantha winked.

'Come on, there is a cup of tea with your name on it.' Suzie pulled Sharon towards the direction of the station.

'Next time we can do a shorter run, maybe five miles,' Samantha informed them.

Christine and John appeared from around the corner as they were a few paces ahead 'Well done, ladies. Very inspirational running twelve miles on a very cold Boxing Day morning.' Christine rubbed her hands together as she spoke to try to get the blood circulating again. 'That was such fun, ladies. Thank you.'

'Lovely to meet you all.' John shook each girl's hand in turn. 'Best of luck for the big day. You will fly through with ease, I am sure.' John handed Samantha the Santa hat.

'Thank you for the inspiration,' Suzie said. 'We are certainly going to need it.'

'Are you getting the train back with us?' Samantha asked Christine and John.

'We thought we might go and see if we can find some food first.' John was turning, searching for a café that may be open.

'Another twelve miles, to add to the *Jogging Buddy* log, this really is adding up.' Samantha smiled.

Chapter Forty

The temperature gauge on the car was reading minus five. 'Why are we doing this?' Samantha asked Suzie as they drove to the boot sale.
'Because you promised to raise some money for your charity.'
'Yes, but it is so cold. I don't think I have ever felt this cold before,' Samantha snivelled.
'Oh, come on, it will be a laugh,' Sharon said. 'I have had a huge clear-out of old toys. I am going to make some huge amounts of money for my charity.'
'Have either of you done a car boot sale before?' Samantha asked.
'Hell no!' Suzie screeched.
'Yes, loads of times and they are great fun,' Sharon chirped.
'We can leave it up to you then, Mrs Young, to take the lead.' Samantha laughed.

They were directed to an area on the car park and told how close to park to the other cars. 'Gosh, I am glad I have lost some weight, otherwise, I would not have got out of my door,' Samantha grumbled.
Suzie looked horrified. 'What are all these people doing around your car?'
'Get away.' Samantha waved at them to move them on, but they did not take any notice and opened the boot of her car and started removing items,

holding them up, asking how much, throwing them into the boot and carrying out the process again.

'Just leave them to it,' Sharon advised. 'They can at least unpack the car for you.'

'I feel very uncomfortable about this. What if someone steals something?' Samantha asked.

'Being a solicitor, you can sue them.' Sharon laughed.

'How much?' A pair of shoes were shoved into Samantha's face.

'Twenty pounds.' Samantha smiled proudly.

The shoes were thrown back into the boot and the buyer walked off making a loud tut sound.

'They cost me one hundred pounds,' Samantha called after him. 'How much do people wish to spend?' Samantha raised her eyes.
'Ten pence, usually,' Sharon remarked. 'Bloody hell, I would rather give them to a charity than let these vultures purchase them for ten pence.' Samantha set her eyes on a young mother who was riffling through the black bags in her boot.

'Do you have any children's clothes?' the young mother asked.
'I am sorry, I do not. Sharon, do you have any?'

'I do – only boys', though. If you are looking for girls' clothes, I am sorry.' Sharon took pity on the three-year-old girl who was in tow.

'Wow, this is amazing.' Suzie held up Samantha's wedding dress. 'How much did this cost you?' Suzie squealed.

'Too much.' Samantha sighed. 'Most expensive piece of clothing I have ever purchased.'

Sharon took hold of the amazing dress. 'You have never mentioned your ex-husband. Was it that bad?'

'Worse. Bloody idiot.' Samantha dismissed the question. 'He was selfish.'

'Aren't they all?' Sharon commented.

'I suppose they are, which is why I have never looked at another man since.'

'Until now.' Suzie laughed.

'Hopefully, Mr Sex God is not as selfish as my Brian was.' Samantha patted her stomach to demonstrate Mr Sex God's six-pack. 'When I was in labour,' Samantha started, 'I asked Brian to go and run a bath, as I was in labour.'

'He didn't do it?' Sharon asked.

'Oh, he ran a bath all right. I crawled up the stairs on all fours as I was in such pain, struggled into the bathroom, expecting to get into the bath but he was sat in it.'

'Oh my God, that is so cruel, but also so funny. I can understand why you divorced him.' Sharon laughed.

'Why was he in the bath?' Suzie enquired.

'Because he knew that he would be at the hospital a long time if I was in labour.' Samantha gritted her teeth as she spoke.

'What did you do?' Suzie probed.

'I took the keys to his Aston Martin and told him I was driving myself to the hospital and not to blame me if I gave birth in the car.' Samantha held her head high as if she had won an argument.

'Wow. What did he do?' Suzie asked cautiously.

'He chased me up the road, with a towel wrapped around him, as I drove away at high speed.'

'Oh wow. Jeremy Kyle eat your heart out.' Suzie punched the air.

'Never mind Jeremy Kyle. What happened next? Sharon asked.

'I got to hospital and left the car parked in the area for ambulances and screamed as I crawled into the hospital.' Samantha was recreating the crawling motion as she spoke.

'The car? Did it get towed away?' Suzie was concerned.

'Not sure. It was ruined anyway. My waters broke on the way.' Samantha laughed.

'Result,' Suzie called out. 'What happened after that?'

'I had Garth. When we finally went home, Brian was gone, car and all. Better off without him.' Samantha sighed. 'That was the final straw. He was such a selfish twat.'

'How much for the wedding dress?' a young girl called out to Samantha.
'Make me an offer,' Samantha called back. 'I'll give you a fiver for it.' The young girl held out a five-pound note.

'Deal.' Samantha held out her hand, shook the young girl's hand and exchanged her wedding dress for the five-pound note.

'Wow, that must have cost you a small packet and you've just sold it for a fiver.' Sharon gasped.

'Didn't bring me any luck though, did it? Hope it brings her better luck. Good riddance to bad rubbish.' Samantha chuckled to herself.

Once the sun came out and the vultures had calmed down, the boot sale filled with genuine buyers, expecting to pay more than ten pence an item.

Samantha totalled up her takings. 'I have over two hundred pounds,' she announced, waving her wad of notes in the air.

Sharon looked horrified. 'Put it away. You will be mugged for a tenner around here.'

'Shit, sorry. I will stuff it in my bra, like a real woman.' Samantha folded the bundle of notes and stuffed them into her bra.

'Love the padding.' Suzie laughed. 'Well, I do need some, especially after losing so much weight from all the training. My bras are feeling rather saggy.' Samantha shook her boobs.

Sharon held her hands over Samantha's boobs to shield her from passers-by. 'Gosh, you are embarrassing sometimes.'

Suzie gathered her bag. 'Anyone want doughnuts and coffee?'

'Sounds great. Thank you.' Sharon handed over a five-pound note. 'Milk, no sugar.'

'No panic about the money, I will get it.' Suzie started walking away from the makeshift stall. 'Samantha? Can I get you a coffee and doughnuts?'

'Please, anything hot and wet will not go a miss at the moment.' Samantha stamped up and down on the spot to get some life back into her feet.

Suzie returned with the three coffees and three bags of doughnuts, using an old piece of cardboard as a makeshift tray.

'I would have helped if you had asked,' Samantha remarked.

'Shut up. I am totally capable of handling a few cups of coffee and some doughnuts,' Suzie said. 'Tuck in. It will either kill or cure you. I don't rate the cleanliness of the coffee wagon. I was going to have a breakfast roll, but wondered if it came with free salmonella.'

Sharon asked, 'Do you mind if I take a wander around? I do love a boot sale.'

'Of course. I will take a walk when you get back,' Samantha announced. 'Just remember you are here to get rid of stuff and try and not purchase anyone else's crap.

'Hang on until I've eaten my doughnuts and I will come with you.' Suzie shoved an entire doughnut in her mouth, then removed the sugar from her fingers by brushing them on her scarf and grabbed Sharon's arm.

Samantha started looking at all the other stallholders and wondered why the stall opposite, run by a gentleman, was getting an awful lot of customers. She was also confused as to why men were parting with several twenty-pound notes in exchange for a box of dog treats. Bloody expensive dog treats, she thought. Not long after the thought entered her head, two police officers arrived at the gentleman's stall. They asked some questions and started removing the boxes of dog biscuits and placing them into one big bag. The gentleman was soon put into handcuffs and led away. Everyone stopped what they were doing and started to look at the commotion that the gentleman was now causing. Soon crowds of people were gathered around the stall, watching as the gentleman was screaming and shouting, asking why his stock was being removed. Sharon and Suzie returned a short while later.

'What's going on?' Sharon asked. 'No idea. The guy opposite is being arrested and all his dog biscuits are being removed.'
'Seems harsh,' Suzie noted.

'I have seen this on a TV cop show that Gary watched once. They do not contain dog biscuits,' Sharon informed them.

'Oh really? What do they contain then?' Samantha was confused.

'Drugs. I bet any money they contain drugs,' Sharon remarked.

'Well, that might explain why a box of biscuits was costing several hundred pounds each.' Samantha twigged.

'Bloody hell, I didn't expect this today,' Suzie said. 'I will come more often.'

'So brash, some people have no scruples. That is the reason I became a solicitor – you will never be out of work as there will always be criminals. Just glad I don't work as a defence lawyer. How can you stand there in court and defend the actions of a criminal? I have enough trouble fighting over the custody of a bread maker.'

'Really?' Sharon choked.

'It is a long story and I cannot possibly comment on confidential client matters, but yes, I have a client who is asking me to fight with his ex-wife's solicitor for the bread maker back. I have explained to him he could purchase ten bread makers for the cost of me writing him one letter, but he will not have it. I have a duty to inform a client if an action is not commercially viable, but he is so stuck on arguing with his ex-wife.'

'Probably why he now has an ex-wife.' Sharon laughed.

'Well, it is funny you should say that, as I did wonder myself.' Samantha placed her finger over her mouth as if to signal to keep it a secret.

'Do you have Jeremy Kyle on speed dial?' Suzie joked.

'No, not yet, but I am considering it.' Samantha rolled her eyes. 'Still, it pays the bills for me and my rather demanding university student son.'

Around one o'clock the footfall had almost slowed to a stop. Sharon started packing the few remaining items into black bags. 'I think we should go. I can't see any more people coming in now.'

An elderly lady shuffled up to the stall. 'Hello ladies,' she greeted them. 'Have you anything interesting?'

'That depends what you consider interesting,' Samantha said.

'I have heard there has been a drug bust this morning. You are not selling dog biscuits, are you?' the old lady asked.

'Absolutely not!' Samantha was outraged. 'The gentleman across the way was. He has gone now – off in handcuffs, to be precise.' Samantha put her wrists up to demonstrate what handcuffs were.

'That was him. My son. I told him he was a bloody fool for selling drugs at a boot sale, but he thought he knew better. Do you have children?'

'Yes,' all three ladies replied in unison.

'Well, I do hope they don't bring you as much grief as mine do.' With that, she turned and walked away.

'Well, how strange was that conversation?' Sharon said.

'Little rascal – she has stolen a DVD off the table!' Samantha said.

'Really? What? Her? That little old innocent lady?' Suzie spun around to see her talking to another stallholder.

'Well, where does her son get his criminal mind from? Not from watching *Inspector Morse*, I can tell you.' Samantha let out a loud tut.

'Go after her, Samantha.' Sharon egged her on.

'What? For ten pence? It is not worth the aggravation. Let her have it, if it is going to mean that much to her.' Samantha looked at the old lady with pity.

They finished packing away and Samantha reversed slowly out of the space. She drove slowly through the remaining buyers who were weighed down with bags of other people's junk.

Chapter Forty-One

Samantha was feeling very apprehensive as she entered the building where the 'Meet the Experts' day was being held. She was afraid that she would stick out like a sore thumb amongst all the elite athletes that would be there. As she entered, the reception room was full of average people, some no fitter than herself. The first thing she saw was a map of the course, which brought about great panic as she looked at just how far it was from the start to the finish. There were many people wandering around looking lost. A young lady soon made conversation with her. Samantha realised she was from the sports drink stand, and the lady offered her a sample. She thanked the lady and started to look around at all the other stallholders that were there. The sponsors, Virgin Money, were there to give advice on raising funds for the run. A sports company were there in a huge hall where they were selling all the running kit you could want for. They had a rather interesting way of determining which shoes were best for your running gait. You ran across a mat and then a computer assessed where your feet pressed the most and figured out which shoes would be more suitable for your feet. She decided she would look around the hall later as she wanted a cup of coffee first and to try to talk to some other runners about their reasons for taking part. On entering the ladies' toilet, she heard two girls talking about how scared they were. Samantha joined in their conversation. 'How is your training going, ladies?'

'Not so good,' the young blond answered. 'We have only managed one long run and that wasn't very long, about six miles, I think.'

'That's okay. We have got just over three months yet. I only ran twelve miles on Boxing Day – that is my longest run so far.'

'Wow, you're keen,' the dark-haired one said. 'I was nursing a hangover on Boxing Day.'

'By the time I had finished, I wished I was nursing a hangover, but I am glad I managed it. Only another one and a bit miles longer and that is half the marathon distance,' Samantha announced smugly.

'Thanks for reminding me,' the blond girl remarked sarcastically. 'So what is your reason for running? You must have a reason. No one would volunteer to run twenty-six miles for any other reason.'

'It is a long story,' Samantha said. 'Let us say it is to impress a guy.'

'Oh really?' The dark-haired girl squealed. 'That's why Trisha here is doing it. A guy who she fancies the arse off said if she runs it, he will wine and dine her.'

'Very similar. I have been offered afternoon tea at the Ritz if I run it, by a rather fit solicitor.' Samantha told the story.

'Wow.' Both girls stood open-mouthed. 'Some guy. No wonder you are so keen to go running on Boxing Day. I think I would if I was being taken to the Ritz. Best of luck, honey.' The dark-haired girl patted Samantha on the back. 'Let's hope you get your promise, if you know what I mean.' The girl winked and nudged Samantha in the ribs as she spoke.

'Well, I do hope so. He is really gorgeous. I'm not normally a man-eater, but he is too good to resist. If you know what I mean.' Samantha nudged the girl in return and winked.

'Joanna is my name.' She held out her hand to shake Samantha's. 'This is Trisha.' Trisha held out her hand, too.

'Samantha. Pleased to meet you. Any idea where we can get a cup of coffee from? I am absolutely gasping.'

'Trisha and I were just saying the same thing. Come on. Let's go and look.' Joanna pulled Samantha and Trisha's hands.

It didn't take long for the girls to find a cafeteria selling refreshments. They all decided to go for a large slice of chocolate cake as they needed to load up on carbohydrates for their training.

'Delicious,' Samantha said whilst stuffing more chocolate cake in her mouth.

'This is the only decent thing about all this training. You can have cake and chocolate and not feel guilty as you can just go for a run and work it all off.' Joanna struggled to talk with the large piece of cake in her mouth.

'Absolutely agree there, Joanna.' Trisha nodded, whilst shovelling the cake into her mouth as if it were the last piece of cake on the planet. 'I had steak and chips the other night – it was the best steak and chips I have ever eaten.'

'What time is the first talk?' Samantha asked.

Joanna got her itinerary out of her bag. 'Eleven o'clock is the first one, it's the Marathon Chief Executive giving an outline of the Marathon and it's charity work.'

'Once we have eaten this, perhaps we should go and get a seat in the theatre?' Samantha suggested.

'I'm up for that,' Joanna and Trisha announced together.

They found three seats together and made themselves comfortable. They listened to all the seminars, which they all found useful: how not to overexert themselves in training, what foods to eat, how to tail off their running before the race day, where the toilet and water stops were along the race. Samantha made a note of the toilet stops for Sharon, as she was worrying about where she would wee along the race. One thing she had not considered was the fact that with almost forty thousand people running the race it would take them over thirty minutes to cross the start line. They would have to go to the ExCel in London the week before the race to collect their race number and pack. Within the pack would be a bag with their race number on in which they could store all their personal belongings. This would then be stowed safely on a bus and they would claim their bag at the end of the race. Any racers could get free travel in London on race day – it was nice of London to do something for free. Once the seminars were finished, Samantha went to purchase several new running items: tights, tops, and a fleece. She had her running gait analysed by the very impressive electronic running mat, so she purchased some more appropriate footwear that the salesman advised for her. She was really excited to meet with the others and give them all the information she had learnt that day. She said goodbye to Joanna and Trisha and wished them luck on the race day.

Chapter Forty-Two

Samantha was proud of her new shiny trainers and they felt as though she was running on air.

'Did you get them at the event?' Sharon enquired.

'Sure did. They had this amazing running mat that measured the position of your feet as you run and they recommend the best trainers for your running style,' Samantha told her.

'I do hope that changing trainers this close to a run doesn't cause you any problems,' Suzie announced. 'We were talking about this in class the other day – that if you change trainers too close to a race, you may get an injury.'

'That is not what I want to hear, young Suzie, but the man did look at my running style,' Samantha announced.

'I hope so. Just something to be cautious of. I don't want to say you will get an injury – just sometimes it can cause an injury.' Suzie started blushing as she felt she had upset Samantha.

'No one is getting injured. We are so close, with just under two months to go until the big race day.' Sharon tried to calm the situation. 'We are all anxious and very nervous now, but we have come this far. Nothing is going to go wrong—' Sharon yelled as she fell over a loose paving slab, straight onto her knees. Samantha screamed and Suzie laughed. 'Are you okay?' Samantha said, holding out her hand to help Sharon up.

'I'm fine. Nothing is going to go wrong, remember.' Sharon brushed herself down as she got up. 'It's fine, really.'

'So what information did you find out at the running event?' Suzie asked.

'I know where the toilets are situated,' Samantha informed them.

'That's all I need to know. Thanks.' Sharon smiled.

'Oh, I can't use them Portaloo things,' Suzie remarked.

'Well, they are not the nicest, I admit, but if you have to go, you have to go.' Samantha looked confused.

'There is a reason. One of my friends got trapped in one once.'

'Trapped? However, did that happen?' Samantha was shocked.

'He was at a concert in Hyde Park and got so drunk, he fell asleep in one of them things. Can't think of anywhere worse to fall asleep.' Suzie pinched her nose to signal the stench of the portable toilets. 'He woke up several hours later and couldn't open the door. He panicked and then realised he was moving. He thought it was from the alcohol he had consumed, but it turns out the toilets had been loaded onto the back of a lorry, with the doors facing each other so they didn't come open in transit, and were travelling along the M25 towards Kent.'

Sharon laughed. 'Bloody serves him right for falling asleep in one then.'

'How did he get out?' Samantha was intrigued.

'He phoned the police. Thankfully, his battery had just enough juice in it to be able to make a phone call. He said it was at least an hour later that he heard sirens and the lorry pulled over to a stop and he heard the police talking to the lorry driver.'
'Did they get him out then?' Sharon asked. 'No, not immediately – they were on the M25. They had to give them an escort off the motorway and then lifted the toilets off to find my mate trapped in one of the toilets.'

Sharon laughed. 'Oh my God, then what happened?'

'Well,' Suzie continued, 'my mate was rather embarrassed, hundreds of miles from home, no money, stinking like a shit house and the driver lost his job for not checking the toilets first before loading them onto his lorry.'

'There is an easy solution to the problem,' Samantha commented. 'Do not get so bloody pissed in the first place.'

'I can safely say he has never got that drunk ever again, or set foot in one of those portable shit houses.' Suzie laughed. 'Buying Christmas presents for him was easy that year – anything to do with toilets and poo. He got given toilet paper, fake poo, toilet fresheners, a book of toilet jokes, toilet games and other equally as funny items.'

'Blimey, you never know when your time is up. Can you imagine if there had been a crash? He would have been covered in shit.' Sharon laughed.

'That thought has never left him. Stupid twat for falling asleep in one in the first place,' Suzie commented. 'Which puts me off going in them also, thanks to him.'

After two laps around Finsbury Park into their twenty-mile run, Samantha started limping. 'Hold up, girls,' she shouted. 'I think I have got something in my trainer. It feels like a stone.' She sat down, removed her trainer and shook it. 'There is nothing in there,' Samantha said whilst peering into the trainer to take a better look.

'Try walking without the trainer and see if it feels the same?' Suzie asked.

'What? You think it's in my sock?' Samantha looked confused.

Suzie tried to reassure her. 'No, it could be an injury. We studied common injuries the other week in college.'

'I am not common!' Samantha was horrified.

'I know you aren't, but it could be one of the common joggers' injuries. It's called planty-vasis-what's-it or something strange like that.'

'You cursed me.' Samantha laughed. 'You need to stop running and get it seen to, otherwise, you won't be going to the Ritz for afternoon tea,' Suzie joked.

'Oh, girls, I am sorry. Please, go on without me,' Samantha begged, sounding like a wounded soldier.

'We are all in this together. Suzie and I are not running without you. Come on. Let's take a slow walk to the nearest Tube station. Get that seen to tomorrow and all will be okay. We can run our long run next weekend.' Sharon gave her advice whilst supporting Samantha's arm.

'Thanks, girls. I do hope it is nothing serious and I will be okay for next weekend. I feel a right failure now.' Samantha was almost crying from the pain.

'You are not a failure. We didn't think we'd get this far. We've done so well. Chin up.' Sharon put her arm around Samantha to reassure her.

'I'm the one who should feel bad. I was only saying about the new trainers can cause injury and there you are hobbling along.'

'Well, you have obviously learnt a lot since being at college. I feel robbed now buying these trainers and listening to that salesman from the sports company.' Samantha lifted up her good foot to highlight her disappointment.

'What's done is done. There is no going back. Come on, let's get you home.' Sharon sounded as though she was consoling one of her boys, not a well-to-do solicitor older than herself. 'Where is the nearest Tube station from here?' Sharon was twirling around to get her bearings.

'Finsbury Park is just up there.' Suzie pointed in the direction of the Tube station.

Samantha held on to Sharon and Suzie as she hobbled towards the Tube station, wincing in pain every time she put pressure on her foot.

After arrival back at Angel and Islington Tube station, Sharon and Suzie walked Samantha to her door, before parting company.

'Take care and put some ice on it,' Suzie advised.

'Thank you, ladies. I will get straight on to booking to see someone tomorrow first thing and I will send a WhatsApp message to let you know how I get on. That is going to ruin my *Jogging Buddy* running log.' Samantha sighed.

Suzie chewed her fingers. 'I feel awful. If I only hadn't mentioned that stupid injury.'

'The only thing that hurt Samantha was her pride, not you. Maybe she should have asked you before she shelled out on the new trainers, could've saved herself a couple of hundred quid and excruciating pain.' Sharon hugged Suzie. 'You need to take a nice long soak in the bath and forget about it. There is nothing you can do. She'll get it sorted tomorrow – you know she will,' Sharon said soothingly.
'Thanks, honey, I'd be lost without you.' Suzie had tears in her eyes. 'I will ask Brett to run me a bath. Only I know he won't jump in it before I do, unlike Samantha's husband.' They both fell about laughing before they parted company to walk towards their own homes.

Brett was there to greet Suzie after she had climbed the stairs. 'What happened? You never ran twenty miles in that time.'
'No. Samantha brought new trainers. I think she has one of those injuries we talking about in college the other day and I feel terrible as I was telling her the danger of changing trainers mid-training, but she bought them at the event she went to as they assessed her running gait. She wasn't to know, but it doesn't make me feel any better.' She gave Brett the huge cuddle that she needed.
'I'll run you a hot bath. You go and get a cup of tea. Chelsea is watching a film, she is happy,' Brett reassured her.
'Thanks, babe, what would I do without you?' Suzie walked into the kitchen, switched the kettle on and then went up to the bathroom where Brett was running her a rather bubbly bubble bath.

Chapter Forty-Three

Samantha hobbled into the office using a walking stick she had found lying around the garage. She was walking more like she had crapped herself rather than injured her foot. The first person to bump into her in the corridor was, of course, The Sex God.

'Morning, Samantha, what on earth have you done?' Greg seemed genuinely concerned whilst eyeing up her foot and walking stick.

'I went for a twenty-mile run yesterday with the girls and only managed ten and my foot is really sore. It feels like I have a stone in my shoe.' Samantha grimaced as she spoke.

'Painful. I've had that before myself.'

'Really? What is it? How long does it last and will I still be able to run the Marathon?' Samantha was anxious.

'I had acupuncture and it worked a treat, back running in a few days. Cinderella, you shall go to the ball.' Greg laughed at his own joke.

'Do you have an acupuncturist you can recommend, please?'

'I'll get the details from my office and I'll ping them over to you.' Greg excused himself. 'I've got another builder going through hell as he changed the designs of the house as per the owners' instructions, but nothing in writing, so the owners are now suing. I wonder when builders will ever learn?'

'If they did, you would be out of work,' Samantha called after him, but she was not sure he heard her as he seemed preoccupied with the builder's case he was working on.

True to his word, Greg had 'pinged' an email over with the name and number of a physiotherapist that he had seen. Without wasting any time, Samantha called the number.

A calm male voice answered. 'Hello.'

'Yes, hello, my name is Samantha and I have been recommended to you by a colleague for some acupuncture. I have an injury on my foot.' Samantha rambled on.

'Can you come to the clinic? Then I can assess your injury.'

Samantha hesitated and then replied, 'Of course, when are you free?'

'I am free now, if you are?'

'I am on my way.'

The physiotherapist worked from his converted garage. Samantha knocked on the clinic door and the friendly therapist appeared. He held out his hand.

'Pleased to meet you. I am George'

Samantha copied the gesture.

George looked at her walking stick. 'You are in pain?' he asked. 'Is it your foot?' He pointed to her foot.

'Yes.' Samantha held up her foot. 'Like a stone.' She was taken aback by the inside of the garage. It was a fully kitted out therapy room, with exercise equipment and a treatment couch.

'Yes, yes, please lie down.' George gestured to the couch.

He started asking her questions. 'What were you doing when it started hurting?'

'Running!' Samantha shouted as George pressed hard on her foot just as she answered.
'Has it happened before?' George asked.
'No.' Samantha grimaced.
'Good.' George took her foot and inserted acupuncture needles. Samantha screamed.
'Does it hurt?' he asked.
'No, not really,' Samantha said, and then screamed some more.
'Okay. Give it fifteen minutes. After that, I'll massage your foot and leg.' George left her lying alone, with the acupuncture needles sticking out of her foot.

Fifteen minutes later George returned, removed the needles and without any warning started to massage Samantha's foot and leg. She screamed in pain as he stretched her calf muscles. Samantha shouted for an epidural, but George didn't reply.
'Finished,' he announced. 'Any better?' He looked for a response.
'Yes, thank you.' Samantha grimaced.
'I will show you some stretching exercises that I would like you to do every day.'
George showed Samantha the exercises and asked her to ice the foot after a run.
George advised, 'I would like you to limit the length of your runs – ten minutes today, twenty minutes the next day, thirty minutes the next day, and come to see me the day after.'
Samantha was calculating in her mind which day she was due to come back for more torture.
'Thank you, George. I will see you in four days. How much do I need to pay you?' Samantha started rummaging in her handbag for her purse.
George shook his head and waved his hands. 'No, it is free. You can pay next time.'

'That is very kind, George. I will see you in four days.' George held the door open for Samantha.

Samantha managed to walk to the front of the clinic without the aid of her walking stick.

Samantha was amazed how little her foot hurt now. She got her mobile out from her bag and sent a WhatsApp message to the girls to let them know her progress.

Just seen a therapist. I've been poked and prodded with acupuncture needles and massage. My foot feels a lot better already. He said I must not run for long. 10 minutes today, 20 tomorrow, 30 the day after and then go back to him. Sorry to let you down, girls, but please go for your long run as planned and I will join you when I am recovered.

She had just closed the cover on her phone when there was a reply from Sharon, saying that they would run with her, as they were all in this together. Samantha smiled, got into her car and drove back to the office.

Chapter Forty-Four

Suzie entered the beauty parlour feeling rather nervous, as if she were entering a dentist surgery. She had reluctantly booked an appointment to have her pubic hair waxed, as she had read in a textbook at college that it can be a great help for those participating in running. When she told Brett of her waxing appointment his eyes lit up and he asked if she was going Brazilian. She told him that she was only having her bikini line waxed, but she was intending on having the whole lot removed. She kept that from him as a surprise.

A rather orange-looking lady with peroxide blond hair interrupted her thoughts. 'Can I help you, lovie?'

'Ah yes.' Suzie stumbled. 'I have an appointment for a wax.' Suzie felt really embarrassed to be explaining her most intimate secret to this tango woman.

'Don't look so worried, lovie. It doesn't hurt,' the woman said.

'Is it that obvious?' Suzie felt even more embarrassed now.

'Are you Suzie? You are booked in with Janice. She will be with you in a few minutes. Janice is just finishing with another client. Can I get you a cup of tea or coffee whilst you wait?' Orange woman pointed to the comfortable-looking sofa by the reception desk. 'Please take a seat. I will let her know you are here.'

'A cup of tea, white, no sugar, would be great, if it is not too much trouble.' Suzie perched on the luxurious fake-leather sofa.

'No trouble at all, you just sit and relax. One cup of tea coming right up.' She trotted off in the direction of the door marked 'Staff Only'.

Suzie sat back and breathed in heavily and slowly, taking in the gorgeous smell of aromatherapy oils and nail varnish products. There was a sample of hand cream on the coffee table in front of her. She pumped a small amount into her hand, slowly inhaled the sumptuous smell, and rubbed her hands together. She could get used to coming to a place like this. The orange woman tottered back towards her and placed a steaming hot cup of tea on the table; the tea was in delicate china with two shortbread biscuits on the saucer. 'Thank you,' Suzie acknowledged.

'You are most welcome. Janice won't be long now.' Orange woman tottered back towards the reception desk and the telephone started to ring, which she answered in an awful robotic voice. 'Good afternoon, Sam's salon, how may I help you today?'

Suzie sunk deeper into the sofa as if the person on the other end of the phone could see her cringing. The tea was extremely hot, but that was the way she liked it. She took a bite of the shortbread just as Janice appeared, who was equally orange-looking.

'Suzie, pleased to meet you. I am Janice.' Janice held out her hand to shake.

Suzie dropped the biscuit and shook Janice's hand. 'Lovely to meet you too.' Suzie placed her other hand over her mouth so not to spit biscuit crumbs everywhere.

'Please bring your tea and biscuits. My consultation room is just over here.' Janice signalled to the door marked 'Consulting Room One'.

Suzie struggled to get up from the soft sofa, leaving her cup of tea and followed Janice into the consulting room.

Janice busied herself fluffing up towels and lit an incense stick. She turned and looked her in the face with a sympathetic smile. 'So, Suzie, have you had a waxing before?'

'Never. How much does it hurt?' Suzie was starting to feel unwell.

Janice placed her hand on Suzie's arm to reassure her. 'Do you have children?'

'Yes, a girl.' Suzie was confused by the question.

'Well, my love, you have endured labour – this is a doddle by comparison.' Janice stood up and walked towards the bed. 'If you can get yourself undressed, just the bottom half, and place this towel over you, I will be back to see you in a few minutes.' Janice handed the towel to Suzie and left the room.

Suzie undressed, placed her clothes tidily on the chair that was positioned in the corner of the room, got herself onto the bed, almost rolled off, and then covered herself with the towel.

There was a light knock at the door. 'Are you ready?' Janice whispered through the door.

'Yes, as ready as I can be,' Suzie whispered back.

Janice wheeled her trolley close and removed the towel from Suzie. 'I am going to put the wax on and then place the cloth strips onto the wax, press down and then pull it off, quickly, and it may sting a little, but just take deep breaths.' Janice rattled her speech off as if she were reading from a textbook. Suzie inhaled deeply as the hot wax was spread onto her pubic hair. It was followed by a rather heavy-handed press of the waxing cloth and then, without any warning, Janice ripped the waxing cloth from her private area and then, without any warning, Janice ripped the waxing cloth from her private area.

Suzie screamed. 'Fucking hell! Oh my God, is there any skin left?'

'Hang in there, girl, it gets easier,' Janice reassured her.

'Fucking hope so! Jesus Christ, I had no idea my skin came off also!'

'Do you want me to stop?' The orange colour started to drain from her face and she looked really concerned that Suzie was finding it so uncomfortable.

'No, you've started now. Do you have an epidural?' Suzie panted.

'It is always worse the first time,' Janice informed her whilst adding more wax, placing the waxing cloth and ripping some more.

'It's gonna be the last time, there is no next time, this is awful.'

Janice continued with more haste to finish the wax as soon as she could. 'I am almost finished now, Suzie.' Janice had an element of panic in her voice.
'Fuck!' Suzie screamed.
'One last area, just a few stragglers now.'
Janice ripped away the wax cloth and replaced it and ripped a few more times. 'All done. Wait there and let me add some moisturiser cream.' Janice pumped some cream from a tub on her trolley rapidly and placed it on the area where five minutes ago there was hair – now it was completely smooth. She placed the towel back over Suzie's private area. 'All done, Suzie. Well done. It is always the most painful the first time.' Janice patted her shoulder. 'Please don't get up too soon. I will go

and get you a glass of water. When you are ready, please get yourself dressed and I will meet you in reception.' Janice turned and left Suzie alone in the room.

Suzie lay on the bed for a few moments before taking a look at the damage below. Staring back at her was a rather red private area that was free of hair. She placed her little finger delicately on the area and inhaled deeply. She had no idea this small procedure was going to cause so much pain. She slowly stepped off the bed and got herself dressed, carefully so not to rub her sore private area. Walking as if she had shit herself, she opened the door and shuffled towards the reception where Janice was standing chatting to the other orange woman on the reception desk. Once they both realised Suzie was shuffling towards them, they stopped talking. She had a really good idea as to what they were talking about.

'Hi, are you okay? Here is your water.

Please take your time before you leave.' Janice handed Suzie the glass of iced water and pointed to the comfy sofa. 'Bethany will sort out the payment and book another appointment in for you.' Janice pointed to the first orange woman as she spoke.

'That is very kind of you.' Suzie took the glass of water and drank it so fast the ice cubes flew up her nose. 'I don't know that I can go through that again. Maybe I will come and have a full body massage after I have run the London Marathon in a couple of months.' Suzie was out of breath from guzzling the water so quickly.

'Wow!' Janice screeched. 'That is amazing, well done you.'

'Thank you. This is why I have endured this torture as apparently it makes running easier without chafing. Hopefully, it is worth the pain,' Suzie rambled on.

'I have always wanted to run it. I keep applying every year, but I am not so lucky. How did you get a place?' Janice was deeply enthused.

'I am running for the local hospice, raising funds for them as that is where my mother passed away,' Suzie informed her.

'Oh, I am sorry to hear that. I lost my dad there also. Please stay there – let me give you some sponsorship.' Janice ran towards the door marked 'Staff Only' and soon returned with a crisp twenty-pound note. 'Here, please take this, it is for a great cause.' Janice placed the note into Suzie's hand.

'Oh my God, are you sure? You have only just met me.' Suzie was staring at the crisp twenty-pound note as if she had never seen one before.

'Honestly, I keep saying I must give money to the hospice and what better way of giving some sponsorship money. I really wish you lots of luck and maybe I will look at running for them next year.' Janice placed a reassuring hand on her shoulder.

Suzie was embarrassed but pleased with the gesture at the same time. 'Thank you so much, I really appreciate it. I will book in and see you for a full body massage after the run and tell you all about it.'

'I look forward to it. It was a pleasure to meet you and best of luck. I must go as I have another client, but I will see you early April.' Janice blew a kiss and turned to greet her next client.

Bethany entered some numbers into the till, which played some happy tunes as she did so. 'That is twenty pounds for today, please, Suzie,' Bethany said.

Suzie fumbled in her jeans pocket, pulled out a rather tatty twenty-pound note and handed it to

Bethany. 'Thank you. Can I book in for a full body massage the day after the London Marathon, please?'

'I have already booked you in. Is lunchtime good for you, say twelve o'clock?' Bethany felt proud of her efficiency.

'That is amazing. Thank you. I will see you soon.' Suzie turned and shuffled towards the door and wondered how she was going to get on the bus without being too conspicuous.

Chapter Forty-Five

Samantha was the first to arrive at the usual meeting place. She was busy warming up by squatting when Brett and Suzie arrived, strolling along arm in arm. 'Hi Samantha,' Suzie called. 'How is your foot?'

'Bloody painful. I am not sure if the acupuncture helped or hindered. It was the most bizarre experience I have ever encountered, and I thought being a solicitor I had encountered most things.' Samantha was wincing as she put her foot down after each squat.

'You need to take it easy, Samantha. Only run for a short period and then walk for short periods, otherwise, you will do yourself some serious damage and you won't be running for a bus never mind a marathon.' Brett gave his best training advice.

'Thank you, Brett, I am glad we have you on our team. The therapist did tell me just that. I feel such a complete twat for getting myself into this pickle.' Samantha was almost crying. 'We have come so far and now these new bloody trainers that I was conned into buying have caused all this pain and upset.'

'Oh, Samantha, please don't worry. All the world's greatest athletes have major setbacks. We are in this together, remember, and together we will get through this.' Suzie was struggling to hold back the tears, too.

'I thought just a gentle run to Finsbury Park and then the Tube home,' Brett advised.

'Sounds like a plan,' Suzie agreed. 'Oh, here comes Sharon.' Suzie turned to see Sharon walking angrily across the park. 'She doesn't look happy at all.'

'Bloody kids.' Sharon was cursing as she walked towards the group. 'I cannot believe how fucking useless they all are.' Sharon was livid with whatever the 'bloody kids' had done. 'David has just decided to do an impression of Batman and gave a "pow" punch to Dennis, Dennis fell over onto the new television we got in the Christmas sales, and the bloody thing fell over, falling onto John's head. Bedlam, three injured children and a broken television.' Sharon was spitting as she spoke, as she was so angry.

'Oh, Sharon, I am so sorry. How is everyone now?' Suzie asked.

'I've got no fucking idea. I just walked out and left Gary to it. I was going to scream, punch someone or something.' Sharon was punching the air to show her frustration.

'When did this all happen?' Samantha asked in a concerned voice.

'Five minutes before I left the house for our run.' Sharon looked at her watch.

'Oh, Sharon, do you not want to go home?' Samantha was slightly alarmed by her actions of leaving the house in a war zone.

'Not a fucking chance. Gary knows that this run is more important to me than anything else, including a broken television and three children now all needing a visit to accident and emergency. I told him to call me when they have all been seen by the doctor. If I haven't heard from him by the time we are finished, I will meet him at the hospital. Bloody place drives me nuts. I am sure the staff are going to call social services on me one day, the amount of times I am down there. The last time I was there the receptionist said, "Hello Mrs Young" – how fucking embarrassing is that?' Sharon was struggling to contain her anger. 'I've had it, had it with them all, so bloody boisterous all the time.'

'Calm down now, Sharon. You are here now. Let's all warm up and go for a gentle run.' Brett retained order in the chaos.

'I am so looking forward to this run. I thought I would never hear myself say this, but this is such an escape from the bedlam at home. It used to be a whole tub of Ben & Jerry's ice cream if I was stressed – now I look forward to going for a run.' Sharon's voice was certainly calmer now; maybe it was the thought of Ben & Jerry's ice cream that had reduced her stress. 'Right then, ladies.'

Brett clapped his hands together. 'Samantha has an injury and can only run for a short distance and then walk for a short distance. Please, though, Sharon and Suzie, if you want to run on ahead, I will stay with Samantha,' he informed them. Brett started the jog and the others, one by one, joined in. After ten minutes Brett called a halt to Samantha's running. 'Can you walk now, Samantha?' He put his arm out to stop her running. 'It is really important that you don't overdo things tonight.'

'Thank you, Brett. It is feeling a little sore now.' Samantha hobbled into a walking pace. Suzie and Sharon slowed down to a steady run so not to be too far ahead.

'Have you ever had your privates waxed before?' Suzie whispered to Sharon.

'No, I have not. Why do you ask? Are you thinking of getting it done?' Sharon was intrigued.

'I had it done yesterday. Bloody killed me and I was screaming for an epidural.'

Sharon started laughing. 'Oh, Suzie, why did you get it done if it hurts that much?'

'I didn't realise it hurt that much. I read in a college textbook that it can help reduce chafing during exercise if you get it done.' Suzie was feeling rather embarrassed sharing this intimate fact about herself.

'Has it helped?' Sharon probed.

'The pain has only just stopped. I thought she tore off several layers of skin along with the hair,' Suzie explained. 'I can see the benefit of not having any hair rubbing down there when you run. I just didn't realise that going for a piss was going to be such fun afterwards.'

'Why? What's the problem with pissing?'

'I now piss in about fifty different directions,' Suzie informed her.

Sharon let out a screeching laugh; she had to stop running to gather her breath. 'Fucking hell, that must be a struggle?'

'Shhhhh, Brett and Samantha will question what we are talking about and I haven't told Brett of my dilemma yet.' Suzie covered Sharon's mouth.

'Does Brett not know you've had it done, then?' Sharon slowly regained herself.

'Yes, he knows I have had it done, of course, he does, I just haven't mentioned the pissing problem and I don't want to mention it either.' Suzie gave Sharon a glare, which Sharon understood as 'keep your mouth shut'.

Samantha and Brett caught the two girls up and Brett was the first to ask what all the laughter was about.

'It was nothing of any importance,' Suzie said. 'Sharon was sharing a personal secret between her and Gary. Women's problems.' Suzie winked at Sharon.

Brett held his hand up to signal time out. 'I don't want to know any more, thanks.'

Suzie whispered into Sharon's ear. 'Mention women's problems to any man and that is the end of the conversation immediately.'

Brett studied his Garmin watch and noted that they had run enough for Samantha and her injury. 'That is all I want you to run today, Samantha. Are you okay? How is the foot feeling?'

'Oh, Brett, it feels okay, bit sore, but I know what you mean. I do not feel comfortable carrying on.' She turned to the girls. 'If you girls want to carry on, please, I will not be offended.'

'*No!*' They both shouted in unison. 'We are in this together.' Sharon told Samantha off as if she were talking to one of her kids.

'Thanks, girls, I really appreciate this. I am going to get myself off and get some ice on this foot, physio's orders.' Samantha explained. 'Then log my miles on *Jogging Buddy.*'

Sharon, Suzie and Brett steadied Samantha towards the Tube station.

Sharon studied her phone. 'I will have to make my way to the hospital as I haven't heard from Gary yet.'

Chapter Forty-Six

Sharon was busy cleaning the house – it was a never-ending task – when there was a knock on the door. She turned the vacuum cleaner off and let out a huge sigh; she hated being interrupted during her cleaning spree. Muttering angrily to herself, she shuffled towards the door. 'Probably just someone selling something I don't want or need.' As she opened the door she realised she was dressed in the most tatty jogging bottoms and a T-shirt that had more holes in it than a portion of Emmental. She was shocked to see her sister Janet standing there. 'Shit, you look awful,' Sharon commented.

'Thanks, sis, you look pretty crap yourself,' Janet retaliated.

'What the hell are you doing here? Why did you not call me first?' Sharon made hurried attempts to brush the dust off her clothes as if it was going to make her appearance any better.

'I've left him,' Janet announced as a matter of fact.

'Wow, that was sudden.' Sharon was now feeling nervous, as she was sure the only reason Janet was standing on her doorstep with a suitcase by her side was she needed somewhere to stay, rather than to visit her and her family with any sincerity.

'Can we have this conversation inside, please? It is the middle of winter and bloody cold out here.' Janet was starting to cry and it appeared it wasn't due to the cold weather; it was more to do with her emotional state.

'Sure, yes, sorry.' Sharon held the door open. 'I was just doing some housework.'

Janet humped her very heavy suitcase into the hallway and removed her wet boots.

'How is everyone?' Janet made polite conversation.

'Well, you know, same old. Never mind about my lot, what happened?' Sharon walked to the kitchen and pressed the button for the kettle to boil. 'Tea or coffee?' Sharon enquired.

'Tea with two sugars, please, sis.' Janet made herself comfortable at the kitchen table.

'So, what is it this time?' Sharon asked sympathetically from behind the open kitchen cupboard door whilst rummaging for two cups.

Janet sniffled and then composed herself. 'The usual.'

Sharon wasn't sure what 'the usual' was, but she was sure she was about to find out.

'Patrick is out all night, every night, drinking and gambling again. He promised me he had stopped, but a friend of mine saw him in the casino.' Janet wiped her nose on her sleeve.

Sharon wanted to say that Janet was working as a cocktail waitress in the casino when she met him – was there any wonder he was drinking and gambling? But she thought better of it. 'Oh, that's awful.' Sharon tried her hardest to sound sincere.

'I met one of my girlfriends in town for lunch the other day. She still works at the casino and she said that he is going in there most nights. He doesn't know that I am friends with her, otherwise I think he would be more careful.' Janet stared blankly at the cup of tea that Sharon had just placed in front of her. 'Have you got any chocolate biscuits?'

'Sorry, no, I don't. I am keeping them out of the house for the time being.'

'Booze, then? Have you got any alcohol in the house?'

'No, I am off the booze, for now, sorry,' Sharon apologised.

'Oh, for fuck's sake, sis, please tell me you are not up the spout again? Heaven help us. Is it not enough you have five boys already?' Janet turned from sorrow to anger.

'No, I am not "up the spout" and I don't have five boys, I have six-well, seven if you include Gary,' Sharon snapped back.

'Sorry, why else would you be off the booze and chocolate biscuits?' Janet stared at her tea again so she didn't have to look her angry sister in the face. 'Well, if you aren't pregnant, have you joined some ludicrous religious outfit then?'

'No, I haven't. I am training to run the London Marathon,' Sharon informed her proudly.

Janet spat her tea out in horror. 'What the fuck? What are you doing that for?'

'Because I want another baby and Gary said if I prove to him I can run the London Marathon then I will get my wish.'

Janet laughed like a hyena. 'I don't expect Gary was thinking you would actually go through with this insane task, that is probably why he said it.'

'Exactly. He will have to eat his hat after I cross the finish line.' Sharon smirked.

'Don't you need shit loads of training?' Janet was now interested.

'Yes, I have been training, me and two other mums, who are also extremely unfit and running it for the first time, are training together.' Sharon pulled up a picture on her phone of the three of them that was taken at Christmas with them amongst the snow and Santa suits. 'I met the other girls on a website called *Joggingbuddy.com*.'

'There are others out there, like you?'

'Totally, there are lots of women in my position.'

'Fuck, you are taking this shit seriously then?'

'Without a doubt,' Sharon announced smugly. 'I don't do things by half. In fact, I am off for a run this evening. Join us if you fancy?' Sharon asked.

'How long are you running for?' Janet was keen to know.

'There is no time limit, just we need to get about eighteen miles run,' Sharon stated.

'Bloody hell, no thanks, I will just watch *Hollyoaks*, that is stressful enough.' Janet finished her tea and plucked up the courage to ask her sister what she had wanted to ask since she arrived. 'I need somewhere to stay, sis. Have you any ideas?'

'Not here, that is for certain. We are squashed up enough. I will ask Samantha. She has a huge four-bedroom house and it is only her and her son and he is away at university, so she rattles around there alone most of the time.' Sharon was busy tapping a message on her phone. 'Done. I have sent her a message. She is not very good with technology, so don't expect a reply for several hours. If she doesn't reply I will see her later whilst we are out running and ask.' Sharon's phone made a noise to notify her of a new message. 'Shit, that was quick.' Sharon read the message and smiled and then read it out to Janet.

Hi Sharon, I would love to have some company and help out a damsel in distress. See you at six-thirty and we can chat then. Ps. I have got the hang of this now, in case you hadn't noticed. XXXX

'Damsel in distress – was that what you called me?' Janet sneered.
'No, I asked if she could put you up as you have just left your partner. A damsel in distress are her words. Sorry, I even asked for you.' Sharon threw her phone on the kitchen table in disgust.
'Sorry, sis, I am just feeling like shit. I do appreciate it.'
Sharon had heard it all before.

Chapter Forty-Seven

Samantha really hated the first day back after the weekend. Couples spent so much time together over the holidays that they were ready to kill or divorce each other by New Year's Day. Then by February, they were lining up to start divorce proceedings and this year turned out to be just the same as every previous one. She had two new clients coming to see her to discuss divorce proceedings. And she wished she had not mentioned to Sharon's sister that she was a divorce lawyer, as all she had for the entire weekend was Janet questioning her on divorce proceedings and how she could get it over with as quickly as possible. Janet was a lovely girl, although nothing like her sister; she was very vulnerable and walked all over by others. Samantha needed coffee, and a large mug of it, so she walked into the kitchen to find Greg standing with his back to the door, buttering some toast.

'Hi, Samantha. Did you have a good weekend?' Greg was sincerely interested for his own benefit as with every day that passed it appeared, he was going to have to take this deranged lunatic to afternoon tea at the Ritz, unless she was lying about all her training.

'Oh, you know, busy training, whilst juggling the housework and an unexpected guest.' Samantha tried to make polite conversation without showing how thrilled she was that Greg was asking about her welfare.

'An unexpected guest, that sounds very interesting. Do tell more.' Greg placed the buttered toast into his mouth and attempted to smile whilst chewing.

'Janet, she is a sister of one of the Mums, Sharon. Janet has left her husband and landed upon Sharon's door needing somewhere to stay. I spent the weekend answering questions about how she can divorce this vile man. I do not feel as though I have had a weekend off at all. The only thing that keeps me going is going for a run and I thought I would never hear myself say that.' Samantha crashed the cup on the side with venom, as if it were Janet's face.

'So the training is going well then?' Greg held his hand over his mouth so not to spit the toast everywhere.

'Yes, it is looking like afternoon tea at the Ritz will be very appreciated in April.' Samantha jabbed her finger into Greg's ribs in jest. 'Wow, you have very firm muscles, Mr Horsforth.'

Greg blushed. 'Thank you, that is what running every day does to you. You have lost some weight since training. You must be very pleased.' Greg shoved more toast into his mouth, hoping to chew it before Samantha had finished her reply.

'Of course I am, but did I need to lose any before, then?' Samantha joked.

'Yes, no, sorry, I didn't mean you were overweight, just every woman I have ever met has complained about her weight, even when there has been more meat on a butcher's pencil.' Greg held his hand up to apologise.

'I was joking, Greg. You need to lighten up.' Samantha placed her hand on his shoulder. 'Anyway, I must dash, divorce rates go up during the first quarter in the year.' Samantha poured the hot water into her oversized mug and winked at Greg as she left.

Greg made a note on his phone to book afternoon tea at the Ritz as it was looking more likely that he would have to honour his bet. He had made some extreme bets in the past, but this had to be the most insane of them all. Even more extreme than betting his Porsche that he could last longer than anyone else on a rodeo horse after fifteen pints of beer. Would he ever learn? Possibly not.

Samantha's first client was a middle-aged woman who looked ten years older than her actual age. A Portuguese lady with very limited English vocabulary, she had obviously had a hard marriage. Marcia started telling her about the issues with her husband, Nick, and why she wanted a divorce. All she kept saying was he was into incense. Samantha had never had anyone request a divorce before due to their partner burning incense sticks, but she kept her mouth shut as it was not her place to judge. Besides, Marcia was talking ten to the dozen and Samantha could not have got a word in edgeways if she tried. Samantha made extensive notes and after an hour informed Marcia her appointment time was up.

'Oh, I am sorry to keep going on. He has just really annoyed me, as you can see.' Marcia removed a rather tatty-looking tissue from her pocket and attempted to blow her nose. 'Do you agree with me?' Marcia waited for a reply.

'It is not my place to agree with my client – I'm just here to make the divorce as painless as possible,' Samantha reassured her.

'Of course, sorry, but you surely have to agree sleeping with your own sister is a little out of order?' Marcia's phone buzzed and she retrieved it from her bag and read the message. 'Sorry.' She looked up from the phone in embarrassment. 'Why would anyone sleep with their own flesh and blood?'

'Well.' Samantha felt as though she had missed something in Marcia's ramblings. 'When did you tell me this part of the reasons for divorce?' Samantha could see from the look on Marcia's face that she had explained it and that she had not taken note.

'Incense! It is wrong, isn't it, to sleep with your own flesh and blood? Why would you?' Marcia raised her voice.

Samantha deliberately dropped her pen on the floor and bent down to retrieve it. This gave her time to compose herself before explaining to Marcia that the word she was looking for was 'incest' and not 'incense'. 'Of course it is not right. Have you informed the police?' Samantha asked an open question to give her time to control her laughter that was bubbling to come out and took a sip of her now-cold coffee to mask her smile.

'No, I haven't. I just want out as quickly as possible. I can't be arsed with statements, court and all the hassle that goes with it.' Marcia was very matter-of-fact.

'Where are you staying?' Samantha enquired.

'In the house. He is… how do you say? Shacked up with his sister. That is what he wanted.' Marcia started banging her fists on the desk between them.

'I understand. I will get on to your case as soon as possible. You will hear from me in a couple of days.' Samantha was desperate to get rid of this woman from her office in case she started smashing things up. 'Can I help you with anything else?' Samantha stood up to encourage Marcia to leave her office.

'No, you have been a great help. Thank you.' Marcia gathered her bag, coat, scarf and hat and left without saying goodbye.

'If you book a follow-up appointment in with my secretary for a week's time I can give you an update,' Samantha called after her, but Marcia didn't hear as she was down the stairs and out of the door before Samantha finished her sentence.

Liz knocked and carefully entered Samantha's office.

'Wow, she was in a hurry.' Liz looked towards the door to signal Marcia's quick exit.

'Why is it all the nut bags in London come to me to get divorced? She was continually talking about incense and that is her reasons for divorce and it turns out it was not due to smelly sticks burning, it was incest – her husband has been sleeping with his sister.'

Liz held her hand over her mouth and then fell about laughing; Samantha joined in and felt a hundred times better for doing so.

Chapter Forty-Eight

Chelsea was refusing to get dressed as she didn't want to go to nursery; she had enjoyed their weekend together too much.
'Please, Chelsea. Mummy and Brett have to go to school and we have exams today. Please don't stress me out any more than I am already.' Suzie was on her hands and knees, begging Chelsea to behave.
    'But why do I have to go to nursery? Nursery is boring and everyone there is stupid.' Chelsea crossed her arms defensively.
    'Oh, Chelsea, that is not a nice thing to say and it is not true. You love nursery – you get to paint and make a mess.' Suzie was trying even harder now.
'Painting is stupid,' Chelsea screamed.
'Okay, what do I have to do to get you to get dressed?' Suzie was getting desperate.
    'Can Brett take me? He is my new daddy now, isn't he?'
    Suzie smiled and brushed Chelsea's fringe away from her face. 'If you want Brett to be your new daddy, he is. Now will you get dressed, please, if I ask Brett to take you into nursery?'
    'Yes.' Chelsea turned and gathered her clothes and struggled to put them on, putting her dress on the wrong way around at first.
'Brett,' Suzie called towards the bathroom.
'Yes, honey,' Brett mumbled behind his

toothbrush.

'Chelsea wants you to take her into nursery. Is that okay?' Suzie held her hands together in a praying pose.

'Of course. I will be ready in five minutes. Are you both ready?' Brett was beaming from ear to ear, thankful that he had Chelsea's blessing about their relationship.

'We are – just waiting on you. We will wait in the car.' Suzie raised her hands and thanked God for helping her this morning. 'Come on, little one.' Suzie took Chelsea's hand and pulled her coat from the rack in the hallway. 'It is cold outside and we don't want you catching a cold.' Suzie swaddled Chelsea in her coat and gave her a huge hug and kiss.

'How can you catch a cold if you are not wearing a coat, Mummy?' Chelsea enquired.

'Not now, Chelsea, we don't have time. Later, I will explain later, I promise.' This would give her time to Google search the rather ambiguous saying. What did parents do before Google? she thought to herself.

Brett and Suzie walked into the rather quiet classroom; everyone who was there already was busy doing last-minute revision from their textbooks.

'Here are the love birds,' their cocksure classmate, Charlie announced.

Suzie blushed as always. 'Jealous, are we?' Suzie retaliated rather sharply.

'Okay.' Charlie raised his hand to signal time out. 'I take it there was no shagging for you last night.' Charlie smiled. 'That is what happens when you get too comfortable – the spark goes.'

'Shut it, shitface.' Suzie gave him a look that could kill. 'How on earth would you know? I can't imagine anyone would touch you with a bargepole.'

Brett ushered Suzie to a spare seat. 'Sit down, ignore him, he's a prick.'

'I know, but I don't need this amount of stress before an exam. If I fail, I will personally kill him.' Suzie gritted her teeth.

'There is a long waiting list to kill him.' Brett turned and smiled to Charlie to show he was talking about him.

The tutor came in and asked the students to follow him into the sports hall, where the exam was going to take place. As they walked in you could cut the atmosphere with a knife.

'I am shitting myself,' Suzie whispered.

'If it's any consolation then so am I,' Brett whispered back. He caught the eye of one of the invigilators and started to blush as he felt he shouldn't be talking.

'Can I ask everyone to leave all their possessions at the front of the room, please?' the rather scary invigilator yelled out. 'Please can you ensure your mobile phones are switched off before you leave your bags? I do not want a constant barrage of phones ringing and bleeping.'

Brett took Suzie's bag from her and along with his own placed it on the pile of bags at the front of the hall whilst she found her table.

When everyone was settled the invigilator requested silence. She announced, 'You have three hours from now. Please turn your papers over to begin.'

Suzie smiled across to Brett who was sitting next to her, turned her paper over, and passed out.

Thankfully, Brett saw what was about to happen and threw himself in front of her before she fell to the floor.

'Babe, are you okay?' Brett screamed, concerned. Everyone in the sports hall turned to see what the commotion was.

'Sorry, I feel sick at the thought of an exam. I need some air and water please.' Suzie sobbed.

The invigilator came rushing over in a panic. 'Please come outside.' She took Suzie's hand.

'I am so sorry.' Suzie was crying. 'I've ruined everything now.'

'No, you haven't. If you feel better in a few minutes you can come back in,' the invigilator told her. 'It's not the first time it has happened on my watch.'

'Do you want me to come with you, babe?' Brett asked.

'No, no, please, you stay and finish the exam. I don't want to mess it up for both of us. I am sure I will be fine in a few minutes and I can come back in.'

After Suzie had a cup of sweet tea and some fresh air, she was ready to go back into the sports hall, where everyone stopped writing and stared at her as she entered and found her seat. She smiled at Brett and gave him a prominent thumbs up. Brett blew her a kiss in return.

The time was up and the invigilator announced that they should stop writing. Suzie threw down her pen and stretched her wrists and fingers.
'Are you okay, babe?' Brett asked.

'I am fine now, thank you. So sorry for the drama. It wasn't that bad after everything. Quite easy, I thought.' Suzie smiled.

'I thought so, too. Come on. Let's go and get some food to celebrate.' Brett took Suzie's arm and led her out of the sports hall.

Chapter Forty-Nine

Samantha was busy talking to the camera crew whilst doing an impression of a constipated penguin. 'It is so cold still. I hope on the race day the weather improves.' Samantha jumped up and down on the spot.

'In my experience, it is usually the hottest day of the year so far on race day. You spend all your time training in cold weather, then come race day you are baking hot,' Jeff the cameraman informed her.

'Julie.' Jeff turned to the sound lady. 'Do you remember when I was training for the New York marathon?'

'Don't remind me.' Julie sighed. 'Bloody awful training. It is all through summer and the year I did it, it was the bloody hottest summer on record. Bloody worth it though, such a buzz running in New York. The scary thing is the year after someone blew the finishing line up. I was considering it again that year also.' Jeff had pain on his face as he spoke. 'I had a couple of friends out there running. It was awful waiting to hear if they were okay.' Jeff wiped a tear away.

'You okay?' Samantha asked.

'Yes, sorry. I should know better than to mention it. One of my friends lost a leg. All he has ever done is run and train for marathons. This was his first time in New York. He spent months training and not to mention a fortune on getting there and staying there and came home minus a leg.'

'I am so sorry.' Samantha didn't know where to put her face. Thankfully, Brett and Suzie arrived to break up the conversation.

'Afternoon,' Suzie said happily but soon realised there was a tension. 'Sorry, did I say something?' Suzie blushed.

Jeff turned with a tear in his eye. 'No, I was just remembering a friend who lost his leg in a marathon.'

'Shit, how did that happen?' The colour drained from her face. 'Can a marathon do that to you?'

Samantha put her fingers over her mouth to signal to stop asking questions. 'Jeff has a friend who was in New York running the marathon when the bomb was set off at the finishing line.'

'Shit, I am sorry.' Suzie chewed her fingers.

'Don't worry. It was me that mentioned it. Thankfully, it was just his leg he lost. There were others not as fortunate.' Jeff turned to pick his camera up from the floor. 'Are we ready to run?'

Samantha spun around looking for Sharon. 'We are waiting for Sharon. She has her hands full with six boys, so we expect her to arrive late.' Samantha saw her running up as fast as she could towards the crowd of them waiting.

'Sorry,' Sharon called. 'Bloody kids again.'

'Are they not at school?' Samantha asked.

'Yes, they are, but I got called into the headmaster's office. David had a conversation with another kid and the other kid didn't like it, so I was called in for a telling off.' Sharon slapped the rear of her hand to signal a telling off.

'They told you off also?' Brett asked.

'They may as well have. So wrong, they are kids, they are innocent, they do not realise what they are saying.' Sharon signalled the height of young children.

'Dare we ask what happened?' Suzie chewed her fingers.

'You can, stupid really. Tell me what you think? A conversation went somewhere along the lines of...' Sharon put her hands on her hips to signal a young girl. '"Can I have the blue pencil, please?" David said, "In a minute." The girl said, "If you don't give it to me, I will ask my uncle to arrest you as he is a policeman." David says, "It's okay. My mum has a friend who is a solicitor, so she can get me off jail."' Sharon stood there with her arms open awaiting a reply.

Brett, Suzie, Jeff and Julie stood there open-mouthed and then fell about laughing.

'That is ingenious.' Suzie broke the laughter up.

'That is the same reaction I gave to the headmaster, only he didn't share the same enthusiasm as I. Which is why I was told off.' Sharon slapped her wrist again.

'How old is your son?' Jeff asked.

'Five, going on fifty,' Sharon announced.

'That is impressive for a five-year-old to think of something so clever,' Julie remarked.

'Well, that's what I said also and again I was greeted by disgust from the headmaster.'

'What did you do then?' Brett asked.

'I told him I have a date with a pair of running shoes and left his speechless. I cannot think calling me into his office to tell me off is going to solve anything.' Sharon started to warm up. 'Let's run.' Sharon let out a huge cry and started running ahead.

Once they approached Wembley Stadium, Brett announced they had reached mile fifteen. 'Well done, everyone. How are you all feeling?'

'Bloody marvellous,' Samantha announced.

'Well, that is not the reply I was expecting.' Brett tapped his watch to check it was working correctly.

'I have totally forgotten about Mr Scott and his telling off.' Sharon punched the air.

'Suzie?' Brett turned to see her face all red. 'Are you okay?'

'Never better. We are going to smash this marathon running lark.' Suzie gave Samantha and Sharon a high five in turn.
'Mum Runners!' they all shouted in unison.
After reaching Willesden they had run eighteen miles and Brett called a halt to their running.

'Oh, I could go on forever,' Sharon announced.

'Blimey, I never thought I would hear that,' Samantha said.

'Can we just do a couple more miles, please and please?' Suzie smiled. 'We can run to Stonebridge Park station.'

'Okay, but take it at a slower pace. You have all come this far and I don't want you to get an injury now,' Brett said.

Samantha stroked her hand across her neck. 'No one mentions that word around here. Every time in the past someone has mentioned that word one of us falls down.'
'Sorry,' Brett mumbled.

They continued running until they all fell to the floor outside Stonebridge Park station.

Chapter Fifty

Suzie and Sharon stood breathless outside Samantha's house, taken back by the sheer enormity of the building that she lived in alone.

'I didn't realise how big it was, only seeing it before in the darkness.' Sharon took in a huge breath.

'No wonder she got herself a cleaner, I struggle with my two-bedroom flat. There must be five bedrooms in there at least, not to mention how many bathrooms,' Suzie observed.

'We can't stand outside looking for much longer, it is freezing out here.' Sharon tugged Suzie's arm, walked her towards the door and pressed the bell. For a second there was no sound then suddenly 'Oh! Susanna' burst into life.

'She obviously needs a loud bell.' Suzie laughed. 'Size of the house, she probably can't hear the door on the fourth floor.'

The door flew open and Sharon and Suzie were greeted by Samantha wearing a pink T-shirt with the words 'Mum Runners' written across the front. She turned and modelled the T-shirt, showing them the picture of the three of them on the reverse. They'd taken it only a few weeks ago.

'Oh my gosh – that is why you were keen on getting a picture of us all together.' Sharon gasped.

'I have one for each of us. One of my clients is a clothing printer, so he did me them as a favour instead of sponsor money. I am really pleased with the results.'

Samantha was turning around with her arms out as if she were on a catwalk. 'Do come in. Please do not stand out there much longer – it is freezing.' Samantha signalled for them to enter the house. 'How are you feeling, ladies?'

'A little nervous,' Suzie replied, whilst chewing her fingers.

'I am feeling determined, although I am sure once the morning comes, I will feel different.' Sharon raised her nose at the gorgeous smell coming from the kitchen. 'Something smells good, though.'

'Pasta party it is tonight, girls.' Samantha ran towards the kitchen. 'Do come through, girls,' Samantha called from the kitchen. 'We need to load up on carbs, so I have made tomato pasta, vegetable pasta and a fish pasta. We are going to get through this tomorrow, girls.' Samantha was buzzing.

'It's just a shame we can't have a glass of wine with the meal,' Suzie said guiltily.

'No, not today,' Sharon said. 'But tomorrow, I plan to drink several bottles.'

'What is the plan after dinner?' Suzie asked whilst admiring the beauty of the interior of the house.

'I have not made any plans – maybe just a relax in front of a trashy film and early to bed?' Samantha suggested.

Sharon squealed. 'Oh, yes, can we watch a real girlie film, please? I don't get a chance at home with seven men.'

'Take your pick. I have most girlie films on the market,' Samantha advised. 'Let me take you to your rooms and then we can eat dinner – it should be ready fairly soon.'

Samantha ushered Sharon and Suzie to the first floor. 'Here you are.' Samantha showed them two immaculate rooms. 'They have both been made up and cleaned, so take your pick which one you wish to have.' Samantha pointed to each in turn. 'The bathroom is across the hall and there are clean towels in there also.' Samantha pushed open the bathroom door slightly to display a sparkling clean bathroom. 'Just come down when you are ready.' Samantha ran down the stairs quickly. 'Shit, I need to check the oven.'

Sharon and Suzie looked at each other and laughed hysterically.

'She is a gem, isn't she?' Sharon asked Suzie.

'Bliss. No distractions. Just the three of us getting ready for tomorrow.' Suzie nodded.

'I feel like this is my pre-wedding night, getting ready for the morning. Almost as much preparation and everyone fussing.' Sharon laughed.

'Well, I can only imagine – getting married has got to be easier than this.'

'Hopefully, you will find out soon, if you marry that hunk of a boyfriend of yours.' Sharon held up her marriage finger to show her wedding ring.

'Like I have said before, Brett will never ask me,' Suzie snapped. 'He can do loads better than me.'

'You need to stop doubting yourself, girl.' Sharon placed a reassuring arm on Suzie's.

They put their bags in their rooms and there was a call from Samantha. 'Dinner is ready, girls.'

'Amazing. I am starving.' Sharon was the first to fly down the stairs.

Samantha was placing the three delightful-looking dishes onto the table. 'Take a seat, girls, and tuck in.'

The girls sat in silence, tucking into the wonderful food, eating as if it were their last supper. Sharon broke the silence and held up her glass of orange juice. 'Mum Runners.' They clinked glasses together and fell about laughing.

Chapter Fifty-One

Suzie was the first to wake and was stunned by the silence. Around her block of flats, there was arguing, cars revving and kids screaming before six o'clock. She went to the bathroom, showered and changed into her running gear. She met Samantha on the landing. 'Morning, Suzie. How are you feeling?' 'If
I am honest, I feel really sick.' Suzie chewed her fingers.

'I am feeling a little queasy myself. I am sure that once I have had breakfast and we get going the nerves will disappear.' Samantha comforted Suzie by placing her arm around her and giving her a cuddle. 'We have got this far, something I never thought in a million years I would ever achieve.'

'Thank you, Samantha.' Suzie had tears in her eyes.

Samantha ushered Suzie downstairs. 'Come on. Let's get you some breakfast. Any sign of Sharon yet?'

'I am awake,' came a call from behind the bedroom door. 'I am just listening to the silence.' Sharon was taken in by the lack of noise.

'Excellent. When you are ready, come and join us for breakfast,' Samantha called back.

Samantha and Suzie were tucking into their porridge, nuts, fruit and honey when Sharon entered the kitchen looking rather grey. Samantha looked concerned. 'Are you okay, Sharon?'

'I have just been sick,' Sharon sobbed. 'Please, why do I get a stomach bug today of all days?'

'I don't think it's a bug, Sharon,' Suzie remarked. 'It's probably nerves. Remember what happened to me on my exam?'

'I hope that is all it is. I do feel really rough.' Sharon used the table to steady herself as she sat down.

'Suzie and I are both feeling a little queasy and anxious, so I suspect it is normal. We are all in this together, remember. Let me get you some stomach-settling medicine.' Samantha started rummaging through her cupboards for some medicine to help. 'I know I have some as Garth used it on Christmas Day.'

'Don't panic if you can't find it, Samantha.'

'Here we go.' Samantha filled a glass with some water and a spoonful of the stomach-settling medicine. 'Knock it back and you should feel much better shortly.'

'Thank you.' Sharon wiped her mouth after knocking the drink back. 'That is rough. I can tell you don't have kids at home.'

Samantha looked confused. 'Why?'

'You look as though you are enjoying looking after us.'

'I am loving the company and friendship we have found between us.' Samantha took the glass from Sharon. 'Please go and lay on the sofa for a few moments. We have plenty of time before we need to leave.'

'Thanks. I think I will go and have a shower. Hopefully, that will make me feel much better – by then I am sure I can manage some breakfast.' Sharon hoisted herself up from the kitchen table.

A short while later Sharon entered the kitchen, looking much better than she did thirty minutes prior. 'I can stomach some breakfast now,' Sharon announced. 'I never used to eat porridge before starting this training – now I can't get enough of it.' Sharon took a huge bowl of porridge from the saucepan on the hob and tucked in without sitting down.

'You can sit down, you know. I do not charge.' Samantha signalled to the chair next to her.

'Sorry, this is my normal eating position, standing up. The boys are usually sitting down at the table, fighting, so I try not to get involved.'

'I cannot begin to imagine what it is like in your household.' Samantha raised her eyes. 'One boy was hard enough, without having six of them.'

Sharon finished her porridge and started washing up her bowl – it was normal for her.

'I do have a dishwasher, Sharon. You do not need to worry yourself with washing up. Go and get your bag and let's make a move.' Samantha took the bowl from Sharon and placed it into the dishwasher.

They each grabbed their bags and then took a huge deep breath as they left the house.
'Ready?' Suzie asked.

'Ready,' Sharon and Samantha replied in unison.

Chapter Fifty-Two

The Tube ride to Greenwich station was a squash, worse than a Monday morning full of commuters. It was almost as if all forty thousand runners were in the same carriage. There were runners dressed in their running kit and spectators with their fold-up chairs and picnic hampers. The queue to exit the Tube station was equally as painful.

'Which way do we go?' Sharon looked lost.

'Just follow everyone else, I guess.' Suzie watched the hundreds of people walking in the same direction.

'How observant. Hopefully, they are all going in the right direction.' Samantha laughed.

The journey to the baggage buses took over forty minutes because of the sheer weight of people walking and Sharon needing to run into McDonald's to use the toilet. Once they had placed their bags on a bus, they started to pin each other's numbers on their shirts and admired the scene. A group of people were hiding behind a tree whilst rubbing Vaseline on their private areas. There were so many people from different walks of life: some athletic-looking runners, some who had T-shirts with 'I've lost ten stone' on them, some wearing bizarre fancy-dress costumes and a man who had an entire fridge strapped to his back.

'Gosh, it's hard enough to run the marathon without that extra weight on your back.' Sharon gasped.

They walked for what seemed another eternity until they found the area where they were to be starting from. The athletes were at the front of the crowd and the slower runners towards the back. Everyone seemed to be buzzing, dancing and jumping around to the various types of music that were being played from different directions. 'This is painful,' Samantha announced.

'What is? Is your foot hurting again?' Sharon gasped.

'No, waiting, the waiting is painful. I just want to get going.' Samantha jumped up and down on the spot.

'Not long now.' Suzie looked at her watch. In unison the crowd started counting down from ten to one. Then the starter pistol sound rang out to indicate the start of the race and everyone around them cheered. Nobody moved immediately. It took almost thirty minutes to cross the start line. Suzie, Sharon and Samantha linked arms as they jogged across the start line and cheered in unison.

'Remember: don't go too fast to start with, we need to pace ourselves well,' Suzie commanded.

'If the route is going to be this congested all the way around, then I don't think there is any chance of that.' Sharon laughed. 'It's like the M25 on a Friday evening.'

The crowds of spectators were lined up along the entire run, cheering and calling out to runners who had their names displayed on their shirts. Every so often there was a call of 'Go, Mum Runners, go!' which gave the girls a burst of enthusiasm.

'How far have we run so far?' Suzie asked Samantha.

Samantha held up her watch and signalled with ten fingers.

'The next set of toilets, I will need to pee,' Sharon informed them. 'Here are some. Wait, ladies, please,' Sharon called, running off in the direction of the Portaloo.

'We've come this far together, we are not going to leave you now,' Samantha called after her, but she was already inside the smelly poo station.

'Gosh, that was needed,' Sharon announced on her return. 'Ready?' The girls linked arms and continued to run. They passed groups of doctors and nurses all running together. 'We are okay if we need medical assistance.'

'No one is going to need medical attention,' Samantha replied sternly.

A film crew were interviewing a group of celebrities from *TOWIE*, who were all dressed in the most amazingly expensive running gear and had a full face of make-up and immaculate hair.

'Bloody hell, why go to all that effort to run a marathon?' Samantha made a loud tut sound.

'The downside of being a wannabe celebrity, I suppose. You can't go on TV without your face. I'll just stick to being good old me,' Sharon commented.
'You are not old,' Samantha replied.

'Tell me that in the morning, Samantha. I am expecting to feel like a ninety-year-old tomorrow.'

A TV reporter called out, 'Mum Runners!' They all stopped and waved. 'Please can I have a chat?' the reporter asked.

The girls walked arm in arm towards the TV presenter and film crew. 'Hi.' They all spoke in unison.

'Thank you for stopping, ladies. I am Peter from Sky News. We are just interested to speak to some runners today. I am intrigued by Mum Runners.' Peter smiled into the camera.

'We are all mums who have never run until we started training. We called ourselves Mum Runners for that reason,' Samantha told him.

'Good to hear it. Best of luck with the rest of the run, ladies, and thank you for stopping.' Peter gave each of the girls a high five.

'Mum Runners!' they all shouted into the camera in unison.

'Shit,' Samantha shouted after they left the camera crew and came to a halt.

'What? Are you hurt?' Suzie was concerned.

'I just told the world I have never run until I started training for this marathon. What if Sex God sees it?'

'I wouldn't worry, as long as you get to the Ritz.' Sharon laughed.

'Good point.' Samantha seemed relieved and carried on running.

At mile fifteen there was a glimpse of Gary and all the boys who were shouting out 'Go Mum!' Sharon waved and blew kisses to the spectators.

'Have either of you seen Brett at all?' Suzie looked concerned.

'No, but it is a little busy, to be fair,' Sharon remarked.

'I am sure he is waiting at the finishing line with a huge bouquet of flowers and a huge box of chocolates.' Samantha smiled.

'Good point. Let's step it up a notch. Chocolate calling.'

At mile eighteen there were women standing with the spectators, holding tins of biscuits and tubs upon tubs of jelly babies.

'Thank you,' Sharon mumbled whilst stuffing as many jelly babies as she could into her mouth in one go.

'Oh my, chocolate biscuits. Thank you so much.' Samantha took one delicately from the tin.

'Take as many as you like,' one of the women informed her. 'We have plenty more where they came from.'

Suzie removed several biscuits and a handful of jelly babies. 'Thanks, ladies.' Suzie struggled to carry all the food and run at the same time. 'This is going to be difficult, running with all these in my hands.'

'You will just have to eat them.' Sharon laughed.

'Who would have said that chocolate biscuits and jelly babies would taste this good?' Suzie laughed and stuffed jelly babies sandwiched between two chocolate biscuits into her mouth.

Mile twenty-five was in sight. 'Oh my, we have almost made it.' Samantha wiped away a tear. 'Are we going to sprint up towards Buckingham Palace?' Samantha was excited by the sight of The Mall.

'I think it would be rude not to,' Sharon agreed.

Chapter Fifty-Three

They turned into The Mall and let out a squeal of delight. 'Ready, ladies?' Samantha asked. 'One, two, three, let's go.' They sprinted the fastest they had ever sprinted in their lives.

'Wow, look at the clock! I can see the clock!' Suzie shouted excitedly over the noise. 'Look! It is less than five hours.' The clock was showing 4:57:26.

'Link arms, link arms,' Sharon called. They linked arms and ran over the finish line at the time of 4:58:59.

'We did it.' Samantha hugged Sharon and Suzie in turn.

'Well done, ladies.' A steward ushered them away from the activity of the finish line. 'This way, please. I don't want you getting knocked over after running all that way.'

Sharon was crying uncontrollably. 'Where are Gary and the boys?'

'We have a short walk before we find our families,' another runner commented.

They were ushered to where a steward was handing out their runner's bag. In the bag was a foil blanket, a bottle of energy drink, an energy bar, lots of literature, a T-shirt and their medal.

'A selfie,' Suzie called. They gathered together, arm in arm, and held up their medals to the camera.

They shouted 'Mum Runners!' as Suzie took the picture.

They hobbled slowly along until they passed the line of buses containing everyone's bags. A steward was holding out their bags with their numbers on before they had even arrived close to the bus. After a twenty-minute walk they found the family meeting area. Everyone was there waiting: Gary and the boys, Brett, Chelsea, Greg, Garth. They all hugged in unison and shared tears of joy.

    John and Christine, the camera crew from Boxing Day, came over with their camera rolling ready to get some of the action. 'Well done, ladies. How are you feeling?' John waved to get them to speak into the camera.

    'Amazing, absolutely bloody amazing,' Samantha announced.

    'Okay, I admit defeat, you get your baby.' Gary hugged Sharon.

    'If it's okay with you, I am not up for sex right now, I am knackered.' Sharon poked her tongue out.

'Samantha, you shall go to the ball.' Greg hugged her tightly.

    'I would like to get changed first, if that is okay?' Samantha laughed.

    'I can do more than that. I have booked you into the Ritz for tonight. You can pamper yourself and I will join you for afternoon tea tomorrow.' Greg smiled.

    'Oh my, I don't know what to say?' Samantha blushed.

    'Nothing, please say nothing. Well done, Samantha. I never thought you would have achieved this.'

'Mummy.' Chelsea ran and hugged Suzie tightly.

'Hello, sweetie. Have you been a good girl?' Suzie asked looking at Brett in apprehension.

'She was great last night, although she missed you loads.'

'Ah, sweetie, I missed you loads too.' Suzie hugged Chelsea tightly.

Brett fell to his knees. 'Are you hurt?' Suzie asked.

'Suzie,' Brett announced. 'Will you do me the honour of being my wife?'

Several spectators turned to look at Brett proposing to Suzie.

'Oh my gosh, I never thought anyone would ever want to marry me. Of course, yes, yes, yes!' Suzie screamed and hugged Brett so tightly he almost lost his breath.

'You deserve it.' Sharon hugged Suzie. 'I wish I never sold that wedding dress now.' Samantha laughed.

John and Christine got all the excitement and emotion on camera. 'Congratulations, the pair of you.' John hugged Suzie and shook Brett's hand.

Several spectators clapped and congratulated them, showing their appreciation with a hug and a handshake.

'I will, of course, ask my two new best friends to be my bridesmaids.' Suzie turned to Sharon and Samantha in turn.

'I will be honoured, I am sure,' Samantha announced.

'At least we will look good in our dresses. If you had asked me six months ago, I would have felt a lot more self-conscious in a bridesmaid dress.' Sharon ran her hands down her middle to show how much weight she had lost.

'Anyone fancy a curry?' Brett asked.

'You bet.' Sharon rubbed her stomach. 'There is a very large glass of wine with my name on it.' She took a photo of the Mum Runners on her phone.

Samantha opened *Joggingbuddy.com* on her phone and tapped away. 'I have logged my London marathon run.' She punched the air in relief.

Everyone linked arms and walked slowly through the crowds, in search of a curry house.

Other books by Kathleen Kirkland

Ninety-Seven Days – **adult fiction**. Available in paperback through your local bookstore, or on E-Book.

David is devastated when his wife, Joan, suddenly dies of cancer. He is even more devastated when Sandra, from the hospice where Joan spent her last days, arrives at his house with a letter that Joan had written and instructed Sandra to deliver after her passing. The letter contains instructions for David to go into their loft and open a suitcase. In the suitcase, there is the answer to the secrets that Joan concealed and took to her grave. Joan takes David on a journey of her final weeks and her reasons for not telling him of her illness, whilst organising her affairs so that David doesn't have to suffer alone after her passing. He discovers that she was diagnosed with cancer ninety-seven days before her passing and kept it a secret to protect him. Can David forgive her, even after all her efforts?

Other books by Kathleen Kirkland

Mum Runners Florida Vacation – adult fiction. Available in paperback through your local bookstore, or on E-Book.

Samantha, Suzie and Sharon, new best friends after training and running the London Marathon together, are off on holiday to Florida with their families.
The holiday brings, lots and lots of laughter and many, many tears. The main reason for the holiday is Brett proposed to Suzie as she crossed the finishing line of the London Marathon. The thirteen of them, hire a villa together for ten days, what can possibly, go wrong?

Other books by Kath Kirkland

***The Chocolate Thief* – junior read**. Available in paperback through your local bookstore, or on E-Book.

Billy likes chocolate. All he eats is chocolate. A chocolate thief starts stealing all the chocolate in the town. Billy is accused of the thefts by his classmates, the headteacher and even the police.

Who is the chocolate thief and will Billy be able to eat chocolate again?

Will the police catch the chocolate thief who is destroying the lives of many children?

How to contact Kathleen

If you have any questions for Kathleen, you can contact her in several ways or follow her on Social Media.

Website –
www.kathkirklandauthor.co.uk

Email –
kathkirklandauthor@gmail.com

Twitter –
@kathauthor

Facebook –
https://www.facebook.com/kathkirklandauthor/

Instagram –
https://www.instagram.com/kmkauthor/

LinkedIn
https://www.linkedin.com/in/kathkirklandauthor/

Kathleen is free for book readings and book signings and to attend events and club meetings. Please contact her for details.

Lightning Source UK Ltd.
Milton Keynes UK
UKHW022227030820
367621UK00005B/317